ADHOCACY

ADHOCACY

Reoferron Martin

authorHOUSE

AuthorHouse™
1663 Liberty Drive
Bloomington, IN 47403
www.authorhouse.com
Phone: 1-800-839-8640

© 2011 by Reoferron Martin. All rights reserved.

No part of this book may be reproduced, stored in a retrieval system, or transmitted by any means without the written permission of the author.

First published by AuthorHouse   08/20/2011

ISBN: 978-1-4567-8495-9 (sc)
ISBN: 978-1-4567-8496-6 (ebk)

Printed in the United States of America

Any people depicted in stock imagery provided by Thinkstock are models, and such images are being used for illustrative purposes only.
Certain stock imagery © Thinkstock.

This book is printed on acid-free paper.

Because of the dynamic nature of the Internet, any web addresses or links contained in this book may have changed since publication and may no longer be valid. The views expressed in this work are solely those of the author and do not necessarily reflect the views of the publisher, and the publisher hereby disclaims any responsibility for them.

This book would not have been possible without the influences of my late father Savy Martin

and

my late senior George A. Rebello

and my mother,my sister and my aunt Theresa

and

The Profession of Law

and

The People of India

To whom it is dedicated too

Rohan never had an inclination that his life would turn in such a manner. He always knew that failures are stepping stones to success. But was warned by Mr.Righteous, "Son the more accidents you have, the more difficult it will be for you to drive. You might have a fatal accident, which might not take your life, but you might not loose a limb." For Rohan only remembered the word, 'Might.'

Haven't we all heard our parents tell us something and we have not listened to them and have landed burning our fingers in fire and then learning a lesson that it is fire. Rohan burnt his fingers, but what he landed up with, you will find out.

It wasn't the cause of his limbs. A Supreme Court verdict doesn't change what has been taught in school. Nor does a section of an Act of Parliament.

You won't find any great scriptures. Text of Shakespeare could have been infused, but then you will not read it, being the days of sms and not the 15th century.

This is Rohan's story being told as if in a pub in downtown London or having Lassi or Chaas in an Udipi restaurant at Churchgate.

If examined the first thing, an entrepreneur or an inventor needs to see, if someone has already done what he seeks to do. Thomas Alva Edison at the time of going to the patents office, another inventor from Germany got a patent for his light bulb apparatus. The only difference was Edison's apparatus could be manufactured on a large scale. The events were exactly what happened to Rohan, since no one went about doing what he did. Rohan's struggle and his life is a corollary of the invention of the light bulb of Edison. That is why Rohan's story is being told here, not written.

An Adhocate is born

It was a cold night. A night in late January of 1975. A year, which brought happiness, but would Rohan call it happiness, for one person as him, in retrospect yes, for when every child is born, it is happiness. The age old saying in India, *'Baccha baagwan ka dayn hai.'* So really, was Rohan a gift from God. Was he special or was he just another litter, unlike litter being twelve at a time, with comparison to humans being practically one at a time, unless one were lucky or unlucky, 8 at one stroke. Talk can be about flies, the famous seven at one stroke and here it is eight at one stroke, a miracle of birth, recently reported in the newspapers.

Introspection with the happenings before Rohan was born, put him in a dilemma, which went on for many years and that never really went away as to why was he an unborn, which gave his mother so much of trouble. In later years, was a question, which he pondered on in psychological terms, as did that, have anything to do with the subconscious of the mind. Which definitely, the answer is in the affirmative. What was the reason for his mother to go through such hardship, for he to come out of her womb. There might have been some reasons. Was one of the various ponders, of the years of growing up. Obviously he did not know, what he had done. It was what was told to him, after his body was able to comprehend. But the fact still remained that having been a problem at birth, he was an intricate and an unexplainable question to himself. Rohan's mother, having to go through the various vomiting and bleeding and the question of, "Should I abort or not?" The buck did not stop there, since the question of, "Should I abort or not?" did not stop. But reality is a long train running, with a destination unknown, where truth is concerned and that is why abort did not happen. But the only reason why, from what Rohan came to know later, was because of his mother's mother. "The more the pain, it means it's a boy," his grandmother had said.

Rohan's mother was not a boy scout, but having berthed the train of one passenger daughter, she wanted to berth the train of a son, which was acceptable. But it was his grandmother's words, "don't abort," which made his mother persist and withstand. The outcome of which need not be said. Since the obvious is never mentioned. But the fact still popped up to Rohan, was he a problem, not just a problem, but a problem with inverted comas, was a constant barrage, which hovered round in his head. "Radhika," his sister, "never gave me any trouble, but with you, I had to go through a lot of pain and it is nana who said not to abort. Radhika was out in a split second, but you gave me a lot of pain," something his mother said many years after Rohan was born, to Rohan.

It seemed to be, Rohan was the height of patience testing.

As a child never realizes that the best things in life is usually free, for the very reason a child is oblivious of the strange roll of money, plays in a humans life. Rohan did really need to realize, that since the fact was that no one even cares unless done something, whereby attention is needed and then attention is given. Otherwise the world could be falling apart at the side, and they could not even bother, until done something to get their attention. A wonder can be, as to why babies cry at the drop of a hat. But that wasn't the case with Rohan. He was a sickly child, why he, out of billions of children in the world, had to become a sickly child, never came around to decipher it, until years later, being there is a reason for such things. The reason being, his sister Radhika would just know how to make people dance and that is exactly what she did, made everybody dance in the Joseph's. Albeit every time was a new tune played by her. So the first tune of hers never landed being mastered by those in the Joseph's.

Rohan definitely does not remember, a lot that happened in his life, as a child, but it is accounts that he was told about later. For instance he wasn't a child, who knew he was a sickly child. A lot of exemptions are got, if one is sick. As a child, Rohan just accepted this is what life is all about. The fact remained that he only began talking, at the age of four, had no attributions to the fact that he was a sickly child. In later years, he realized that he was not the one asking for things, unless really required. He did not need to start talking, because he got everything what he wanted, was something he put and still, in terms for understanding himself as a child. However those were lessons, which nature was teaching him. Since obviously having grown, acceptance had floated, as to who he really was and what are his inert ways of thinking. Which apparently did not change, even though embracement of adulthood took place.

"The way you thought when you were first born, is still the way you think, on your first instinct of thoughts are concerned. Unfortunately people do not realize this fact of psychology and live in the wrong

notion that they do not think like a child. They need to realize, that this is the biggest lesson anyone in psychology needs to teach a lay person, that they still think like a child, the difference is, how they act. But it is a question, which I accepted in later years as one, that did not give someone else trouble, unless in extremism. What I would attribute, is knowing how the other felt, without even they knowing I knew how they felt."

"It is rarely, to be able to find solace now that having been born and out in the open and that of being a sickly child. For one cannot change the fact, that you are born with certain inert qualities of your Sun Sign and that cannot change. So however you might want to change that may never happen. As an Aquarian I landed up with this questioning mind that went into trying to open watches and other gadgets like a wall mounted telephone etc. I landed up being known as the mechanic of the house. It gave me a sense of acceptance, but as a true Aquarian, that gave me a sense of being different, a want and trait of every Aquarian. Whether he lands up achieving this want, to the extent of his liking, is a point to be pondered and questioned upon by the author of the book Psychoanalysis through Sun Signs. But the point of opening these various gadgets, such as watches and telephones and which were expensive gadgets in the early 80s, was the start of the questioning mind, as to how these things worked. The questioning mind never stopped, since it became a way of life and at some point of time in later years, dad actually had to try and drill it in my head that, "Don't try and reinvent the wheel." That statement which he made actually got me thinking. I just kept my self searching, for making of what I had in mind a reality," was Rohans view about himself and his life.

It is said, that where Aquarians are concerned, there is a thin line, between geniuses and eccentrics. At one time, being called a genius and at another being called an eccentric. Whether that had anything to do, with what the doctor, who delivered Rohan from his mother's womb, Dr. Adatia of Adatia Nursing Home said, "This is a miracle baby and he will be a genius," had anything to do, with being praised on the one hand and being ridiculed on the other is a point in question. A roller coaster ride. But that is what life is, a roller coaster ride. The only time one gets to enjoy the ride, is when the man managing the roller coaster, takes a break to put other people on the ride or you step out, till your turn comes again. In most roller coaster rides, you pay for it. Here it is free, except there is no warning the roller coaster is going to start. You hop on the roller coaster, on your own free will and the roller coaster simply takes you on to it, out of its own free will and you have no choice but to ride it.

So as a child, Rohan had accepted the fact that he wanted to and would and did in his later years be like Socrates, the questioner. Definitely he landed mellowing down and did not question things as he used to, when he was a child. But the traits, was there and they would always remain there, whether it meant reinventing the wheel.

For an Adhocate was born.

Only those who risk going to far can possibly find out how far they can go.

T.S. Eliot

The Transition

Know thyself and you will the universe and the Gods
Greco Roman Temples

"*It was a gruesome, ghastly and lurid time of life. Why I say gruesome, because the only time of life which is not, is when one is six feet under or back to ashes,*" was one of Rohan's many one liners.

Life is sweet, whether looked at, as half full or half empty, it's a matter of choice. It was the second year that Rohan was in school. Rohan had the great urge to be a sportsman, an athlete, among the others, that of a Pilot and that of a drummer. Aquarians are born drummers. They have a drummer boy beat, at a constant pace in their head. Like Phil Collins of Genesis. He didn't know, that this crazy urge would alter his life.

As a runner, stamina was racked up inside Rohan, of the appreciable sort. But whether in question comparable, whether similar to or superior, was a point, not debatable.

Radhika, Rohan's sister, went to a school, almost but not quite adjacent to Rohan's, had another construction not blocked the building. Radhika would be and will, called a female whose parents would be common with Rohan's.

Oh! A sigh of relief.

An act, Rohan must have committed, the number of days of his existence on this planet, had it not to be named another name than earth.

For there were and are no more, females or males, whose parents would be in common with Rohan.

Pra-th-bha as some would, the act of pronunciation. Though her name, was simply to be accentuated as Prathiba. Was a Bong. Since the people who had begetted Prathiba, as an offspring, hailed from Kolkata. A city, on the east coast of India, whose inhabitants, are to be more intellectual, than the daughters of the soil, having an ability to win medals, in the field of competition, of running races with others. Though the city has the greatest love for sports and yes times change.

Dropped in a similar course of instruction with Radhika, Prathiba proved stamina a slave and Prathiba the master.

In the stages of life, Rohan was three notches lower than Prathiba and Radhika.

An oral exchange, between Sonia and Radhika, put Rohan in the know, that Prathiba was the fastest girl in her class. A term used by all and sundry, of that stage of life. Though the term would not be correct to be used. Since being at that stage in life, Prathiba was the fastest girl, in the course of instruction of Prathiba and Radhika and in comparison, those of many other schools too.

To feel the necessity, for the craving, to be crowned like Prathiba, was every boys dream. The crown of being called the fastest boy, in the course of instruction, was the necessity and a craving Rohan felt.

"There must be something that Prathiba does which I am not doing," was what was going on between Rohan's conscious and subconscious.

All young goats, of the same age, had the same thoughts of,

"My daddy is strongest. My daddy is greatest. I am the fastest."

Was the terminology used by young goats Rohan's age then, so would Rohan.

The next action was, deciphering what Prathiba does, the next course. To be the discoverer of, what Prathiba does, wearing the crown of fastest. Rohan saw no road to be taken. Except the direction was, use his senses, his ear to the phone, to do the discovery act, when Radhika was in conversation with Sonia. As is what is, the procedure of a best friend concept, where Radhika is concerned and Sonia had passed and now fit the best friend tag on the head, as does a hammer. Radhika and Sonia, what a pair. Their vocal glands, were put to use every day, for such long hours. All being of the eve context. Rohan's achievement to be achieved, had no relation to the interaction of, the vocal chords of Sonia and Radhika. Rohan had only one goal to gain success of, an achievement of that being, the discovery of the development of what Prathiba does, which gave her the crown of fastest.

Rohan was the Eddie Murphy in Stakeout. Except Rohan was not just staking out, but had to be an eve's dropper, in the true sense.

"You know that girl Prathiba, she is the fastest girl in the class and faster than everyone till the 7th standard," was the exchange between Radhika and Sonia on the phone, which was very important for the discovery.

"And she has won 5 medals at sports day and has come out first," was Sonia's reply.

"Have you seen how she runs?"

"With her head up."

"No one runs like that."

The errand Rohan was carrying out, was heading in the right direction.

"I got it," excitement, euphoria had to let Rohan let the cat out of the bag and Archimedes was outside the bathub.

"Swine you Rascal," Radhika went running into the other room, where Archimedes was. Except here, Archimedes was Rohan, who had said the word Eureka only once.

Archimedes had felt like a king, when he uttered the word Eureka.

But Rohan?

All he knew was that the word caught, was labeled to some part above his eyes.

"You were on the extension hearing my talk."

"You cheapstake," was Radhika's reaction, to Rohans's action verbally and physically, was hit by bound sheets of paper which had an impression of, that for which a little of a book could have been given.

Was that the finale of the confrontation?

No.

Mr.Righteous was definitely to be dealt with, in correction Rohan would have to be dealt with by Mr.Righteous.

Gleam in Rohan's eye, being apparent, made Radhika ire and with rage. But an opponent, she was not.

Knowledge which she had was all that Rohan wanted to procure. Which he did, through an act of dropping on eve, but the noose fell.

What was to follow from the discovery was unknown. But one act, which altered the course, of life of Rohan and the man named history.

The gleam stuck.

Now the test of the hypothesis had to be done with the fire, with the knowledge sopped in Rohan, after the discovery.

"Aaj mere yaar ke shaadi hai, aaj mere yaar ki shaadi hai,"

"Pank Pank Pank,"

"What are these sounds?" was a bell which rang in Rohan's head.

"What are these sounds? These sounds have to be from a wedding procession."

Ran Rohan, did towards where the sound was coming from. Carl Lewis had not yet hit the sheets. But the brain has a weird way of rearranging things, with what information it has soaked. Carl Lewis being a part and will always be, of Rohan's running speed, since he did the front page of the Time magazine.

"Pank Pank Pank," went the trumpets again and Rohan knew it was coming from the Gateway.

The pier, which everyone depicts for Mumbai, with the Taj Mahal Hotel and Towers in the back ground.

When the procession reached Gateway, the procession had only passed the Radio Club. Rohan began walking alongwith the procession.

ADHOCACY

One end of Gateway is where the stone structure is, to commemorate the arrival of King George V.

The end is where, the structure jutting out in the sea of the Bombay Presidency Radio Club. The structure jutting out in the Ocean is like the V shape of the end of a vessel. The structure became famous after the Act of Kate Winslet and Leonardo Di Caprio's pose in the Titanic.

An Indian wedding is a large procession, with a band on the streets, with trumpets and the bride and bridegroom on a horse. The British have always said India is a land of horses, bullock carts and elephants in the streets.

What a connotation? But the fact remains, that this procession, was like many other of the connubial state, of two people and both sitting on a horse each in the streets. They were the son and daughter, of two of the wealthiest people in the world and both would have taken Cadillacs, Rolls Royces, Limousines to follow the entourage, with the daughters and sons to the social gathering, to celebrate the connubial state, which was to happen at the Taj Mahal Hotel in grand splendor. But the groom was sitting on a horse and behind the entourage. Exactly what the British had said about India, about horses and elephants in the streets.

The 21st Century has made witnesses, of the wild and sleek Jaguar and its sister the Land Rover, which has always been living, in the U.K. and now with a parenteeship of Sir Ratan Tata today. But the bride and bridegroom shall roam the street adjoining the pier of Gateway riding on a horse each. Having embarked on this journey, from the excursion elucidated and at the end of the journey, the fact will emerge of the reality.

Had Rohan to have had a compass, he would have been told, that he was half the Gateway stretch. The halfway mark, to the Taj Mahal Hotel.

"*Rohan are you going to go, to Timbuk 3 with the process?*"

"*What are you going to do, if the process goes to Timbuk 3?*"

Rohan had not heard, of a place called Timbuk 3. But he thought, there can be a place called Timbuk 3, since his teacher at school Miss Alira would say, that she would send any bad student to Timbuk 2. So there could definitely be a place called Timbuk 3.

"*Rohan you have already gone out of the building compound which you are not supposed to do. You better go back, in the building compound, lest you make everyone begin to search for you,*" was Rohan's thoughts at that moment.

The wink of an eye was felt.

"*Now,*" said a voice.

"*Now,*" and again a voice was heard.

What voice, where, whose voice, but hasn't there been, one impression of human nature that has been consistent that multiple nature, is what man is and expressed mythlogically, philosophically and religiously.

"*Yes now, yes now, test Radhika's strategy now,*"

"*Now here at Gateway.*"

"*Yes Rohan.*"

"*There is no better place or time. If you don't now, you will never know, whether Prathiba's strategy works with you or not.*"

"*But this, on the road?*"

"*But!*"

"But, if you don't now, you will regret later."
"It's time Rohan, now."
"OK!"

A contract, Rohan concluded and he put to use the moment he said its time.

Rohan began running and looking up after changing gears and gaining pace.

Wonder comes to mind, questioning the amazement of passerby's, of the evening walk goers, standing and leaning at the promenade. Sounds Rohan was oblivious of, with his head looking up, to the Gods and running. What happens next, remains as a mystery even today for Rohan.

Running Rohan was, in the middle of the road of Rohan's left hand and in his reality the sky, there was no traffic.

A hilarious sight.

If Rohan was an adult, he surely would have been given the apt name of *'Yeda.'* Running in the middle of the road with his head up.

"Something must be wrong with this guy," is what people would have said watching Rohan.

One sound and the train changed tracks.

"Thud!"

A dull, but a sound it was and not from a comic. It was derivative, it was reality and it sill resounds in Rohan's ears even today.

One sound and one thud, changed Rohan's life and that of . . . .!

The sound, *"thud,"* came from Rohan's head, banging the scooter that was right in front of Rohan, that Rohan saw suddenly, when Rohan put his head down, from running with his head up. If one standing or sitting at the Gateway parapet, they would have thought, the scooter was a bull and the other bull Rohan. Bull Rohan and the other bull the scooter were both running towards each other. The scooter head long, while Rohan head up and then head down.

A gathering of people was Rohan surrounded with, after a brake which the rider of the scooter did. Rohan wasn't unconscious but was nearly getting, since Rohan didn't know, what had happened. Rohan's head was hurting, as if the drums in Rohan's head could not be controlled and everyone else was taking a go at his drums, though the drums were Rohan's, at one go.

"Rohan, you were not supposed to go out of the compound. You have messed up big time. You have proved your mom's words right."

Fear of what had happened and what it had done to Rohan's head, was moving waves in his head.

"Beta, there are cars coming at very very high speeds, anything could happen to you," was what was told to Rohan, as a broken record, by Mrs.Sonal Modi Joseph.

Here the anything was Rohan's head, which hurt due to the beating of it all, at one go.

"Tum teek ho bachha?"

"Paani lekar aao?"

"Tera mummy daddy kahan hai?"

"Tumhaara naam kya hai?"

Was the words, Rohan began to hear. Words were distant and none came from Rohan's mouth, since blood was oozing out, from his head like a fountain. Blood was Rohan's friend. He had played with blood, when blood came out, through wounds on his leg. Rohan had a motto, 'play with blood whenever a chance pops with wounds on legs and hands and blood will never be one to be afraid off.' So it did not matter, it was just his red friend, who was coming out, even though it was coming out from his head, where his drums was stored. At least that is what Rohan thought, where it was stored, since from there the drum noise was coming from.

"Mein wahan rehta hoom Radio Club ke peeche," is what Rohan heard, himself saying.

Rohan was walked back to the building by the man from the scooter, alongwith another person, who took hold of Rohan after Rohan was made to drink some water.

"Rohan Rohan what happened?" that was Radhika on seeing Rohan.

Radhika went hysterical, on seeing the blood and began to cry. *"Why people have such an aversion to blood,"* Rohan always wondered.

Blood was Rohan's friend, he was not going to do anything.

"Reena Reena come fast see what has happened to Rohan," was Radhika running to call Reena the Joseph's maid.

"What happened?"

"Radhika why are you crying?" was Reena's reaction to Radhika's crying.

At first, Reena had thought something had happened to Radhika.

"What happened to Rohan?"

"Rohan is hurt and blood is coming out from his head."

"What?"

Mr.Righteous was called on the phone and he alongwith Mrs.Sonal Modi Joseph came straight back to the Joseph's abode. Rohan was taken in the car to the famous Dr.Mistry of Bazaar Gate street.

"Rohan today your head, will have to undergo, one big operation, since you got a hole in it. One solace, you will not have to go to school for a couple of weeks," were ideas running through Rohan's head.

But some small particular powder, cotton gauze and a bandage strapped round Rohan's head through his chin, is what Rohan got.

Since the Kuwait invasion or Bush firing into Afghanistan, had not taken place, a wounded soldier, prisoner of World War II is what Rohan was.

What actually took place through this accident is like an ECT. The medical terminology of an ECT is the administration of a strong current that passes through the brain to induce convulsions and coma. Better known in layman terms, as shock treatment.

The mind of a human has a conscious and a subconscious. At birth the conscious is empty and it keeps growing and attains the highest state when one is an adult. At old age, the wearing out of the conscious state happens. The conscious has a life span. The subconscious doesn't.

What took place through the accident was the permanent disability for the conscious to be at the forefront and made the subconscious a driving force. A similatity to many a clairvoyant.

The transition happened.

You can only achieve success by understanding your trueself,
Your subconscious.
Psychoanalysis through Sun Signs

Known Chupa Rustom

Living in the building Shradha, situated in the bylane, between Radio Club and the sea, stopped short by another building, called Sidhi, before the stop at the Chota Gateway was the Joseph's. Better known as the wall, in the hay days of Strand Cinema, in the 70s and 80s. The wall had been witness to the hippy life of Bombay (now Mumbai) had to offer then. Now it watches the entry and exit of the hifi of the city of Mumbai, going in and out Athena now Prive. It's a strange phenomena of big cities, once upon a time, everything was done in the open; today everything is done in closed doors.

The building was full of Sindhi's. Whether all spurt out of Sindh Pakistan, always a mystery till history came to Rohan's rescue. There is a saying if one sees a snake and a Sindhi kill the Sindhi first. Rohan obviously did not know the phrase then. He learnt it the hard way and at times looks at himself, having been thrown in a very very large beehive or wasp area, a feast on the Queen bee and all the other bees put together. Fortunately or unfortunately whether a Queen Bee in the many beehives of Shradha and Sidhi stung Rohan or not, Rohan was never known to have dawdled with any of the Sindhi bees then, before Rohan could, Rohan landed out from Shradha.

The fourth out of the nine was where the Joseph's family abode was. The Joseph's could be called the outcastes, due to the stipulation of only Sindhi's then.

The abode, a flat of Mr.Mansukihani, who did a division of his flat and gave the Joseph's two rooms and a balcony. One was made into a hall. The other a balcony, into a bed room, where Mrs.Sonal Modi Joseph and Mr.Righteous slept. The last room a kitchen, from where Mr.Mansukhkihani's flat was connected, but was locked through a door. At the kitchen, the second door to Mr.Mansukihani's flat became the Joseph's entrance by default. The hall which the Joseph's called was a room of around 200 square feet and was exactly a square. When you entered the room exactly at seventy degrees, a cupboard could be found, though some called it an Almarah.

The cupboard was where all the valuables were kept, since it had a huge safe. It had a glass mirror on the left, which was the mirror used by all and sundry in the Joseph's house. For Radhika and Rohan, it was for making their practice face making sessions. Something all children do, except they, at the time of their doing their face making sessions, think they are the biggest face in the world. Till wisdom dawns on them, instilling in them the knowledge, that every kid has made faces in front of the mirror. If their was a fortune, yes there was, that dawned with the mirror, being a scarcity and a luxury at one point of time.

Be it Mr.Right Sebastian Joseph, or the ever accepting Mrs. Sonal Modi Joseph. An intriguer to everyone that Mr.Righteous's name was Sebastian Joseph and Rohan's mother Sonal Modi Joseph and everywhere came a Modi.

In fact Rohan was always asked, "Rohan why does your mother always write her name as Sonal Modi Joseph, why can't she write her name as Sonal Joseph?"

Rohan had no answer then, but today, "Marriage is a culmination of love, let it be throughout and so the surnames." Is Rohan's perpetual answer.

With everyone's mother, their surnames came to go to a journey, where no man has gone before, oblivion, extinction. But Rohan's mother still had her surname and so came the saying, marriage is a culmination of love, let it be through out and so be their surnames.

Reena from Mangalore, Rohan's maid did her Sunday dance of pleats, before embracing the Lord Almighty, was what was told before her pleat dance, before the mirror.

With Rohan's vivid imagination, came the enlightenment, *"I want to be a mirror in my next birth."*

A question which Rohan cannot answer. A simple reply about the next birth, since Rohan's dad was a slave to Christianity and his mother a slave to Hinduism and he in the middle.

Does the mechanism of rebirth happen?

"Please do not ask me. Come to me after you die and you will tell me," is what Rohan would say.

With Rohan's thoughts of wanting to be a mirror. He surely wouldn't need any playboy or Debonair, when the net had not been integrated with something so important as 'inter'. It has taken years for the acceptance that females are humans too.

"Isn't me if I was a woman entitled to want to be a mirror," is what Rohan would say about the question of equality.

Ms.Radhika and master Rohan, were the face makers of the mirror.

"Rohan yours and Radhika's names are not Christian names are you Hindu's or Christians?" was what Rohan was asked everywhere he went.

If the game of riddles were to be played, anyone would win. They were kept by Mrs.Sonal Modi Joseph. So Rohan and Radhika were a fusion, with their first names being that of a non Christian and their surnames being that of a Christian.

So when Rohan said his name to anyone, their question to Rohan would be, "Rohan are you a Hindu or a Catholic?"

"Both," was always Rohan's answer.

"How can you be a Catholic and a Hindu?"

"On Sunday we go to Church first and then to the Mandir for Hanuman Darshan and then the following Sunday, we go to the Mandir first for Darshan and then to the Church for Jesus Darshan."

"But your surname is Joseph."

"But My first name is Rohan."

Rohan's answer was a formulation made, in the second standard, which stood as his reply, at the point of time of this nib being pierced into the fabric made of wood.

To Rohan, the world was a tug of war, since he didn't know which side to fall from the fence and was always asked,

"Rohan what do you want to be, a Christian or a Hindu or a Keralite or that of a Gujarati with a Goan upbringing?"

He was always at the pivot, since the anomaly never got solved and realized in later years, the anomaly would never reach solvency and went on to build his own identity, happening out of default, by calling himself a Bombayite and later out of compulsion and later out of acceptance, a Mumbaite.

This didn't have an impact though, as to why he was called a

Chupa Rustom.

But on that fateful Sunday, one of the many fateful Sundays, when he was in the second year of school, in the afternoon he played his act.

He saw the Almarah, the cupboard, the Godrej cupboard, whatever it may be called, whose doors were ajar, not even to a span of a palm.

"Where is Rohan?"

"Where is Rohan?"

"Where is Rohan?"

Was what Rohan could hear Radhika, Mrs.Sonal Modi Joseph and Reena saying.

"Where could he go, has he gone down? I will check in Prickus house."

"Rohan they are going to check in Pricku's house they are in for a surprise."

Radhika came back, "Pricku's has not even seen Rohan all Day."

"Where has he gone?"

"Where has he gone?"

"Where has he gone?"

"What you mean you don't know? You were in the kitchen. If he opened the door and went out, you would have seen him going," was Mrs.Sonal Modi Joseph blabbering to Reena. Poor Reena did not know what to do.

"Radhika did you fight with Rohan? You are always fighting with Rohan, tell the truth Radhika," here came the Rightful Mr.Joseph, screaming and shouting on top his voice.

The paternal species seems to take a crash course of shouting and the maternal species of stop shouting, to pass the paternal and maternal exam. At least they seem to land up doing so, when children are born. If the paternal species do not shout, they are termed as part of the Chimpanzee clan. If the maternal species shout, they are as one who doesn't have maternal instincts.

To Rohan, achievement of his want was at hand, victory.

A search warrant was issued and a search was made everywhere. Even under the sofa, under the bed in the bedroom, which was the balcony, as was the building built.

"Lambhu Rohan ko dekha kya?"

"Sanman tumne Rohan ko dekha kya?"

Mr.Righteous questioning both liftmen, if they had seen Rohan

"Nahi," was their obvious answer.

No suspicion of any kind arouse that Rohan could be in the cupboard.

Why?

The cupboard was purposely kept open, in exactly less than the span of Rohan's palms. Everyone in the house was kept running. Normally one could come out. But Rohan stayed and stayed even though, chaos were happening outside the cupboard.

What a live movie?

Rohan should grow up to be director.

That particular scene had its roots built for bigger chaos. For when bigger chaos were happening, Rohan stayed in the cupboard.

It was 9.30 since Mrs.Sonal Modi Joseph was going hysterical. Maybe she was just seeing all the trouble Rohan gave, when Rohan was in her womb going down the drain in a jiffy. But it was Mrs.Sonal Modi Joseph being a Virgo and Virgos tend to race with the brain when in a crisis. Besides, running the race is always in the negative, till another puts positivity, whereby the aim achieved of passing on responsibility, which makes the crisis even bigger and that is exactly what happened.

"What if Rohan is kidnapped?"

"What if he has had an accident and lying in some hospital?"

"What if Rohan is bitten by a stray dog downstairs?"

"Seby go to the police and lodge a complaint."

That was Mrs.Sonal Modi Joseph putting ultamatums to Mr.Righteous.

"Wow Rohan you have become so important. If one wants to become important, all one has to do is disappear and go into a cupboard of one's own house."

Years later Rohan realized that if Rohan had an endurance power, was because of such incidents. The whole house was upside down. No one could find where Rohan was.

Mrs.Sonal Modi Joseph, Radhika, Reena, and anyone who was not part of the Joseph's house and if present, would have been part of the chaos theory of the day and would have gone beserk, like everyone else in the Joseph's. But Rohan sat still for 5 and a half hours.

"Seby go to the police and lodge a complaint," Mrs.Sonal Modi Joseph must have said this 100000 times to Mr.Right.

"Sona, we have to look everywhere before we lodge a complaint," Mr.Righteous obviously trying to make Mrs.Sonal Modi Joseph hold and trying one last effort to find Rohan. Something which all fathers land up doing, the one thing telling their wives to hold. Which obviously, psychologically is the wrong thing to do. Imagine telling a drunk person to hold and don't drink more. Would he listen?

Not that it means all wives are drunk without getting drunk. Why because the same applies to husbands whether they drink or not.

Rohan came out at 9.30. For five and half hours Rohan stayed inside hiding. While the whole house was in chaos. Why because this was an episode of a training a rehearsal and a discovery of an inner quality. A quality to live in chaos.

The height of surprise was the outcome on the faces of Mrs. Sonal Modi Joseph and Mr.Righteous.

Rohan had no intention of starting a new religion. But before a part of the rays of the Sun could be seen, there had to be a cross to be nailed on and Ram had to go to Vanvas.

"The School"

Rohan would have been in a relationship for 10 years and finally tying the knot with an S.S.C. certificate. But landed with a relationship, because she beckoned him that is ICSE, though he didn't tie the knot. But who cares, the knot is something society had brought about, to bring contractual terms in a marriage. Here without the ICSE marriage certificate, the relationship was extra ordinary. It gave him everything that one would want in a ten year relationship. Ten years is a long time, to be in a relationship and not get married, when you meet each other from 9 a.m. to 4 p.m. that is a lot of time spent together. Rohan always thought distance makes the heart grow fonder and too much familiarity breeds contempt. Meeting each other from 9 am to 4 pm was definitely too much familiarity, but contempt, don't know, because he did not know the meaning of the word then and later it just became a habit, with St. Ignatius Loyola School. Known for its imparting of academic intelligence. Which it did and still does.

The year was one, where he had already failed the 7th and now doing the final of the 7th standard. The first one was a practice session.

It was the last day of the exam. Rehan and Ismail, bold as they were, landed up being the only ones remaining with him. Rohan calls it, the fateful day of the 19th of December.

The first class Rohan failed was the 7th standard. Which meant, he was 1year behind the others. What could he do, Mrs. Sonal Modi Joseph was sick, at the time of the exams, was the only excuse he would give then. Today it is thank you to Mrs. Sonal Modi Joseph. He would have passed the 7th standard and he would have passed by, his first visible in society stepping stone.

It now being the 19th of December afternoon and something had to be done, since the exams were over. Ismail, known to be a rascal in some language, cunning in another and in another shrewd. He was known as the runner in the class. Anyone seen him running, would mistake him for a deer. In fact it was a rule in the class, when Ismail ran everyone joked and said, "see see that Hiran running."

"Lets go in the classes and open the cupboards, they are not locked now," said Ismail.

Rehan was the normal Bawa. Spoke with a sloppy accent. Unfortunately no one out of Mumbai, running up to Gujarat, would understand Bawa, his accent was different. Since the whole Parsi community is concentrated in these two states.

"Che che yes yes," is what Rehan said.

"What che che, you Bawa can't speak English without saying the Guju translation first. Instead of having your surname as Toddywalla or any walla, it should be prefixed as translator Rehan Toddywalla or better Rehan translatorwalla," Ismail said with, "Give me a five."

Rohan burst out laughing. The joke which Ismail cracked was so practical. For Rohan practical jokes is what gets him really binging on laughter. Rohan had learnt when Mr.Righteous told him the most practical joke, "A man prayed every day to God, to make him win a lottery, but he never won one. One day the man got angry and told him he is not going to pray to him any longer. God slapped him hard and told him to go and buy a lottery." Rohan began believing in lotteries and in practical jokes.

It was then, that he realized that he was not like those, all the others. Since every girl his age, was reading *'Nancy Drew'* and every boy *'Hardy Boys'* and both put together *'Archie's'* while Rohan was reading *'First Among Equals.'* He didn't know whether he was way ahead or way behind. But he knew definitely, he was not on the same plain.

"I will hit out," Rehan said swinging his right hand at Ismail. The Hiran was too quick for words and backing his reputation he ducked. He caught Rehan at that time and all three went with their two fingers saying

"Peace!"

Peace, was the funny Playboy bunny rabbit sign, which was the craze of the 80s, with Michael Jackson coming out from anywhere and showing his two bunny rabbit fingers, the index and middle. *"Playboy must have definitely been paying these iconic figures to promote their logo. The world doesn't realize, that every time one showed their two fingers, meaning peace, they were promoting Playboy,"* is what Rohan would say.

Playboy got free publicity in the 80s, with everyone showing the peace sign, the bunny logo of Playboy, whether Rohan looked at it in that way, can be pondered.

"Ok lets go," said Rehan and Rohan followed with Ismail.

They went through all the classes from 7th to the 3rd spanning the A+B sections, opening all cupboards and drawers of the teachers. The cupboards had all sorts of items, which had the lost and found too. There were some good items in the lost and found. The craze of the time was Staedtler. Anything Staedtler made the guy a stud. Rehan couldn't resist, even though he was rich enough to buy a mansion full of these items. His father was the CEO of Beinette Shipping and Protection and Indemnity Club Ltd. in London, Captain Ronsi Toddywalla. Rehan had everything, one would need or want, from a Fiat 1100 to a Cadillac, with a house in Cuffe Parade and a Mansion in Napean Sea Road. When Rehan got fed up of Napean Sea Road, he went to Cuffe Parade. Wonder whether that's what he did with his parents too. Unfortunately Mr. and Mrs.Toddywalla was never in Mumbai. They were in London or traveling around the globe. You cannot be CEO of a shipping company, nearly as big as Lloyds, which had its own parallel Beinette Shipping registry and be staying in Mumbai taking care of Rehan. Besides Rehan's mother Farzana Toddywala had her own couture label in London's Bruton Street called 'Farz.' Even though, the street is known for art galleries.

"What you doing Rehan?" Ismail asked.

"It is lost and found, so I found," went Rehan.

"See Rohan, he has not taken things like you, beside your pop is so filthy rich, he has more ships than cars. Why are you taking these?" asked Ismail.

The Beineitte Shipping Company did own 487 motor vessels and 156 motor tankers and 23 luxury cruise vessels, which was more than the cars captain Ronsi Toddywalla had.

"Rehan Ismail is right you are filthy."

"I told you it is lost and I found," said Rehan.

Surely Rehan could finish his sentences, with putting an it, at the end of the sentence, but he didn't because that is what people do, when they want people to back off, like talking with grinding their teeth. It felt as if comas were being used in his speech. It sounded as if he ate words but it landed up being correct.

"It is just translation from Gujarati to English," Rohan said to Ismail and they both burst out laughing.

"What is so funny Rohan?" asked Rehan.

"Nothing translator," Ismail and Rohan chuckled in unison.

Rohan too had taken some things from the lost and found but Rehan was doing the raiding.

The building of the school was an 18th century structure. It had three floors. If the white, yellow, red and blue paint was stripped off the building, it would look like any other British structure. The blue and red looked like ribbons round the building. The building was divided by a hall in between, which was called, the assembly hall. Where everyday the senior students had to line up, for what was called, a lecture to emphasize that all are cattle and the teachers are the cowboys, whether male or female, it didn't matter they were just cowboys. The whole exercise of the school, was about the cowboys making the students, walk within the herd. If a student walked out of line, the cowboy gave a swank. Even though all are humans, a civilized lot, with a subconscious unlike the cattle. Which is better left to the neighbour's next imagination. That of the cowboy, the teacher shouting "click click click" for the students to move in line with the herd, was their designated work, for which they got paid. But maybe doing this is what makes all, a civilized clan.

So here they were Rehan, Ismail and Rohan plying through the teachers cupboards of classes 7 to 3 and shifting through the lost and found. Something which students should not be doing. They were like the three musketeers, or could be named as the three thieves. But that won't be appropriate, since Rehan's line shall apply, finders keepers loosers weepers. Nothing wrong in wearing that hat. Everyday they had to go through the grime of the cowboys telling them what to do. They were beating them at their own game, opening their drawers, checking their belongings. It is the only day the cupboards are kept open, since the papers are kept in the cupboard and collected by Ramy the head administrator.

"What the fuck are you doing messing with the papers?" Ismail questioned Rehan and gave Rehan a tole. It was a hard shot and Rehan landed catching his genitals as if he was going to fly.

"Basket," was all that Rehan could say, still holding his genitals. He couldn't even say the word bastard. Since he was so much in pain. But that got Rehan messing with the answer sheets further. The answer sheets were kept neatly together, roll number wise and Rehan inquisitive, wanted to catch the papers of Ketan.

Ketan was the brat of the 7th[th] standard but of the other division and he could cut anything with a knife, except it wasn't a knife, it was his mouth. He had a tongue which was as sharp as Lotya Patan from Tezaab. He had a built not like Lotya Patan. But was large compared to others. He had already failed twice.

The 5th and the 6th. But he managed to pass the 6th the second time. An accepted phenomenon, for happening of events, he had spent 9 years in school instead of 7. He was the bull eye of the school.

Ketan had actually made Rehan's life miserable. It was Ketan who on one evening, being still at school, even though school ended at 4 pm got onto Rehan.

"Hey you filthy nerd," Ketan shouted at Rehan in the Back garden. A ground used by a consortium of schools. This was exactly 4 days before the exams had started. Exactly two weeks later, they were acting as spies. There were six of them at that time, playing the game of attackers and defenders, with Rehan as the sloppy goal keeper, for the defenders.

What had got Ketan's attention of Rehan, was his sloppy attitude. But more than his sloppy attitude was his squeaky voice with which he would speak his Parsi Gujarati dialect.

"Tanni Maini Bosdo," was Rehan's standard line and this must have been the 10000 time Rehan must have said the phrase that day. Obviously a very important one, since it was being said not just with a Parsi accent, but with a device which had a squeal, a reproduction amplified by an amplifier attached to the larynx of Rehan. The squeal of Rehan would kill the sound barrier. If an experience of Rehan's squeal is to be felt, the equalizer needs to be put to minus 100db on left and plus 100db on the right and the volume needs to be pumped to an imagination level.

All six of them stopped attacking or defending and stood motionless. It was the first time Ketan had barked at Rehan.

"Yeda Parsi milavat," was the bark which Ketan gave. They all understood yeda Parsi. That didn't matter, but the word

ADHOCACY

milavat, was Greek, even though they knew the meaning. Mr. and Mrs. Toddywalla were both Parsi's so where was the question of milavat. The silence was killing, except of the sound of the Koyals and the birds. To see Koyals, Parrots and other exotic birds while studying join The Loyola School.

There was no one else, but the six of them Ismail, Akanksh, Mohan, Prakash, Rehan and Rohan standing still in front of Ketan. It felt squirmy, just none of them knew what Ketan meant by saying milavat. Normally they might pull Rehan's leg, but that was part of the game of growing up and studying together. But they would never say a word called milavat. Parsi's put spice into people's lives. A story was heard of one Parsi, who was so worried about his new car getting hit on the sides, paint falling on to it, kids making scratches on it, that he wanted to sell it, because she, the car was getting hurt everytime and he didn't want to get her hurt. We are only humans.

It was the 7th standard versus Lotya Patan.

"Don't Don't I will do whatever you say," is what Rehan kept screaming in Pain.

Where and when Ketan got a pen and began poking Rehan in the ass was a mystery. Even the crows began to craw, just at that time and the sound of their crawing was irritating. The whole thing happened in a jiffy.

"Don't even insult the Gujarati language you Parsi's are outsiders and have spoiled the Gujarati language."

It was strange what Ketan said and they all knew that Rehan was in pain, with a ball point poking into his ass and his white shorts were oozing with blood.

"Remember what I said milavat, you will not speak in Gujarati you heard and if he speaks all 6 of you will have poker," said Ketan and with that was the release of Rehan's ass from the clutches of the sword, which on that day was a pen.

"I will not speak in Gujarati again sir," was all Rehan could say. How Ketan became Rehan's sir in such a short time, on a guess, it was because of the pen. The pen was mightier than the sword and that it can do mighty things, was heard many times by Rohan. But at that very moment, the pen was doing mighty things to Rehan's Adams apples. All six thought that it was good that Rehan called Ketan sir. It had such an effect that Ketan released the pen from Rehan's apples instantly.

"Sir I am sorry sir," Rehan said again, as Rehan understood that saying sorry got the pen out from his apples. They thought it wasn't sorry, but calling Ketan sir, did the trick. But they were in for a surprise. Alongwith his plea, Rehan had tears falling like a tap left open, which had no water and which was suddenly infused with water and could not be stopped.

"I am not your sir, I am your sire, say it," said Ketan and just then ramming the pen in Rehan's apples again.

Rehan screamed in pain. The word sire is part of the oblivion city. But too much learning of Shakespeare, made Ketan infuse his talk with words of the 15th century.

"Yes sire I am sorry," Rehan had no choice but to say it.

Rehan wouldn't be called a Yeda Parsi, since he averaged with good grades of 65%. He only landed failing, because his grandmother who he was very attached to, expired that year. Which had an adverse effect on him. The effect was so bad that he became the last bencher, even though he didn't sit in the last row, but in grades that year. So Fr. Hercules the Principal even though he wanted to, could not push him to the next class.

Rehan solved the puzzle by saying "Yes sire."

"Yes I am your sire, say it again that I am your sire," Ketan barked.

"Yes you are my sire," Rehan kept saying it.

They didn't solve the puzzle, they realized later that it was just the squeal, is what saved Rehan. The way in which Rehan said sir with his squeal landed as sire.

"Stop searching for Ketan's paper," Ismail told Rehan.

They were in Ketan's class 7B. Rehan was still standing holding his genitals, whether one wants to call it his vitals is a case in point, with Ismail and Rohan having just done the hi five, as if Ismail was the bowler and Rohan the wicket keeper and Rehan's vitals, the stumps.

Never understood the concept of the tole, but it was the act of the times. It was part of the school adjacent to The Loyola School at the Back garden. Whether it was part of the acts of the other schools cannot be said. In fact it definitely wasn't, since another school, which would be termed in the same category of St. Loyola, as the school came to be called or Loyola School in short, was a coed. The guys may have, but imagine a group of boys and girls and a guy gives another a tole, but it lands up being Jayshree, Mona, Sonal, Rehanna, Sundari, Pragati instead of a Chandan, Ronny, Laksh, Debashish, Kavish, Rohit.

"I am sure the words stay free, was implanted there so the boys could stay free, otherwise the boys might just find themselves botched in red," is what Ismail would say.

"I till date have never given a tole where women are concerned. It wouldn't be a tole in the right sense, since they don't have genitals sticking out like men do," is what Rohan had said when remembering what Ismail had said.

"How the fuck do you know, I am searching for Ketan's paper?" Rehan squealed grinding his teeth together. He actually wanted to say, 'what do you know what pain I have gone through.' Around 90% of the times, one says things but wanted to say something else or mean something else. If one can understand that something else, that is the meaning of understanding somebody, where their feelings are concerned. There would be no psychiatrists, if everyone said what their first thoughts are.

"Everyone knows you have been made a rat, after what Ketan called you a milawat. You are a milavat, you are a milawat," said Ismail, who can really hit below the belt in actions and in words. But Rohan joined in too chanting with their hands up in the air, which got Rehan burning with anger.

"I will hit out, I will hit out," was Rehan's slogan whenever he got to the anger level. In fact he did get to the anger level, when Ketan called him a milavat, at the Back garden but he just couldn't do any thing. Not because he was a coward, but because Ketan was a bully and one doesn't become a bully unless he knows to instill fear. After all, fear is nothing but your own imagination, caused by unrealistic conversations, between your conscious and your subconscious. All of that time in the Back garden they had succumbed to the unrealistic conversations between their conscious and their subconscious and they just let Ketan call Rehan a milavat. Only Ketan could come up with something so simple yet so harsh. When Ismail and Rohan called Rehan a milavat, it made no sense. But when Ketan did, it was different. Besides they said it, only to get him to say, 'I will hit out' and would make this funny action which was hilarious. He would punch his fist in the air, like a blind man trying to find the person to punch but lands up punching thin air.

Whether Ketan had an inferiority complex of being a Gujarati vis a vis Parsis or had suffered some humiliation, where Parsi's of his locality are concerned cannot be ruled out. Even though Parsi's are, in all practical terms a peaceful lot, is what anyone would say and if not they aspire to be the commander, like Sam Maneckshaw. It was this calling of Rehan milawat by Ketan that made Ismail dissect the Mehta's family secrets. The Mehta's family, being that of Ketan Mehta.

Ketan Mehta came from a broken family. His father Mr. Anil Mehta owner of a cloth mill, situated around 30 kms from the main city of Valsad was a family inheritance, which goes back a 150 years or more. His father was the only son, with six sisters, Ketan's aunts. Mr. Anil Mehta being the only son inherited the family estate, by which time all his 6 sisters were married, through mammoth contracts of marriage, without any written agreements, in Court arguments it would be called dowry. But with the business of a size of a mini empire, scanning not only Gujarat but running into Mumbai, Maharashtra, with a confectionery and a dairy. With metal factories in Kolkata, coffee and cardamom plantation next to Coorg. With mining locations around Goa and Belgaum with a chemical factory in Bhopal and others unheard of, which meant those which Ismail hadn't found out about.

Mr. Inherited businessman, Anil Mehta's biggest problem, was not being allowed to marry his childhood crush, turned love, Mahbanu. A Parsi girl from school, who befriended him in Mumbai. His father Bhimchand Mehta ensured that Mr. Anil Mehta married a popular Gujarati from Gujarat which landed up being Anilaben from Ahmedabad Ketan's Mother. The outcome being Mr. Anil Mehta never stopped his commaraderie with Mahbanu and since Parsi's marry late Mahbanu was not yet married. Mr. Anil Mehta with all his escapades landed up in the hands of Mahbanu, leaving Akilaben, Ketan's mother. Out of which sprung the term milavat on Rehan and how many other Parsi's had to go through the venom of Ketan calling them milavat is unknown.

It's strange what GIGO can do, even though humans are not computers.

Rehan being called a milavat by Ketan, the outcome was Rehan walking like a Doberman, as if he had a baton stuffed up his ass. It looked funny, but it reminded them of the scene that made it happen and Ismail and Rohan could only look at Rehan, doing the Ass Jingo while walking. Rohan has done the bounce like Johnny Nagareli but doing the Ass Jingo was something else.

They were now in Miss Mahek's class. She would give anyone a turn on. She wore the most tight fitting Salwars and Kameezs. The baggy fashion had just set in for the guys, but Miss Mahek stuck to her sparkling greens and sky blue tight Salwars. It became an everyday affair, to guess which colour Salwar Kameez she would wear. Usually in offices, it is always which colour of the day, has been worn by a colleague. But everyone was quite content with guessing the colour of Miss Mahek's Salwar Kameez. At times one did get a glimpse. Since every contour was fit with a filament, which hung, as if there was a gravitational pull. The force was so high that one would feel the fibers, would just give way to freedom.

Here they were probing through her class cupboard. The cupboard, which like the Godrej cupboard, but wasn't the Godrej, had a safe on the right hand side of the cupboard. Every safe of all classes were locked. All classrooms had a cupboard and all of them had a safe. The safe was exclusively given to the class teacher and that was a part of what was given to the school teachers, besides the locker in the staff room. What the teacher kept in the safe was his or her private business. The rumour which ended as a joke that went around was, about Mr. Saranand the Marathi teacher, was that he robbed people and he kept his loot in the safe. He was always seen counting money, when the safe was opened. But there was nothing to show that he had made huge sums. Rumours will remain rumours.

It was Christopher Columbus's discovery of the safe, being Ismail's discovery of Miss Mehek's safe. It wasn't really a discovery. But all three of them turned and gave each other a hi five. Which has been kept as a symbol of victory, in cricket playing countries. Being a slap of one person's hand, to that of another in unison, above the height of the shoulder of that person. A hope to get the definition right. Why Christopher Columbus, since he went to Columbus College in Ohio. Yes an after thought.

"Abra, Abba, Kadabra, Dabra, Khul, Khul, Khulja sim sim," Ismail goes with his shrill voice. Rohan had no idea that Muslims had a Shia and Sunni sect. Rohan had put all Muslims to be as one. Till Rohan came to know that there being Sunni, Shia and Ismail being from none of them, but being a follower of Aga Khan a Khoja Muslim.

It was after the safe door could be opened the voice, "Who is there?" was heard.

Where the voice came from, they had no idea and it sounded as Miss Mahek herself, as if Miss Mahek was inside the safe. The whole situation turned eerie.

The three of them, for the first time realized after the initial fear that they were in no mans land and they should not be doing what they were doing. The teacher's desk was strewn with Christmas gifts, all open in the third standard.

"What are you doing here? Who allowed you to open the cupboard?"

"Who allowed you to open the cupboard?"

"Who allowed you to open the Christmas gifts?"

This was Miss Roma and she was firing questions, as if she were in a rapid fire question answer session and they were to answer the questions, except they did not know the answers and were pressing pass every time.

"Show your bag," she plucked Rehan's bag and found all the lost and found items, pens, rubbers, pencils, geometry instruments and every other item one could find in a lost and found at school.

Just then Ismail gave the order.

"Run!"

Rehan grabbed his bag and ran along with Ismail. The first floor of the building was as good as any second floor. Rehan and

Ismail ran to the balcony. They knew they were caught stealing. Rohan wouldn't really put it as stealing, since just as Rehan put it, it was lost and then found. But never the less, they were in a soup. Rehan and Ismail jumped from the first floor, which meant jumping from the second floor because of the height. Ismail was an athlete, but for Rehan to jump was a feat, since he was Mr.Podgy. He might have definitely made a hole in the Back garden. Rohan was left to the slaughter.

Ismail and Rehan both pulled Rohan to run. Rohan wanted to, but Miss Roma stayed a building away from his building. One can run away from many things in life. But how could Rohan run from Miss Roma, who recognized Rohan, obviously she would.

Rohan was taken to the Principal's office and was made to spurt out Ismail and Rehan's names, since the dagger was put in front. They were going to be rusticated. The word rusticated, is enough for one to want to commit suicide, the moment Rohan came out from the Principal's office. A truce was reached the next day that all three would not be rusticated, but Rohan had to own up as to who the other two boys were. If Rohan didn't, once the others were found out all three would be rusticated.

In life certain situations which pop up, you either take or the trigger shall be pulled. It seemed fair, as long as no one was going to get rusticated. The Principal kept his side of the bargain, so no one was out of school, but were on the verge. Any other incident and they would be rusticated. But they could not eat at the canteen, no visual instructions, no extra curricular activities of school, except physical training. Life goes on rustication averted, which led to coming to know girls as friends.

The biggest education you can ever learn is 'WHY?' and the answer to that question is Socrates the father of education.

Pychoanalysis through Sun Signs

COMING TO KNOW GIRLS AS FRIENDS

"What is this?"
"Take it fast, I have to go the bell has rung."
"But what do you want me to do with it?"
"Fill it."
"What?"

Rohan was wondering, 'Fill what?' For a split second, going into oblivion territory and then coming back into reality, Rohan realized he was holding the book, which was not one of the normal books. It was neatly decorated with stickers all around it, on the cover. It was little bigger than the size of a phone book and on top it was written 'My Slambook.' Rohan read it as my slap book. It was just the way Rohini had written it.

Doing the sticky act was the craze. Archie's, Betty, Veronica and the others. Those whose pappy's had seen the daylight of richness, would surround themselves with stickers everywhere. Even though tattoos had not penetrated the world of school, but the odd male putting a sticker on his hand and the girls on their T shirt besides their hands, were the order of the day, not just the rich pappy's kids, but kids since, the cost of stickers have eaten a snake in the game of Snakes and Ladders.

Fusen gum made hordes of money, just like any Japanese company then. It was the only gum imported, which sold one piece at a time, at least the hawkers did. Just like the millions like Rohan, who have been brought up with a little of everything, wanted everything in small quantities. If a 'Spout' was bought there would be seven pieces to spout with. If a 'Hubba Bubba' was bought, which was good for the bubbles, the first one out, four would be left. Fusen served the Indian concept, just fine. If the shop keeper had to deal with the remaining of the Fusen, that was his problem.

Fusen gave a wrapper, at the back of which was the infinite tattoo, which was different every time. With a little water the wrapper gave a tattoo. Trust the Japanese to do their innovation. Tattoos were still not such a big craze, since the vernacs as they were called, a term which is extinct today, thanks to MTV, Channel V, Star TV, Zee TV, NDTV and the list goes on. If the word tattoo was said, they would say, "Ya tattoo," which means a sissy, which may not be in the unisex phraselogy. No non Vernac would use the word tattoo with a vernac.

Talking about the onslaught of the channels, then everyone was only exposed to DD1 and DD2 better known as DD Metro. Whether one called DD as "Desh Drohi" or "Desh Darshan" which would go as one of the Hindi movie names of those days, is a matter of choice.

Rohan was fortunate to meet a Newsweek publisher, being in the 7th Standard then at an extravagant restaurant called "Outrigger" at The Oberoi and in conversation with Philip Lim, his name, he informed there were fifty channels in the U.S. Today when Rohan looks back at that statement, the U.S. definitely have been outrigged where channels are concerned. If a wonder is made, it is not that there weren't channels, there were private cable operators. But it's the secret of India's channel flight which took a flight of fancy. *"The only thing is that India is playing hide and seek, chuppa chupi or crystal maze with its own success,"* is what Rohan would say.

So Rohini goes after instructing Rohan to fill her slam book and Rohan was left in the Back garden staring at her, walking back to her school gate. Girls when they walk, they move in a rhythm motion like Simba the lion and that is exactly what Rohini did.

Rohini had these features, which were striking. She had jet black hair with curls. No the curls were not those curls of curlers, as if curlers were still on. Obviously girls don't put curlers in the 8th standard, at least in those days. They were natural curls.

She had all the features of Kelly Mcgillis. The world had just woken, to the sphere of Tom cruise, the era of Top Gun. The resemblance was conspicuous. No one changed their appearance, to that of the stars, in school. One Rohini's uniform was, a full white blouse and a full white skirt. It wasn't only Rohini's uniform, it was the uniform of the whole school of the Immaculate Conception convent for girls. To me it sounded as a vent, for all the con people. With Radhika going to another convent, it made sense, since Rohan always got conned by Radhika, is what Rohan would say.

The question which arose in Rohan's mind was why some of the girls of the Immaculate wore something which he later came to know is a habit. The uniform of the Immaculate was a full white blouse and skirt and so did the nuns, who ran the convent alongwith a habit. Now if the girl of the 9th or 10th standard was a little full rounded in a figure, she would pass of as a nun without a habit, was the boy talk of St. Loyola.

The answer to the equation here was that those with habits were big conners and those who only wore a white blouse and skirts are budding conners. The equation seemed right. After all the nuns of the Immaculate were so strict, they put Hitler to shame and Mussolini had to put his tail between his legs in front of them.

As a kid in school his thoughts didn't have brakes. Rohan definitely has the utmost respect for the habit, who toil to teach and have taught the women of India. Since it's a known fact, that the girl child lacked education, due to the faulty thinking that since she is going to get married, why make her study. The trend was similar to simple traders and businessmen which had the notion where their sons are concerned. If he is going to carry on a family business why make him study, instead let him start learning the business as early as possible. Unfortunately even though the habits have been teaching the women of India.They still have had to succumb to atrocities. Change the equation and there would be a question mark.

So what was Rohan doing with a budding conner girl, with a white skirt and blouse in the Back garden and taking a book from?

Which book? He had no idea since he knew nothing about slam books.

"Ok fill it baby," was Rohini's words before she entered her school gate.

"What?"

"You're my baby no?"

"I thought babies were only in the cradle."

"But you're my big baby no," was Radhika who loved saying the word baby. In fact Rohan might just pass, for her baby. One she was in the 8th standard and Rohan in the 7th. Two, because she looked like Kelly Mcgillis, taller than Tom Cruise, so she was taller than Rohan.

Today Rohan's reply to Rohini would have been, "yeah whatever." But this was 1988 since the creator of whatever, had not yet created whatever.

Obviously Rohan had to say something.

"Ok cool."

"Give it to me at the lunch break," was Rohini's orders.

"Cool."

Sometimes you are in a witness box and asked a question and the only answer would be yes. Rohan just said cool.

"You're my choclate no baby."

"Yeah!"

Rohini going back and smiling at Rohan and doing the Simba configuration, which is like a hallucination today for Rohan. Since that was the start of coming to know girls as friends.

Rohini was the last to go inside the gate. The watchman looked at her as if she was an alien.

"If I was the watchman, I would have been looking at her too as if she was an alien, waving at me, as if I was going to Dubai to work and was not going to get to meet each other for a year," is what Rohan's thoughts were.

All this was part of the recess, which was a twenty minute recess. Rohini, was already late reaching her class. The recess was after three lectures better known as periods. Rohan had to know about the facts of adolescence and the word period was one of them. *"So what if the boys were girls and had to pass through three periods one after another, which happened, only then did the recess come. Well that's what lectures were called in school period right. Wouldn't say all periods were bad, some were good some were bad. Each period was for forty minutes. Each second of those forty minutes were like being kept in a jail, with thirty nine other students and each word of the teacher being like a drop of water falling my head."*

"Except these droplets didn't fall on your head, but through your ears, into your ear drum in the form of words. A term I defined as word torture through your teacher," is what Rohan would say about the whole act of having to listen to the lectures of his teachers in school.

Droplets could be dropped on the head by oneself, since the hands of the students weren't tied. But there has been no clever person till date in the whole wide circumference of the planet earth, who has been able to wade off the words of the teacher. If a computer was made to wade off sound, trapped is what the act would be, in a silent room called ones name, with two people in it, called the conscious and the subconscious.

"The only way there is an acceptance of life is hearing third party sounds besides the conscious and the subconscious."

Some days later Rohini gave Rohan a Dictaphone in a similar manner again at the first recess and asked him to record his voice. He had no idea what he was supposed to do with it. He sat with the Dictaphone at the last bench and and kept wondering, "Why did Rohini give me the Dictaphone."

"Tell me all the reasons, why you love me," was what Rohini had told him.

What was he to do with the instrument? He had no idea. The Dictaphone wasn't even of the walkman size, it was smaller. The tape in it, was smaller than the usual. This wasn't one which was available easily. In hindsight, good he did not record his voice in it. He just landed up giving it back to Rohini two days later. Though he did record a few tracks and gave it back to her. But what transpired was she got caught with the Dictaphone by the principle of The Immaculate and was asked to leave Immaculate. She did and so was the start of the journey, but the end of Rohini-Rohan.

Failed PNG

I t is hard to apply oneself to study wisely and thoroughly.

Lord Buddha
Part11 Of the beginning of the Path to Enlightenment
of the twenty difficulties to overcome.

Rohan landed up being one who failed the 9th standard. "I shall give you a school leaving certificate as pass, if you take Rohan out from the school. However if you wish to keep him, he shall have to repeat the 9th standard," was the words of the Principal, Fr.Hercules.

Those words, if you wish to keep your son in Loyola School, he shall have to repeat the 9th standard, were a double edged sword, which meant to Mr.Righteous your son has failed the 9th standard and Rohan realised that he had failed the 9th standard.

Those words didn't make Rohan get into a remorse state. Rohan realized not then, but later, that he already had the subconscious in the forefront. Obviously nothing affects the subconscious. It was Rohan's second experience of failure. But today he calls it not failure but a paradigm shift. Mr.Righteous decided to take Rohan out of Loyola school and put him in National Open School. The fact that Rohan had only five subjects to study changed Rohan's life.

Unfortunately the world looks at a failure as an untouchable. Rohan having lived all his life in Colaba and having failed the 7th standard, Rohan did feel ridiculed as an untouchable. But suicide didn't come on the agenda. The irony is that with the new curriculum, Rohan wouldn't be allowed to fail. If Kapil Sibal was a minister then. Life would have taken a different turn. Rohan simply wouldn't have failed the 7th standard.

No one will explain failure better than Rohan. The hare and the tortoise, what an apt para for Rohan. Where the hare is Rohan the failure and everyone else are tortoises. The only difference is, people who are tortoises do not know to stop they have to keep moving. When they see the hare moving at such a fast a pace, they get jealous. But when the hare sleeps, the tortoise moves forward and wins the race. Life is all about, while you were sleeping tortoises have gone forward and how to wake up and catch up with the tortoise. Since driving at 300 kms per hour, you are bound to have to stop at some time and rejuvenate. The race called life is so long that the hare can keep his regular interval of sleep and get up and drive at 300 kms an hour which is something the tortoise can never.

The first lesson failure taught Rohan, who Rohan really was, just like an alcoholic having to accept that he or she is an alcoholic.

Rohan realized he might read great self help books. But the greatest help Rohan understood is understanding himself, his subconscious.

Rohan knew that if he had to reach success, passing of failure was eminent. Though success is a relative term. The Tortoise was travel and tours, the company was marketing the International Business Travellers' Club, Executive Travel Card. The card being a brainchild of Mr.Righteous, which he started in 1987 in partnership with Mr Naeem Shehzaan. A Bhori muslim. It seemed the only thing left to be infused in Rohan's life, was a Singh, since Hindusim was filled through Mrs.Sonal Modi Joseph, Christianity through Mr.Righteous and the Muslim way through Mr. Shehzaan. The void was filled by Dimpy Singh. There are some things peculiar of everybody, like the impys of the Punjabis, the anis of the Sindhis. After all, each and everyone, have their own identities and yet as Indians have the power to shift from the fifth gear, without going into the fourth or third or second to the 1st. "What an exceptional phenomenon. One of the Peculiarities of India," is what Rohan would say. There is definitely the peculiarities of the Punjabis and Sindhis and on and on and on. But what is the peculiarity of every Indian, is the fact that each and every Indian can change from the fifth to the first and and back and forth without any difficulty while speaking. Giving them the uniqueness of being able to run two machines at the same time, one in the first gear and the other in the fifth. Except if the machine is not a car, since one can't drive two cars at the same time. The first lesson of learning to play the drums is, about moving your palms one clockwise, the other anticlockwise. Something which comes naturally to every Indian while speaking. Not the playing of drums, since drums is not an Indian instrument, but the application.

The mornings were filled with an everyday escapade, of a journey to a land of subjects and in the afternoon Rohan worked, which gave Rohan a sense of pride of being independent and a sense of his worth. Unfortunately the year was 1990 and the liberalization had not even started. Though you could call it, the final year of non liberalization. Rohan had a meager income of Rs.300 per month. Why meager, it was actually pittens in this day and age and the days and ages to come, even if the Rupee gets revalued to the dollar.

Life has a peculiar way of making you start at the bottom. It resembles the game as children that one played, called snakes and ladders. Everyone has learnt the saying, to reach the top you have to start at the bottom. But the saying doesn't say that on the way you will have to climb ladders and at times, besides ladders you will meet snakes, who will bring one down. Not back to the start, but that cannot be ruled out totally and then back to the top to stay permanently at the top.

"So beware that along with the saying comes the disclaimer," was Rohan's caution to all and sundry.

Rohan's escapades with his friend Entrepreneur, started with marketing of Gaware Sun Control films. Rohan's world whose circumference was restricted, at that stage to Bombay today, Mumbai, had not seen the shades of dark colours on car windows. Very difficult acts if done, was to be able to cover ones white windows of their cars, from the rays of the sun. The times had not come for the windows of the cars, to be pre filled, with that of tints. The need for the tint had a market then and the one company which manufactured this tint was Gaware and popularly marketed as Gaware Sun Control Film.

It was a little help from a friend of Mr.Righteous, Mrs. Poonam Bijlani. She was the head of the latest show case of hotels in Goa.

The Renaissance, unfortunately pronounced by many as, 'Rain and Sands.'

"If you cannot pronounce the word simply say the English meaning," is what Rohan would tell the many who couldn't.

The answer Rohan would receive would be, "Rain why and salt."

"Didn't they say English is a funny language and you and I are indulging in funniness," is another answer Rohan would get.

Poonam Bijlani's husband, had an agency with the Gaware company, for the fitting of the sun control film on the windows of cars and buildings. From there came the sub agency to Rohan Joseph. A 15% commission on the sales of sun control film fitted, where cars are concerned and a 20% where windows of buildings were concerned. A contract letter for the commission was executed to Rohan Joseph. Rohan was 15 and already with a business contract. Not that Rohan had not done some sort of business earlier. But this was serious business. Besides sky was the limit, as far as orders were concerned. If business was made, commission was made and so was profit.

"I started working at the age of twenty, Rohan has started working at the age of 15," was what Mr.Righteous would say to Rohan's mother. Rohan didn't simply call Mr.Righteous, Mr.Righteous. Mr.Righteous had printed a leaflet with their home address and telephone number, which Rohan could distribute to those in cars parked at signals. Whenever Rohan sees children or teenagers selling books at signals, he visualizes a Rohan in the eyes of each of them.

ADHOCACY

In that same year, one of Rohan's friends had a contact, who had surplus shirts, which normally would have been exported. But for some reason they were not. The areas around Regal were already selling export surplus. A very dignified name given, in terms of clothing scientific technology, it would mean seconds. After a court battle, these vendors were given a whole road which began from the O.C. Police booth and closed just further from the Cross Maidan gate. Rohan picked up around 200 shirts which were properly packed on credit at Rs.20 per shirt and sold it for Rs.30 in a span of 2 months. A profit of Rs.2000 was made. Whenever Rohan carried out a transaction and made a profit he was lifted up in his own eyes. This was a start of a training, which MBA students land up having to endure during an internship. Rohan was getting a hands down training at the age of 15. For which Rohan had Mr.Righteous to thank, for making him embark on the road, learning the ropes to make profit from transactions, by simply polishing his shoes. The Rohan's journey to Entrepreneurland began and with his friend, Entrepreneurship.

The sale of shirts, did multiply into a second consignment of Benetton T shirts. But there were other things in the market to be sold.

"These are good and not expensive, you have actually sold 400 shirts," mentioned Kaizad, who was introduced to Rohan through another friend.

"Why don't you sell Halogen Bulbs, there is a person who has Halogen bulbs and wants to sell them in bulk, you can pick that any invention has to be viable for mass production and utilization. Unfortunately empty refills are not available. Yes Rohan could use the same refill by filling it with ink. But the ball point has a shelf life and the refilling is a process. Otherwise everyone would be refilling ball point refills and not ball point pens with refills.

Now the year being 1991, Rohan had already begun to work for Mr.Righteous's company in 1990. The work he was doing of delivering parcels and documents everyday on cycle was definitely more than Rs. 300 as salary. Mr.Righteous was the head of the company and he was doing the work of a courier boy. Not that he had any qualifications, he was only 15 years old.

But?

But Rohan knew he could do better.

He came to know about the, 'Learn while you earn program,' of the 'Times of India.'

Just like Robert Ingersoll said "In the republic of mediocrity, genius is dangerous." Wouldn't say Rohan was or is a genius. Rohan simply knew he was ahead of time.

Entrepreneurship demands the ability to think independently and act courageously. The opening up of the hem needed courage, since it was counter prevailing to the prevailing accepted beliefs of the time 1990.

Being ahead of time is all about exploring the roads not taken.

Coming to know of the learn while you earn programme was by chance.

"What are you doing these days are you still working?" asked Shitesh, who used to live in the same building as Rohan.

ADHOCACY

"No."

"Why don't you join me at the Times of India?"

"What do I have to do?"

"They will tell you everything at this meeting at 4 o'clock, they are still recruiting. It is for 40 days and you will learn how a paper is actually printed and sent to everybody, and at the end of 40 days, you will earn 1200 bucks. Isn't that cool man?" asked Shitesh.

This seemed good to jump from 300 to 1200. Except the month of May had 40 days not 28,29,30,31. That was ok with Rohan, he was going to get to learn about how a newspaper collects news and transforms it, for everyone to read. Which better newspaper to learn from, but the worlds most read newspaper, 'The Times of India.' Rohan was 16 years, he did not know of any other newspaper but the, 'Times of India.' Yes Rohan did know of the Indian Express, but the Times is the Times recording and telling you the real Times of India. At least that is how Rohan saw it and he as an individual, was entitled to have his own dictas.

To him the thought of getting an entry into the iconic building opposite V.T.Station, now renamed as C.S.T, was an excitement by itself. Whether anything materialized out of it made no difference. The fact that he was getting to enter the Times of India building was all he could think off. Till date, he had only gone to the ground floor, where a watchman sat more like a policeman of the British era and delivered documents and parcels. But even the act of delivering courier documents, to the Times of India building was an excitement. They were taken by the Britsh era policeman look alikes, besides the other staff, who would assist in taking the documents.

What Shitesh did not say, is that Rohan would have to sell the Independent newspaper, thinking that if he told Rohan, he would not go the next day. India had not come to the United States level of acceptance of the dignity of labour. So, if Shitesh was to tell someone else that the job was to go around in a plastic brief, case supplied by the Times of India to sell the Independent newspaper, with Independent written on it. It would be telling someone, to go jump in a dry lake everyday for 40 days and they shall pay you Rs.1200. It would actually be so bad, as jumping in a dry lake.

1991, and everyone knows that newspapers are sold by the newspaper Bhaiya. Today these ideologies do not matter any longer. It never mattered to Rohan. If he could be a courier boy, he could definitely do sales of, 'The Independent.' They definitely do not know English except the footballer, son of the newspaper vendor at Electric House outside the shop Rajshri brothers.

The meeting at the 1st floor of the Times of India building was at the Response section in a hall and there were many other boys and girls. All were above 18 years from what Rohan could see. It was then that Rohan learnt the programme was, 'Learn while you earn.'

There came a short middle aged lady, from what Rohan could guage. She seemed stern and was wearing a yellow kameez with a white salwar in the style the Punjabis wear. Which looked good but it also meant she, 'meant business.'

"I believe you all are here for a job. My name is Simran Singh and I am the COO of the Independent newspaper and of this Project. The programme which will run for 40 days now 38 for you since the programme started 2 days ago. You will receive an

ADHOCACY

amount of Rs. 1200 minus Rs. 60 for two days. There will be an induction for 2 days and after the induction, the job shall start."

"The job shall be to go around your designated areas, which shall be assigned to you and give free subscriptions to prospective subscribers for one month and at the end of the month, go back to them and ask them if they would like to subscribe. The concept is of getting them to try the Independent, see the difference, the benefit they would derive and they will begin to subscribe."

"The Independent newspaper is a newspaper launched by the Times of India group."

"As if we don't know," Rohan heard one of the boys in the room say. But Rohan didn't know, until then.

"The newspaper has exceptional reading material as the articles are written by some of the best talent available and is headed by the Editor himself Mr. Anil Dharker," she carried on.

She takes out a copy of the Independent newspaper and raises her hand in the air with it.

"The newspaper besides having excellent reading material, is printed on imported newsprint paper from Canada, for better quality reading. The paper is so thin and still the print doesn't overlap itself, on the other side."

She was speaking so fast, but some how Rohan managed to catch on. It sounded like an order to him, since for Rohan anyone who spoke fast and emphtically sounded like an order to him.

"Your induction starts from tomorrow. Please note you have to have a college id."

There were many questions asked but Rohan's was a simple one.

"Maam, could I get a copy of the newspaper to take home to read?"

For a moment, Rohan felt funny, no one had asked such a question. But Rohan was known for asking funny questions. Everyone asked all the normal questions.

What time they would have to work till?

What time they had to report back?

What would happen if they felt sick?

With Rohan's question, everyone went into silent mode.

"Sure here take this copy itself."

Everyone wanted a copy following like, follow the leader.

"One more thing I presume, all of you are 18 years."

Yes came the answer from everyone. But Rohan, he did not know what to do. He was 16 and it seemed he had lost the opportunity.

"Maam I am 16."

All eyes turned to Rohan, as he was below 18 and was caught watching a movie in a mini theatre with an 'A' certificate.

"For you I will make an exception. I want you more, than you want me, I mean this job. No one has asked for a copy of the newspaper. Besides asking, you want it, to read it, if you know the product you are selling, you will make good sales," said Mrs. Simran Singh.

Rohan was overwhelmed. He was 16 and below the age and getting to do what others do, when they are 18. Besides he felt so good, for being praised for wanting to read the newspaper. People always believed in academic accolades and always land up having a hard time with their boss. Rohan believed its better to get accolades from your boss, than academic accolades which are only theoretical accolades. Not that one should not have academic accolades but your academic accolades should have a practical usage. At the end it is, 'Joh jeeta wohi sikandar baki sab bhandar.'

The next day induction was a tour of the Times of India building. Explaining how the news was processed from the time, it was received. How the editing was done and articles formulated to fit a particular page. Why articles were on a particular page and why not on other pages. Right to going down to where the printing press is and that only the non English dailies are printed there, such as the Nav Bharat Times. In those days there was no internet to transfer information and the group was shown how data was transferred from the Times of India building to the suburban press at Kandivli through a special machine. All in the room were fascinated. Since none of them, could fathom then that data could be transferred in such a machine.

It reminded Rohan of the excursions that he went to at school such as The Mafatlal Cloth Mill and The Shangrila Biscuit factory learning exactly how cloth was made and that the cloth mill being one of the nosiest places in the world and how biscuits are made.

The next day was a visit to the printing press at Kandivli. In all the time spent, one thing Rohan learnt that it takes parts from practically every major developed industrialized nation to put together the 4 colour printing machine, which was the state of the art available then. Something he will never forget, thanks to the Times of India. The four colour printing machine was mainly used for printing sections such as the, 'Sunday Review.' The, 'Bombay Times,' had not yet seen the light of day. Nor had the everyday front page, of newspapers seen the light of colour. Things that are taken for granted.

Rohan went on to do a robust sale of The Independent Newspaper. Why, simply because of the knowledge available through Mr.Righteous. Even though his territory was assigned Colaba, Nariman Point and Cuffe Parade, he got orders from all parts of the city. All he did was contact all the Libraries in Mumbai and that was it, bingo. Unfortunately the Times of India had set the programme only for exactly 40 days.

One thing he didn't expect was Simran Singh's acceptance since he was 16 sweet and way ahead of time.

The one tragedy that took place at that time was on May 21st 1991. The last time Rohan heard a similar news was in the year 1984. But this was terrible. He had prayed at that time, to bring Rajiv Gandhi back as Prime Minister and on that fateful morning to learn of the news from his very own Independent newspaper, of what took place in Sriperumbudur was saddening. He never wanted to again. He wanted the glory, which he felt as a child with Rajiv Gandhi as Prime Minister. Even though India was a nobody vis a vis the developed nations. What Rohan knew was he had a dynamic captain. Someone like Kapil Dev. Who from nothing made a 175 against Zimbabwe and then the glory of winning the 1983 World Cup.

Unfortunately his captain died. So did his hopes of India as a country winning, like the 1983 World Cup. He will never forget the Dynamic Lion the suave Leo, Rajiv, 'The Gandhi.' Why would a St.Helena happen as Sripreumbudur when the battle of the horacious Nelson had not yet been fought, nor did the retreat of Russia take place.

My only wish the Barrack of Obama doesn't meet St.Helena in such a manner. Even if he does I am sure Rohan would be praying that he be saved.

The D. J. and the Jobs

Mr.Righteous had a nephew Lenny, who was part of a partnership which had started the disc 'Xanadu' in the late 80s, which was housed in Hotel Horizon. It was the most happening place to be in. Except in those days the word happening, had not yet sprouted to acceptance. The glitter and glitterati, actors and actresses would be found at Xanadu. It was where page 3 photographers would go, to play with their shutters, digital cameras had not bulged out then. Even the connotation 'Page 3' had yet to stem to fruit and was hiding in the roots.

One fine morning Mr.Righteous gets a call

"Lenny has had an accident and is in Hinduja hospital and is critically serious," that was Mr.Righteous's brother. Mr.Righteous rushed to Hinduja hospital. Hinduja Hopital is known to give birth to those who seem to be losing the light of day, which is what happened.

What had transpired was, when Lenny was coming back from Xanadu in his Maruti Van an Ambassador rammed into his van. It wasn't an accident. It was later found out that it was the underworld trying to do its activities, which it has to, for protecting its reputation. Except the purpose was to achieve the outcome of Lenny's van and Lenny, but of another van and some other person. Lenny was in hospital for 6 months and lost his hair, though he gained it later.

In 1990 at Open school is where Rohan met a group of friends, Reginald Gracias, Loyld who turned to be DJs and there was Ryan Beck too but not part of his clan. It is then that Rohan began bearing the ropes. Then Djs used LPs or DATs. Since Mr.Righteous was dead against Rohan having to do anything where 'Djing' is concerned. Rohan had to do it on the sly, for parties and at pubs and discs of the time but only as a guest Dj and he never let anyone know about his Djing.

Then there was no scope for Djing. A very good friend, a model who modeled with Lubna Adams once told Rohan in 1993 that Djing is for Loosers. Today a Dj is a celebrity. Then a live band made more sense compared to Djing. Going to a disc only meant for the high flying and for actors and actresses. Some what, how calling from a mobile phone in the 90s was Rs.16 incoming and Rs.18 outgoing and today its in paise. No one would have accepted such a revolution and no one would have expected Djing to become a profession. Whenever Rohan made a mention to an uncle or an aunt that he is a Dj in those days, they would reply with, "What." But if he was to say he was a guitarist or that he played the tabla, "Oh you are guitarist, oh you play the tabla," is the reply he would have got in admiration. Today playing the guitar or drums isn't what it used to be. The Dj equipment in those days had to be imported on a made to order basis. Today one can go to Lamington Road and pick up Dj equipment and go to a venue and play. Even though that's not how Djing is done. Spare styluses had to be kept in those days and they had to be constantly bought from overseas.

Rohan's love for music actually brought him to the realms of the music industry in the 8th Standard. When he began to spend his time, at a music store on the causeway called Melody Saloon. It is no longer visible, since it's no longer operational. Everyday after school and on Saturdays he would spend his time at the counter. There were no CDs available and no internet to download music from. He wasn't working at Melody Saloon, but the notion crept. Then the only music companies in the circuit of International labels were Music India Limited (MIL), which everyone terms the short form for mother in law, His Masters Voice (HMV), Columbia Broadcasting Service (CBS). The labels available were limited. For instance Madonna was not available at all. It was then the new company bringing in Warner Records (WEA) came in and a host of labels such as Madonna and Tracy Chapman. Gradually the revolution began to take place.

Rohan was in the 8th Standard and knew all the available tittles right from Pt.Hari Prasad Chaurasia, Pt.Zakir Hussain to Merle Haggard besides Willie Nelson in country and of course the Bollywood flicks to solo labels of Mohammed Rafi. That stint of spending time at Melody Saloon made him meet some stalwarts of the time, in the music label industry like Bashir Sheikh. Djing could not become his career since he wanted to stay in the Modi's and Josephs home. So it could only be done at a time when Lloyd was Djing at Leopold the famous café after 26/11 terrorist attacks. Not that it wasn't famous earlier, but became world famous by making those who didn't know about Leopold come to know. Café Royal hit to fame since President Bill Clinton visited it with the Ambanis on his Mumbai visit. That was opportunity. But calamity has surely brought opportunity to Farhang the owner.

ADHOCACY

Opposite Leopold is a store Lacoste then in 1991 it was 'Benetton'. Liberalization had just started. But the foreign labels had yet to come in. Rohan had a friend who was working at the Benetton store and he asked him to join him in sales. It seemed good Rs.2000 a month. Just like how everyone joins a call center today. Rohan was still under age 16. But it didn't matter he was on.

The store had a mezzanine floor and at the rear of the mezzanine, a store room. The manager was Grover. His mom a Parsi and his dad a Punjabi. Rohan got along well with him, and landed up being nearly, if not always with him, handling the mezzanine floor and the store below. He was an Aries and had one hell of an authoritative spree. Though he was shorter than everybody.

The store was doing well and cracking a sale of 100 to 125 pieces a day. It was a newly opened store giving the other Benetton stores such as the one at the Oberoi and the biggest Benetton store at that time in Asia Vama at Peddar Road a run for sale.

Grover as everyone called him, even though that was his surname and Rohan having befriended him, his drug habit had to come to light. He was a brown addict. Drugs then were not sophisticated as of today and then cheaper. At least brown was nothing compared to prices of today. Besides Brown is gone out of style, white is in.

Brown was an addiction which killed a person as a slow death and Grover was on it.

He would come in the morning and say "I am going to the loo for my morning crap, take care of the shop till then."

Rohan knew his morning crap was a morning chase. It so happened that trying to get him out of the drug habit made Rohan taste the chase and life was on a high mode. It had happened at an area on the steps, which today is a disc called Prive. Then there was office space, with a stair case to the first floor on a heavily raining night and the patra covering the staircase was the shelter.

Alcohol does not, but drugs is basically a tool which helps to go out of your conscious and to go into your subconscious or bringing your subconscious in the forefront. The subconscious is like a genie and what you ask it to do, it will do. In a drugged state that is exactly what happens. The subconscious is like Google, there is no control. If you make a search on Google for anything. It will pop up hundreds and even thousands of options. The same is what the subconscious does, in a drugged state. But that's an illusion. It is why many already take Google to be a Genie.

Though Grover tried, one chance was all it took. Yes Rohan just didn't think he needed an illusion. The transition had already taken place years ago.

Singapore Airline crew would be at the store since they were housed at the Taj Mahal Hotel. Rohan always believed, do what the Romans do in Rome and speak in whatever extent Latin, Italian to Roman's and you will get your way and still does.

"Do you have a smalla?" is all what the Singapore crew would ask.

"No only largela and mediumla is sold out," would be Rohan's answer.

Very soon Rohan became friends with the crew members and every second night he would be at the 1900s with them. It seemed good to get a free entry, since one could enter 1900s only with a membership and out with a new crew every second day was great. Didn't need to be part of an airline. Rohan was 16 and part of the Singapore Crew already, at least when he went to the 1900s, without flying with them.

"Where is Rohanla?"

"Who is Rohanla?"

"I want to meet Rohanla."

"I want to speak to Rohanla."

Was what every new Singapore Airline crew came and asked at the store, who had not met Rohan.

Even the colleagues who were jealous began to call Rohan, Rohanla. The only thing that Rohan could tell them was, "Fuck off la."

Grover had to resign and leave to join the rehabilitation center. Which gave Rohan the opportunity to become manager of the store. To Rohan the feeling was exhilirating being manager of the store at 16, with all the others above 16. Managers are supposed to be always above the age of those below them, if not at least not 16 years which was below the age of majority. A minor was the manager of majors.

"Do you have a small in this?" one of the customers asked Sanjay, one of the major salesmen. The customer had already open T shirts from 10 different racks and didn't seem to be inclined to buy anything. Whenever Sanjay asked him, whether be should keep a particular T-shirt aside, when he said he liked it.

"No I am only looking," is what he would say.

The only looking customer had spent two hours at the store already, made Sanjay go up and down bring smalls, if a small wasn't there on the racks and then say.

"No the T-shirt doesn't seem good in small, it only looks good in large or medium," is the answer the customer would give. Sanjay was totally pissed off. He could actually kick the guy in his ass and throw him out of the store. But when in sales the customer is God. That is why that customer didn't get a kick up his ass, since how can one kick God. But there are other things that one does to God.

"Array is pagal ko issme chota chaiye, zara dekle isme chota hai ki nahin," that was Sanjay cursing God. Kicking God might not happen, yes everyone, maybe even the priests of every religion might have cursed God once in a while.

"Tumne pagal kisko bola," that was the customer. The question of why the customer was insisting on small was because he was Japanese even though small wasn't his size.

"Pagal," and now Sanjay got a slap.

"Sir I am sorry," This was Sanjay folding his hands. This was reality drama. A Japanese speaking impeccable Hindi slang. Just then the Japanese kicked Sanjay on his ass. Sanjay was a well built guy, 5 feet 10 inches. The Japanese 5ft 4inches. It was a mirth scene to see that a puny guy hitting a well built Sanjay, whose biceps were well toned and if Sanjay was to take one swing, this puny Japanese would fall, may be even land up unconscious. But as the saying goes, never hit God. You might hit a customer though. It reminded Rohan of a flick he saw 5 years earlier to the incident, when Bob Cristo kept saying, "Bhagwaan marte bhagwaan marte," in 'Mr India'. The slap and the kick happened so fast, there was no time for Rohan to go and plead with the guy along with Sana the salesgirl.

"You know who I am, I am the head translater and interpreter of the Japanese Consulate. I can speak twenty five languages . . . .," And the Japanese began speaking in Hindi, Marathi, Gujarati, Tamil, Punjabi, Bhojpuri, French, Italian, Malayalam, Mandarin and Japanese and stopped. It was hilarious and Rohan wanted to laugh, but the situation he was in, he had to keep his mouth shut.

Now this was Rohan at his best.
"First I apologize for my colleague Sanjay. Sir, he didn't mean any harm. He was actually abusing the peon on top to get you a small. I am sure it is only a misunderstanding."
"So you agree he was abusing," the Japanese asked.
'If this guy was not stopped our store would be in the newspaper.'

JAPANESE CONSULATE TRANSLATER INSULTED BY BENETTON STORE STAFF AT COLABA
"Yes sir, but it's a misunderstanding sir, I am sure you have seen the latest set of T-shirts." Rohan took a small of the samples, which were staff surplus. Rohan was treading on slippery ground.

But it was a shot. He had ransacked and seen the whole store. There was nothing left for him to see or for Rohan to show.

"I have never seen this design before. Its simple but says so much on it," is what he reacted. The colours were pale green and the others yellow and red.

"You like it sir?" Rohan asked.

"Yes Yes, how much is it?"

"Sir for you this is a gift as an apology from the store. Its free for you sir."

"How could you give a free T-shirt to the Japanese and not me, I don't mind being a Negress if not a Japanese or whoever. Besides he has already kicked Sanjay's ass" Rohan saw in Sana's eyes.

It wasn't just her eyes, since that is what she said later after the Japanese left. Negress impossible, she was fair as milk. She would be called a fake Negress, besides the words Negro and Negress have travelled to oblivion territory and have made it to No Mans Land.

"That is very kind of you and I am sorry for hitting that salesman."

"Sanjay sir, Sanjay is his name."

"My apologies Sanjay, I just got carried away."

"No problem sir."

"And what is your name?"

"It's Rohan Sir."

"Rohan Joseph."

"Which part of India are you from?" asked the Japanese.

ADHOCACY

Rohan guessed he definitely knew more of India, than he did, since he knew more languages than him. But Rohan was only 16 sweet which the Japanese did not know.

"Sir I am from Bombay, but my dad is from Kerela and my mom from Goa, but she is a Gujarati, originally from Gujarat settled in Goa."

"You speak Gujarati?"

"No sir."

"Malayalam?"

"No sir."

"Konkani?"

"No sir."

"Marathi?"

"I can sir, after all I am from Bombay."

"Hindi?"

"Beautifully, after all I am an Indian."

"I like that."

"Next time you wanna learn an Indian language come to me."

"Yes sir."

"Give me 25 of these T-shirts, 5 in each colour. They can be in small or medium."

"Yes Sir."

It was a good day, a bad day and a lucky day all in one for Rohan.

"What is the total amount?"

"Rupees Three Thousand only sir."

"Yes only. The other T-shirts would have cost me Rs.7000. You are a good salesman."

"Sir I guess that is why I am the manager sir."

He gave Rohan the money.

Rohan thanked him and said do come again. But the fact about why the Japanesse wanted 25 T-shirts was hovering around in Rohan's head.

Rohan had to find out.

"Sir one thing I do not get, why do you want to buy 25 T shirts?"

"It's because I am going to meet a Chinese delegation next week and they wanted the T-shirts in 5 different colours and identical. In Shanghai the rate would be three times these, they are made and imported from Italy," said the Japanese.

It never struck Rohan that is why he was ransacking the full shop. Just how the Singapore Crew would always make a purchase, since the price of a Benetton T shirt in Singapore would be three times the amount.

Rohan never thought he would be able to crack this one. As part of the Japanese Consulate he Yahamoto, his surname Rohan hasn't an idea, enjoyed immunity. A slander by Sanjay would have landed him in a lot of problem. Especially with the Colaba police station being just the next building after the boundary. But it was good selling 25 pieces all in a days work. These T-shirts were received free for the staff.

Giving competition to Vama was causing havoc. The store was selling between 100-150 pieces on normal days and upto 200 on other days. Jaya Patel from Vama who owns the building

Kanchenjunga had to do some thing. That was, call Rohan and that is what happened. She offered Rohan a job. An amount of Rs.1500 as a stipend. But 1% commission on sales. Rohan took it and was at Vama. Again the question arose, that he was under age. But the rule applied. She needed Rohan, not he her. What roll Rohan was put on, no idea, maybe a swiss roll, but he was not put on the pay roll.

The first days of the first month, Rohan did no sales and on the 15th Jaya hits Rohan, though verbally.

"You have not sold anything except Ten thousand. You don't make any sales you won't get any pay. You have to make a sale of 1.5 lakhs to get your basic pay," she said smugly.

"Yes maam, that's ok," is what Rohan replied.

"What you mean that it is ok? Anyway thats Upto you," she said and she walked away.

Rohan clocked a sale of Rs. 1.5 lakh that month, but the next month Rohan called this Iranian to Vama who bought huge amount of merchandise and sold it in Tehran in his shop. A sale of Rs. 7.8 lakhs became a reality. Since the Iranian himself brought merchandise worth Rs. 4.9 lakhs. The rest Rohan did himself. However Rohan was not willing to stick around, where fights took place between salesmen because of commission. But what he definitely does miss is the escapades with Sarah from the building being Kanchenjunga who was the daughter of a man with one of the families accredited to one of the Consulates.

Though it was the constant fights which took place, there was another reason, exams were round the corner. They having got over, it was time for Rohan to get back in action.

Croissants was where everyone went to in the early 90s. The picture of Barista and Café Coffee Day had not propped up. Milk shakes, salads, burgers, submarines, chocolates, pastries, croissants, brown bread, white bread, garlic bread were the friends of the shelf. Everything one could want from a Patisserie, which you could not get somewhere else, was available. Then exotic cakes weren't available and the Dutch Truffle which Rohan and the others called D.T. was the most sought after and used cake language. Black Forest was available, besides the Ananas Krokant, the pineapple cake. But the D.T. did the deal everytime.

Rohan's interview was taken by then General Manager of the Ambassadors Flight Kitchen Aspi Nallaseth. It happened that Rohan was appointed counter staff of the Juhu outlet. The Juhu outlet was a small outlet just opposite a store called Foodlands, adjacent to the Ramada Palm Grove hotel. Rohan had seen film stars at Discs while Djing or when Disc loitering. But here they were in their casuals.

The charmer that Rohan was, landed up making him do all sorts of things. There are two famous schools at Juhu both ICSE schools.

"Hi," this was Nisha, obviously he didn't know her name, when she walked into the outlet.

"Hi," was Rohan's reply.

"I want a choclate truffle pastry."

"Wouldn't you like a D.T.?"

"What?"

"Most of you love it."

"What you mean most of you love it?"

"Girls from M.C.E."

"I maybe from M.C.E. but my tastes are different."

"So which class are you in?"

"9th."

"So Shakespeare is your friend or not?"

"What?" her what was so loud that everyone in the store heard and Rohan had to pacify Dinesh the cashier and manager that they were just talking, below the counter.

"You have Julius Caesar for your boards right?"

"How do you know that?" Nisha was just doing her what with words.

"I studied at Ignatius of Loyola."

"You really studied at Ignatius?"

"Yes."

"Then what are you doing here in Juhu?" Rohan definitely wouldn't count the amount of times she said, "what" but he did. Maybe that was her, but all the others had this phenomena called what, at least where the girls were concerned. So whenever it was heard from a guy, saying what, he was labeled as a panzee.

"Working."

"Why your parents do not have money?" said Nisha. Today that statement would seem absurd since that question will not pop up, when everyone is working in a call center and if not, hope studying at that age.

"No, just thought doing something constructive besides studying," was Rohan's answer.

Rohan didn't give her time to answer and obviously prod and ask further questions about working.

"Ok let me guess your Sun Sign," Rohan had not even asked her name but was going to guess her Sun Sign. She was still in her uniform and it reminded him of Radhika's uniform. Girls from school in uniform is a real high. She had this straight hair, with a parting from the left, which took her hair from the left to the right and on the right her hair would fall on her face and partially on her eyes. Those are girls and when they become women, you wanna cuddle them just as a Lassa Apso or a Fox Terrier mix.

"You wana guess my Sun sign?"

"Yes I get three guesses."

"Ok!"

"Are you a Capricorn?"

"How did you know?"

"Because you have this lean stature like that of a goat."

"So you calling me a goat?"

"No I am not calling you a goat. I am calling you a Capricorn."

"By the way my name is Nisha."

"Hi Nisha the goat, sorry Capricorn, I am Rohan."

She laughed with a giggle. There are three things in life which do not change, one: birth, two: death, three: Sun Sign. Everything else has been left to play with.

Rohan and Nisha landed up taking a walk on Juhu beach that day, since he was doing a morning shift and it got over in the afternoon.

"So tell no what you know about Capricorns?" she asked as they were next to a private property leading to the beach.

ADHOCACY

It was a construction site now 'The Marriott.' The board read 'trespassers will be presented' actually it should have read prosecuted. It didn't make a difference. It reminded Rohan of the 'Hotel Marine Plaza' building, when the hotel had not watched the waves lashing against Marine Drive's promenade.

"Well this is something you will not read in any Linda Goodman, or any book for that matter," Rohan was doing the making of faking.

"Then I want to know all the more."

Rohan had no knowledge about Sun Signs. All he knew about Sun Signs was from this book Psychoanalysis through Sun Signs. By whom it is, is difficult to remember, the author has the most unique name.

So Rohan played, "Capricorns have their ruling planet Saturn. The planet has two rings round it and that differentiates them form others, from the other planets and Capricorns from others. Normally one will never find the Capricorns moody. If you are then you have retreated, not into a shell, but outside the planet earth, where for you it is Saturn into those two rings. When you are on these two rings you are moody and irritable since these rings are made of tiny particles, moving round Saturn in a gravitational path. Therefore you are now in one of those particles and are practically alone on a marooned island away form the world. You then rejuvenate after making some resolutions and come back into the fray, the world with renewed vitality. The Capricorn doesn't venture out into the world unless you are really cheerful."

Rohan stopped and looked at Nisha. She didn't say a word and gestured to him with her hands to go on.

"Does it make sense to you?" Rohan asked.

"A lot, carry on I want to know more."

"Basically before I go on about Capricorns you need to know as to why, each Capricorn is different from the other."

"Your Sun Sign is only 50% of you. The next 50% is broken up with 10% being your genes which could come from your father, mother, great grand father or grand uncle, the next 20% is the influence in your life of your mother and father which is called parental ascendance. This doesn't mean only your parents, for instance if your mom and dad expired and you were brought up by your aunt and uncle then the parental ascendance influence would be that of the sun signs of your aunt and uncle. The next 10% is the environment in which you are brought up."

A recent study has named the behavior memes. Memes is a recent study but Rohan had put forward this in 1992.

"The last 10% is the present situation being Nisha and Rohan are talking. Your brain functions in a manner in which your first thought will always be of your Sun sign. Just multiply the next 5 and you will get to know how a person thinks."

"I never knew this, this is so interesting, tell me more no, tell me more."

"It's always a pleasure miss Nisha memsahib."

"Don't call me memsahib," she said it with such a smile which actually meant I like it. If it was some years later Rohan would have said thy ladyship Miss Nisha.

So Rohan carried on.

"Ok, the Capricorn as I said is a goat, the first thing it does is butt. Even if you are their best friend. Which makes them at times very cynical. They aren't really cynical, that is just the way they are. You can change many things but you cannot change your Sun Sign. If you see pigeons it actually moves its head back and forth as it moves forward one step at a time. The same is what a goat does. As I said you can change many things but you cannot change your sun sign."

"So how did I butt you?" was her question and she was fast on the draw.

"Good question, do you remember when I asked you "wouldn't you like a D.T." you said, "what." that was your first butt. When I said "most of you love it," you replied, "what you mean by most of you love it," that was your second butt. When I said "girls from your school," you said, "but my tastes are different," that was your third butt."

"I never knew those were called butts."

"Those aren't, since that is just the way you are."

"Ok tell me more, I like listening to you."

"Wouldn't you want to leave some for some other time. It is seven o clock, wouldn't your mom and dad be looking for you?"

"No they think I am at Sneha's place, my friend, I was going to go to Sneha's and then I met you and I like listening to you."

"You do, I thought I was boring."

"If you were boring, would I have spent four hours listening to you?"

"Good question."

"Ok lets meet same time, same place, don't forget. And don't call me madam."

"Can't resist you going back in that Merc and I in a 100 seater taxi to Juhu Station and then in a thousand seater taxi to Churchgate and back in a hundred seater taxi to Colaba or I might just walk, now who is the madam and who is, if not the memsahib."

"Shew, didn't someone tell you, you talk too much, lets meet tomorrow same place, same time don't forget, I want to know about Cancerians."

"Why you got a crush on a Cancerian?"

"No my dad, you idiot, I have a crush on you, you dumbo," with that she left, not before landing a peck on Rohan's cheek. It was then that Rohan realised that he had met Nisha 3 years ago, when she was in the 6th standard and Rohan in the 9th. They had not been introduced. She had a cousin, who stayed at Shradha and who Rohan had played with, even though 3 years younger to him. She had known him all along.

They met regularly.

"I Guess I was a dumbo and did not recognize her. What fun it was driving her pop's Merc," is what Rohan would say about the Nisha episode, which was done without a licence. But Nisha's father decided to transfer their residence to Sydney for some reason since all his Sindhi relatives were already there.

On a perspective on some later date Rohan realized he can't live with Sindhis and can't live without them. What a love hate relationship.

What happened on the 6th of December 1992 changed the face of everyone's lives. At least that's what Rohan thinks. But for Rohan traveling to Juhu was not possible and that became the end of Croissants for him.

At the end of the 2nd year Rohan joined the Art Gallery at Sophia's college, 'Sophia Deutschne Art Gallery.' The experience was to be that of being confined within the four walls of the gallery. Rohan had strict instructions. He couldn't converse with any girl from the college. Though errands had to be carried out as that of going to the famous artist Jehangir Sabavala's residence off Pedder Road to the Alter on the mount road. This carried on for some months. Playing of Carom at the back of the art gallery was fine. But Rohan wasn't such a carom freak. At the back of the gallery is a quadrangle where the girls play basket ball and yes boys from the Polytech. All Rohan could do was watch them play. But he couldn't, not when he knew something that he could teach them. Since he had been playing basketball and seen some National level players play at YMCA.

"Hi!"

"Hi!" these were from four girls from the college, all said hi in unison.

"You girls are simply throwing the ball to the basket, and I can show you a game."

"Ok, what is it called?"

"2s and 4s,"

"What?" all the girls went of, in unison.

"2s and 4s,"

"Ok what are the rules, and how do you play it?" Rohan knew they did not know 2s and 4s if they did, they would have been playing 2s and 4s just like attackers and defenders in football.

"If you basket from the D, the points your team gets is 2. If you basket from the quarter line you get 4 points. Did you get it?" Rohan asked after showing the D line and quarter line and taking the ball from them and shooting a basket.

"If we basket from the D line, that is this line, we get 2 points and if we basket from the quarter line you get 4 points," One of the girls asked after going to the D line and quarter line and making sure she had got the lines correct.

"Ok got it," the other one said.

Rohan began playing with them, he had not even asked their names. Some thing he believes in refraining from.

"Girls do not like being asked their names by boys and boys always seem to ask girls their names. It's a simple psychological rule. If you do not ask a girl her name and talk to her as another human being, she will respond. But if you ask her name. Her instant reaction will be a repulsion, since that is the first action which puts the differentiation between a boy and a girl. It's always easier for the girl herself to tell you her or their names." Is what Rohan always says about asking girls their names.

Just within a couple of minutes there came a call from top, from the first floor from the back entrance of the Art Gallery asking Rohan to come on top to the gallery. He did and he was asked to go home. Rohan just thought that he did teach the girls 2s and 4s. From what Rohan learnt later everyone started playing the 2s and 4s at least the girls but Rohan was, 'Gayab.'

ADHOCACY

There were other jobs which Rohan did. But doing three at a time was difficult, even though one being attending college, but why not. This was his last year of college and doing an attendance was needed, which Rohan did. But by 12 o clock he was at Worli and at the art gallery,'Galleria'selling etchings of Daniels till evening and the night over another assignment.

The call centers had not yet started their barking, but was on the verge off. On star T.V. products used to be displayed but could not be purchased. Interwood Marketing from Canada came to India with a collaboration with Mirchandani and Co Ltd. better Known as India Book House. Since they needed someone to take calls in the night and Mr.Righteous knowing them, Rohan got the assignment. It was good and bad for Rohan since the Joseph's residence number was flashed all over India in fact Asia. But those in India would call.

"Hello!"

"Hello!"

"Is this Interwood Marketing?"

"Yes Maam, how can I help you?"

"I want to know what is the price of a Contour Pillow?"

"Madam its Rs. 2950," would be Rohan's answer.

"I want to know the price of an AB isolator."

"Maam its Rs. 4950."

"I want to know the price of a double burner."

"Maam its 7950."

"How do I pay the amount?"

"Maam you can give me your name address and telephone number our staff will call you in the morning and inform you, how you can pay through cash or credit card."

"How will the product be delivered. Will we get doorstep delivery?"

"Yes maam you will get doorstep delivery and the product will be delivered at your convenience through courier."

When Rohan looks back, the pitch is the same except wordings are different at all the call centers. Rohan did that too, five years, 1995, before the flood of call centers

"College"

The shop for a college, stopped at, 'The Elphinstone College.' Rohan did have an interview with the then Principal of St. Xavier's college but in vain. So Elphinstone landed having Rohan.

The college is an 18th century heritage building, which Rohan had to enter day in and day out. But fortunately it was a Government College and being a Government College, they weren't strict on attendance. The rationale being, this has not yet been decoded. But had he had to adhere to the day in and day out principle, surely Rohan would not have been able to have practiced, the profession of jobs at the same time.

Since he wasn't an adherer to the rule of attendance. The concept of knowledge reaching the spongy material called brains, did not take place. He was always a loner at class, where elementary school was concerned. Since the transition took place in the second standard itself. Rohan had to do a paradigm shift. He had to invent someway in which to pass the F.Y.B.A. How was it going to be a reality?

Let's dissect what is needed at the exams. All the exams need is, to throw out what has been given, earlier in notes. There doesn't seem to be any logic to the whole thing. If the exams simply amounts to, throwing out what has been given in notes by the professor, then where does the concept of idea and conflicting idea and the students bringing about a synthesis in the paper. The essence of learning and the essence of everything in life is, an idea and a conflicting idea and bringing about a synthesis of the two, by fusing the idea and the conflicting idea and in the process, creating a compound not a mixture. The theoretical terminology being, a thesis and an antithesis and bringing about a synthesis of the thesis and antithesis. Unfortunately the exam was all about remembering the notes given and throwing it out on paper. This amounted to a mixture not a compound. The essence of education is, when there is fusion of an idea and a conflicting one, with the help of ones own ideas, thereby bringing about a synthesis of the two, which would amount to a compound not a mixture.

If what is written is a mixture in exams, that is an outccome of mugging. A mixture is nothing new, it is like an embryo moving up but not fertilising. It's like a Member of Parliament being a member, but under a special legislative law, cannot speak. Why would reproducing notes amount to a mixture, because the same notes can be dissected and traced to the teacher. So what the student has done is basic transportation. Like a courier boy.

Rohan always said, *"If I was the education minister, I would discontinue that exam F.Y.B.A. and would ask the students to do as much research and write a thesis with regards to whatever subject. When a student has to write a thesis, the thesis will be that of the views of himself. That amounts to a compound. The compound can only*

ADHOCACY

happen, when there is fusion, which takes place between your conscious and subconscious being an idea and conflicting idea." Something Rohan read in www.relcoach.com.

Unfortunately the F.Y.B.A. exam was about creating a mixture not a compound. With the transition, there was no way Rohan would have passed. The reason being, to be able to reproduce matter at the time of the exam, there is the need for the conscious mind to be in total control. Any extra poking by the subconscious, would amount to a hindrance. The transition had already taken place, where Rohan was concerned. Rohan had under any circumstance to perform a paradigm shift, an invention. Since this producing of mixtures was an inappropriate system of the present reality. He could not succumb himself to this concept of bearing how to make mixtures. To simply produce or reproduce. But reality is reality, which professes destruction of any sort of utopianism.

Definitely Socrates the father of education, as at least Rohan would call him and the contemporary of Plato and Plato being Aristotle's contemporary would be crinking in their graves. All three might just be listening to the reading of this writting.
Why?
Why, is the word which Socrates taught the world. It has not been realized Jesus died and Christianity spread. Ram experienced Vanvas and enlightened a whole subcontinent and beyond. Socrates was made to have the cup of poison and die and education became the biggest business of the world.

Without pegging the turnover of the business of education, it is the biggest in the world.

"Educational institutions should begin to start giving Ceasar his due. Except here Ceasar is Socrates the father of education. In every educational institution Socrates should be glorified just like Bapu, Mahatma or if as is called by many, the father of the nation India or Abe, if the nation was the United States. Though there is no right to state Abe, instead of Abraham Lincoln. Just like Mohandas Karamchand Gandhi will be found on every Rupee note of India. Since no education institution would be prevalent, had Socrates not to have started the revolution called, 'Why?'

"If you ever want to know, why I call Socrates as the father of education, don't go to an Encyclopaedia or to a public library, go to Google and Wiki will pedia you."

Was Rohan's ideas on education.

So Rohan had to be like Lochinvar, his was not to question why, but to do and die.

Mr.Righteous had these note pads given as gifts, from doing some marketing of IHT, the world renowned newspaper, 'International Herald Tribune.' They were sky blue in colour and had the great, International Herald Tribune logo on it, at the bottom. They were leaflets attached to a leather pouch and the leaflets could be replenished in the leather pouch. The leather pouch had these gold edges, the pronunciation of regality, 'International Herald Tribune.' Rohan had nothing to do with the leather pouch. To him, the note pad was the most important, for the invention and for the paradigm shift to take place.

Having passed the F.Y.B.A. the spade of production on demand being exams did not seem to stop. After F.Y.B.A. came another spade of production on demand called S.Y.B.A.

There were six papers. Five had already gone. One to go. The notes with the International Herald Tribune was already tucked in Rohan's jean pockets and kept at the bottom. Jeans had to be worn. If trousers were worn, these important steroids were sure to fall. They were neatly wrapped as puddies, as if the family doctor had given him steroids. In fact you can call them steroids, since it did the work of steroids.

"The spade of production on demand was always a 3 hour ordeal or raw deal. How this three hours ordeal came to be decided, that the authorities could decide your fate, the ability to be able to produce on demand what they wanted, which was put down in the form of a question paper, is an anomaly. This act of sudden death can only be accepted in the game of soccer. But even in the game of soccer the teams are given ample time, first half, second half, extra time and then an act of sudden death is applied. If one was playing a game of snooker, the black ball comes after considerable deliberation with other balls. In the game of tennis, the question of deuce takes you to advantage and then a sudden death is applied. Besides the fact in a decider net, you can keep going to deuce, advantage, deuce, advantage. However the spade of production on demand decides your fate in the form of sudden death, even without any warning. Ever wondered why the spate of suicides have arisen, that the government had to catch the bull by the tail and put the helplines dedicated to old people with that of students requiring immediate help before the suicide act is committed. They want to get the donkey to the water and then say please do not drink the water, a helpline will prevent you from drinking the water. It is the concept of

spade of production on demand which should have a solution, not make the student, come to the verge of suicide and then apply the brakes," Rohan thoughts, never seemed to have the lever called brakes.

One can rave and rant about what should be, but Rohan had no choice he wasn't living in the 18th century to be Abraham Lincoln who did his education in a log cabin or that of Thomas A Edison who was taken out of school. Both changed the history of the world and are still changing the history. For instance had Abe not fought the civil war, the United States would not have culminated to elect their first Black President. Thomas A Edison still lighting up the world with the light bulb. Abraham Lincoln and Thomas A Edison being Aquarians something Rohan learnt from www.relcoach.com.

"The world will come back by taking a full circle of Vinyl records, long play, LPs whatever you want to call it. Since I am sure a record plays after a 100 years. I am not sure whether a compact disc will or a hard disc. Besides a 100 years has not passed since the compact disc was invented. The record companies brought their own folly. Till date duplicating a record is the most difficult thing thanks to Thomas A Edison. The question of piracy would be history," a food for thought is what Rohan would say.

But in this point of time Rohan was sitting in room No. 19. A rectangular room on the second floor. Why not first, since the first floor was occupied by the Archives Society. If ever sketches are needed of the Murud Janjira fort where his highness Chatrapati Shivaji Saheb had hood winked a many or of Sawantwadi traced, the first floor, right of your left hand side should be visited.

ADHOCACY

The long rectangular room No 19 has the professors' desk at 90 degrees. A classroom, which can seat more than 200 students, were full with benches to seat three students totally. But this being an exam, only two sat. The benches were made of metal pipes and wooden planks, were put on top of the metal pipes. One plank for the book rest and the second to seat an ass, the third to rest books or at this juncture the question paper and answer sheets and the fourth was in front and the fifth was under the plank.

The paper was AIC or Ancient Indian Culture. A paper, which did need a sort of paradigm shift or invention intervention.

Rohan had not used the invention in the last 5 papers. This was the 6th and the last paper, with 2 and a half hours already passed. The last half hour of a paper is known as the last 10 meters of a 100 meter race. The most difficult.

Everything was going according to plan. The invention was working.

"Whose paper is this?" went an invigilator. With a 100 road rollers rolling in Rohan's stomach he did not know, whether he wanted to shit, pee, or pee from his asshole. Though Rohan had never done that and would never want to know how.

"Whose paper is this?" again went the invigilator.
Again came the grind, now he wanted to defecate from his mouth, which usually people call vomit and pee from his eyes, which people call tears.

"Give me your paper?" the invigilator went picking the students papers in front of Rohan.

"Give me your paper?" the invigilator picked the students paper at the side of him.

"Give me your paper?" the invigilator now grabbed another students answer sheet and she went on grabbing students answer sheets all around Rohan. It was as if Rohan was in a plane that was crashing and was in a tail spin, losing altitude rapidly.

In life there comes a time when a decision has to be made, how many martyrs will be called martyrs.

Rohan decided he was not going to be the one and let everyone else go down. The inconspicuous firing, of the engine, of the invention, which discharged some paper as waste material, having already been used and production taken place, with the help of the pen touching the answer paper. The waste material, the discharge of the invention having fallen out of the grasp of the engine Rohan and on to the floor, which the invigilator saw and picked up. The question of fate, of the product of the invention, was in serious trouble.

"Maam please don't take these answer sheets of these colleagues of mine, that paper is mine," Rohan couldn't believe what he had said. He had actually already made up his mind that he was not going to give in.

What a martyr, but there weren't any options, the plane was going to crash and the tailspin in which Rohan was, had to be

ADHOCACY

stopped. Besides he had other waste material of the application, lying with him in his pockets. He could not let these fellow colleagues, even though they were just students, go down with him, because waste material of the application of the invention, fell down on the ground. The Municipal Corporation in Mumbai, the commercial hub is never prosecuted for the waste (garbage) lying around at various parts of the city. But unfortunately he wasn't the BMC. My apologies since bad habits die hard MCGM. Though MCGM does a great job, but again bad habits die hard.

He was in the middle of the classroom and everyone was looking and glaring at him, that being 200 students. Though Rohan had not counted the exact number of students who were present, at that juncture.

"Give me your answer sheet?"

"Miss Miss Miss I can explain," Rohan was crying like a baby without tears flowing out, behind the invigilator, as she grabbed his answer sheet. What a Mary had a little lamb scene. He went wherever she was going. The lamb, except he knew she wasn't Mary and that he was going to the Guillotine land, the slaughter house. Which he knew and came to know was the Principal's office.

"Come with me, the rest of you can carry on writing."

"Yes carry on writing and you are going to carry on with the act of the slaughter of the little lamb, which has been following you and which has glorified you, by making you the Mary and I the designated lamb." weird thoughts go through ones head at weird times and the time was weird which made weird thoughts go through Rohan's head.

"Miss where are we going?" Rohan cried.

"You have been copying and you are asking me, where are we going and don't call me miss, you are not in school," she grumbled at Rohan.

He had no choice but to decide what to say in a jiffy.

"Yes maam."

There came a smirk on her face, as if the lamb acknowledged Miss Mary in the right manner.

They had left the classroom and was now in the corridors. The building built in the British era and today a heritage building. Had this loony corridor, with one staircase at the rear of the corridor and the other at the far end. There were students who had finished their paper or those who did not have a paper, at the staircase. It was like a reception, on the likes of what lord Ram got, when he was going to Vanvaas or what Lord Jesus got, when he was carrying the cross to Cavalry. But they, as prefixed here 'Lord' and will be, were to make nations follow them. Rohan was a lamb going to the slaughter house and was obviously not designated to have even one follower.

One thing he knew, that now was the time to empty the other waste of the invention, lying in his left and right pocket. The invigilator was walking in front of him. She was wearing a bright red kameez and her yellow dupatta draped across her shoulders, with the same yellow salwar. It reminded him of the colours of holi. She had this fashionable statement, of draping her breasts with her dupatta in one swangy movement. Watching her for 2 and half hours, while writing his paper was in slow motion.

Now behind her she did it in one swangy motion. Her dupatta sprang across Rohan's face like a slap.

"Rohan some slap in life you will cherish," was the thought which went through Rohan's mind.

What he gathered, she was not part of the profession and was only doing the supervision as an extra curricular activity and that she was only 23 and she looked stunning, like Vidya Balan types in a salwaar kameez or a Gracy Singh but then there was no Vidya or Gracy.

Passing the corridors, he took one set of papers from the right hand side pocket and threw them in a waste basket. The next set, of the left hand side pocket, was from the window while going down the stairs, from the first to the second floor. Which remained there for months. Which he could not do anything about.

The Principal's office was on the first floor inside the college office. Whenever a lamb is being taken to the slaughter house or dragged you will find it crying. Rohan was human and even thought he, wanted to cry like a lamb, but could not.

"What happened Sandhya?" was one teacher asking the soldier teacher, bringing the lamb to the slaughter house and whereby Rohan came to know her name to be Sandhya.

"This boy was caught with chits," Sandhya said.

"You take him to the Principal, she will decide and deal with him. She is in her office, I will come with you," this was professor Rehanna.

Professor Rehanna was known as the Hitler of the college. She was so strict that she could make a drunk ant walk in a straight line. Everyone's first thought was that she was a Muslim. But she was an Iranian who had married a Parsi. When she started, her voice could be heard in Jehangir Art Gallery and could rattle the paintings stacked up on the wall. At least that is what the students in the canteen would make of her rattling and slurping on insipid tea, but the coffee out of this world. The guy who ran the canteen actually hailed from Udipi district, so the canteen was called Udipi canteen. The waiter had the accent which was the typical railway guy bringing coffee at the station. Except here was a stationery station with no train movement called the canteen of the Elphinstone College. The waiter shouting, "Copy Copy."

Waiting outside the Principal's office on the bench, while Professor Rehanna went inside, with the invigilator, Miss Sandhya was a nightmare for Rohan. His head was spinning with thoughts that tomorrow he would be a laughing stock. He would be walking down the road and people would shout like anna,

"Copy Copy,"

"Aye Copy copy,"

He could feel, the whatever in his stomach turning rancid and wanting to come out from any side. Luckily 99.9% of the times peoples wants remain wants, unless they are really wanted. The want of the rancid in his stomach wanting to come out, remained as only a want, since just then.

"Come in," was what Miss Sandhya said coming out from the Principal's office. The doors were like the ones which Dr. Mistry at Bazaar gate street had, before one went in the examination room.

"What is your name?" asked the Principal.

"Rohan Joseph."

"Is this paper yours?"

"Yes but."

"Did the Principal ask you for an explanation?" Miss Rehanna butted in.

"Rehanna let him go on," the Principal gave her, a rejoinder.

"Yes that belongs to me, but that was part of my studying material which seems to have fallen down while keeping my studying material back at the entrance of the class. Believe me maam, I had not taken that piece of paper, nor have I copied from it. Yes I will not deny that paper belongs to me and what has been written on it, is in short forms of the notes taken down at the lectures. It is by mistake that one of those papers . . . . . . "

Rohan, obviously did not want to use the word chit. The word chit seemed to be a bad word and so he used the word piece of paper. As if the word piece of paper, was going to change the situation.

"What are you trying to say, piece of paper, piece of paper, it is a chit and you were caught copying with it," shouted Miss Rehanna. At which time the paintings in the Jehangir Art Gallery would have definitely, rumbled in their hangings.

It was the invigilator Miss Sandhya who came to his rescue.

"He was not caught copying with it. It was found on the ground next to his bench."

"But the fact is that, he had admitted the chit to be his," the Principal said.

"I do not deny the piece of paper is mine," Rohan said.

"Stop going on piece of paper, piece of paper, it is a chit and you have admitted it is yours, and we shall decide what to do with you," Professor Rehanna, fighting for her right as a professor, to prove whatever she says is right. The reason why professors love being professors and teachers love being teachers. It reminded Rohan of one teacher in his kindergarten days, who was filling in for another, saying salee for sally, but what could he do or any other toddler then, if the teacher says its right its right, if she says its day, even though it might be night or it might be day, so be it.

"You can go home, but I want you alongwith your parents tomorrow, at 10.30 in my office," said the Principal.

'AM or PM?' is what Rohan wanted to ask.

Rohan was doomed and actually felt like jumping in a dry lake. He had heard of many stories of bringing someone else as their parents. But there was no one, who was going to fill the parent arena. Besides he could not stoop so low. He was proud of his Christian father and Hindu mother. He had some dignity, at least where his parents were concerned. The chit had the answer pertaining to the life of Ashoka and the battle of Kalinga. There was no question, in the question paper about Ashoka. All the chits were thrown out and there was no detection of the other chits which took part as raw materials, for the invention application. So there was nothing they could prove, whereby he was caught copying.

"Dad I need you to come and meet my Principal with me at 10.30 in the morning," Rohan squeaked to Mr.Righteous.

"What have you done? Is this a repition of your school," Mr.Righteous growled.

Rohan knew this is what Mr.Righteous was going to say.

Rohan had to come up with something.

"Dad the supervisor found one paper on the ground and has framed me for copying," Rohan squeaked again, putting his tail between his legs, like a puppy to his master.

"Did you take the chits to copy and was that paper yours?" asked Mr.Righteous in the same wolf tone to Rohan the puppy.

There was no lies, which Rohan could tell. He had taken the chits and he wasn't caught, the chit was. The chit should have taken care of itself, than get caught. But the chit was his and he owned up to the fact that the chit was his.

"Don't tell me lies, did you take chits to the exam and did you copy?" Mr.Righteous asked the puppy again, with its tail in between its legs still.

There was nothing Rohan could do.

It was like someone asking him, "Is your name Rohan Joseph don't tell me lies, since you have written this on this chit?"

"Yes dad," was Rohan's reply. which Rohan had to give since he had no choice.

"Is this what days, I brought you up to see?"

"Is this what have I thought you.?"

"Why can't you be like all the other boys."

"This is why I work so hard to see you do this and now I have to meet your Principal."

"What if she just throws you out?"

"What you want me to do, beg her?"

"This is why I work so hard to beg your Principal. You will never give me peace of mind," shouted Mr.Righteous.

This was the time when the lamb had to put his tail between his legs and shut up. Though Rohan had never seen one do it. So he stood with the puppy status and it surely wasn't his day. Mr.Righteous wasn't having a field day at Rohan. He was furious.

"What are you going to do, if they rusticate you from college, go and wash toilets?" questioned Mr.Righteous.

Rohan had washed the toilet in the Joseph's, wasn't very difficult though. But he didn't think he was going to get to that level. Rohan had already been a manager at the Benetton store at Colaba. Worked at a fast food outlet. Had been a D.J. and still was at that time and he might land up being one, till his dying day. Sold Gaware Sun Control film, shirts, halogen bulbs, worked at an art gallery. Sold gift items, as customs made leather goods for corporate companies, besides many other jobs, had not the opportunity of being a store manager in Dubai, even through he got selected as 1st out off 400 candidates who applied and was kept on standby, since he had not attained the age of majority. He surely wasn't going to wash toilets. But that was Mr.Righteous's standard line from Rohan's school days. For parents their children never grow up.

"I will go late to work and come with you and you come with me in the car, as if I am dropping you to V.T.Station," then Victoria Terminus today C.S.T. Chatrapati Shivaji Terminus, was Mr.Righteous settling to an acceptance of the situation.

ADHOCACY

"Don't tell Sona or Radhika about this," was an order which Mr.Righteous gave.

"Yes dad."

"I love my dad and I miss him today," is what Rohan says about Mr.Righteous. Mr.Righteous could turn even the most difficult of things into positive. Even though Rohan calls him Mr.Righteous he acknowledges, he is rightly so. For he has always been true to his word.

"Go out and if you face a problem I will handle it," that is what Mr.Righteous would say to Rohan. Which is exactly what happened the next day. Since the Principal and most of all Miss Rehanna had to face no longer the weak and humble Rohan Joseph of yesterday but the diplomat, who played with the streak as if he had already won. Mr.Righteous must have been at some time, the chief of the Chinese army, since he used the Chinese art of war and fought without any weapons at hand, on that fateful day. Mr.Righteous was truly Righteous on that day, just like the fateful day at Rohan's school. Mr.Righteous seated on a chair in front of the Pincipal and Rohan at the side. Miss or professor Rehanna and Miss Sandhya at either side of the Principal. What a moot court. Except this wasn't a moot court, it was reality and reality is a long train running with the destination unknown.

The advocate for Rohan Joseph the accused, was Mr.Righteous. The bench comprising of Her Ladyship Mrs. Shetty, the Principal, Mrs. Rehanna and Miss Sandhya. A full bench.

Luckily in that Court Room even though Rohan was the accused he wasn't put in any witness box. He was seated at the right hand of his advocate.

"Mr. Joseph you know and I suppose are aware that a chit was found below the bench of your son and that your son has accepted that the chit belongs to him. We are contemplating taking action against him. What have you to say in the matter?" the Principal asked Mr.Righteous curtly.

"If you have to take action, you have to take action. But the chit was not found with my son. It was found on the floor. Yes my son has accepted the chit belongs to him. But whatever is written on the chit doesn't pertain to any question, of the question paper. So even if the chit was found with my son, in his possession by mistake for this exam, it cannot be called copying. Since technically he wasn't copying . . . . "Mr.Righteous went on, as if he was a trained orator, in the shoes of Mark Anthony.

There were some words which Mr.Righteous always used which hit the nail on the head one of them was technically, which in this case was the victory goal, a home run a winning stroke. There was pin drop silence after Mr.Righteous spoke. The only noise that could be heard was the overhead ceiling fan. All three judges were stunned for a minute. It was the Principal who spoke.

"In that case Mr. Joseph we have decided to make your son sit for a re-exam and write the paper again. Except it shall be another question paper. He shall have to come day after tomorrow at 1 o'clock and shall have to write the paper in front of Professor Rehanna in her office."

"Thank you madam," was the reply Mr.Righteous uttered without any hesitation or questioning. Mr.Righteous had already prepared himself to make the Principal do this. But he did not say any of it. It's like, hitting a jackpot, even without asking for it.

"You are going to write that paper day after tomorrow and you have to not only pass but you have to come out with flying colours. I don't know about any other paper. In this paper you have to come out with flying colours and if you take any chits with you I don't Know you," that was Mr.Righteous giving his client, his son, instructions, after coining an order in his favour.

What could any son or client say but, "Yes dad."

"Just remember for 3 hours, you will be in front of that mad woman and she will not allow you to go to the loo and even if she does, she will follow you to the loo and if you do some bullshit don't expect me to come to your college and rescue you again.........."

When a dad gets a chance to reprimand a grown up seventeen year old son, he definitely doesn't know when to stop. So all Rohan could do was sit in the car and while the driver drove, was shut up. Luckily Samun the driver did not understand English. Even though he tried to.

"And your mother and Radhika doesn't need to know about this. You know how humiliated you have made me. Having to bow down before that teacher of yours, Rehanna," ordered Mr.Righteous.

Mr.Righteous did not believe in calling teachers, professors. For him they were all teachers.

"She thinks no end of herself, you know what she told me outside the office. "Mr. Joseph your son needs to be rusticated from college, for what he has done. How have you brought your son up. It reflects on the teaching you have given him and on yourself. If I was you, I would have been ashamed to even come here. If Rohan could do something like this, I can imagine what you would have done." She was accusing me of copying. I wanted to slap her there itself. But because of you I had to shut up. Do you know how insulted I felt?" shot Mr.Righteous.

Rohan did not know what to do, sitting in the car. He knew professor Rehanna was a bitch. But he did not know she was like a hyena.

"I am telling you one thing, if you do any gadbad, if you do any nonsense, I will chappal you," Mr.Righteous said.

That was it. The whole night Rohan did not sleep. His mind kept spinning with how did the chit fall on the ground. What if it had not fallen. But there was no use in retrospective thinking. He had a paper to study for and he did not have any time. It felt like as if he was bitten by a hyena Miss Rehanna. All he did was a nap, for an hour in the morning.

ADHOCACY

At 12.30 he was in Mrs. Rehanna's office.

"So the good boy is here on time."

Rohan did not know where to jump. She just degraded him and his father yesterday and today she was calling him a good boy.

"I heard you are very popular with the girls?" she was blushing since secrets were out of the closet.

"Maam."

"Why cat got your tongue?"

"Maam."

Rohan was stumped. She had just bowled a googlee.

"What?"

"Maam," that was all Rohan could say. Like as if she was stripping him or something similar. Well frankly, it actually was in a way. It was as if Rohan had been stripped and there was nothing he could do. He had practically no sleep at all. All he wanted to do was give his paper and get out of that room. It was, as if his past had caught up with him. He thought, the past would remain passé. But no, he was sure Miss Rehanna was going to bring out the whole episode of the near rustication in school and correlate that Rohan is a habitual offender. If it were a court of law, conviction was sure on the basis of being a habitual offender. Rohan felt like going to the loo for what he didn't know. He knew he was not going to throw up, but felt so.

"What has happened to you today?" she asked Rohan.

"Maam," was all Rohan could say.

"You look sick, by me asking you whether you are popular with the girls."

"Maam I . . . . "

"Ok here drink some of my water."

"I am only asking you, because I am Sheena's aunty the girl from St. Johns at Afghan Church. She told me all about you and how you had done all her projects for her. She even told me she knew nothing about boys, but how attracted she was to you?"

"Maam but she is in USA today," Rohan could not even say US being scared of what might happen next.

"Yes son but her parents are in Mumbai for a brief period. You know her father was in the Navy?"

"Yes maam and Sheena had to go to Cochin and then I did not get to meet or keep in touch with her."

Suddenly the thought of Sheena and Professor Rehanna being related and Professor Rehanna, being Sheena's aunty put Rohan at ease.

"So I made you think of Sheena and you are already blushing Baacha. Sheena has such a great impact on you."

"Now I am called son, couldn't she have known yesterday. At least Mr.Righteous would have not got insulted. For all I know Professor Rehanna might have handled the whole thing."

In fact Rohan could see the apologetic state in her eyes.

"Anyway son, I am not bothered about these chits any longer but the situation now is that you have to write this paper. Here is the question paper and your answer sheet. I am not going to keep any time for you."

"Maam."

"You can call me aunty after all I am Sheena's aunty."

"Sheena was like my daughter, I know it was because of you that Sheena came out first in the 7th Standard because you taught her."

Which was true, Rohan could not pass, but he could teach Sheena to come out first. Rohan finished his paper and did not waste any more time. Professor Rehanna could not stay long and after he started writing, she had to go, maybe someone else was caught copying. The plight of someone else in Rohan's shoes made him feel like going to the loo.

"Why bother when you got Professor Rehanna in your lap, sorry aunty."

Rohan's fears were true since he wanted to thank Professor Rehanna but she was with the Principal doing exactly what she did to him yesterday. Except he was sure that whoever was caught did not have a girlfriend called Sheena in the 8th standard.

The Casanova

What has thou done? thou has mistaken quite
And laid the love juice on some true love's right
Of thy misprision must perforce ensue
Some true love turned and a false turned true

        OBE in Midsummer Nights Dream
                  A Shakespeare Play

The word Casanova is depicted with vulgarity. The simple meaning given for the word, 'a lover, who is promiscuous and an unscrupulous lover.' But only if one doesn't have human values, does it turn vulgar. Rohan was termed a Casanova, but had humane values.

It all started with coming to know girls as friends. Rohini was in the 8th standard. At the same time Supriti was in the 6th standard and at the same time Simran was in the 5th standard and Rohan in the 7th. All from Immaculate Conception Convent for girls. The Joseph's had only one telephone number then. The number had flashed as wild fire. Rohan would get calls from girls and they wouldn't tell him their names and land up chatting with him for hours.

'Tring,tring,' Radhika picks up the phone.

"Hello, hello, hello, hello, hello, hello, hello, hello, hello, hello, hello,"

Radhika could have said hello a hundred times and the caller was not going to answer.

"Rohan, it is blank a call you take the call next time, it is definitely your call," would be Radhika's request.

"Hi Rohan," the next time the phone rang this was how Rohan was greeted. Out of 100 calls he would know 3 of the callers.

"Who is this?"

"You don't know me, but I know you."

"How do you know me?"

"Everyone knows you, you are the only cutest guy who wears a denim jacket to school, with a heart on his sleeve, has a crew cut like Tom Cruise and walks like Johnny Nagareli," said the caller.

Rohan knew what she meant, 'heart on his sleeve.' He used to wear a denim jacket to school and wear a badge of a heart beat, not on his sleeve, but on his left top pocket.

"But I am Rohan not Tom Cruise or Johnny Nagareli."

"That is why you are so cute."

"Ok have I seen you?"

"Yes you have."

"Where ?"

"Where, I can't tell you."

"Ok! Which school do you go to?"

"Immaculate."

"So how did you get my number?"

"The bees gave it to the birds, in the trees and a tweetie bird gave it to me."

"Do I know the tweetie bird?"

"No."

"Then how did she, the tweetie bird get my number?"

The conversation went on for more than an hour.

Everyday the same ritual took place. The phone became a menace for Mr.Righteous, Mrs.Sonal Modi Joseph and Radhika. For Rohan it was a daily routine. There were days he would receive close to 100 blank calls, besides the calls spoken to. How the number was found by them was a puzzle, which didn't seem to get solved. Later revelations by some, was the MTNL directory and in the act of trying to find the right Rohan, they even dialled some wrong numbers, before getting the right one.

Mr.Righteous did not have a problem. For him he saw it was, his son starting a journey early. But Mrs.Sonal Modi Joseph always had a problem. Radhika had a problem too, she could not stand the fact that all these girls were calling Rohan. She believed a guy having girlfriends was bad and a girl going after a guy by calling him, was a sin. Here it wasn't one girl or a group of girls, but a number which is still to be found. Rohan just couldn't care about what Radhika or Mrs.Sonal Modi Joseph had to say. He wasn't stealing, he wasn't cheating, he wasn't swearing, all he was doing was interacting with the fairer sex and yes with their consent, with their offer. Which Rohan just had to accept.

The foundation was laid then itself.

ADHOCACY

Rohan always had a rule, that being, to go out of his way to help each and every girlfriend in whatever way possible. The number of girls Rohan has thought history to is a number Rohan doesn't want to count. In fact who ever he did teach history, hated the subject. They were mathematician's. While he had no idea about maths. They hated history and Rohan loved it.

They would say, "Rohan is more loving than history," since history was the excuse of gaining Rohan's love. What they meant by the first sentence was Greek fused with Urdu. The same wordings would be said by all those who Rohan taught history. This was the beginning of learning the psyche for Rohan, of not just how a woman thinks in given circumstances, when things remain constant or similar, but men too.

On one occasion Rohan finished a full journal for Deekshaa who lived at Churchgate. For another, who stayed at Cuffe Parade, he finshed a whole science project, Firozah.

The list goes on.

One fine evening Rohan was outside the Joseph's abode.

"Hello!"

"Hello!"

"Hi Rohan."

"This is not Rohan, this is Rohan's father, Rohan is not in, you can call later."

Mr.Righteous's and Rohan's voice was so similar that there was practically an impossibility for one to detect one from another. People would call and start with, "Seby......................."They would say the first sentence and Rohan would have to say uncle, aunty or whoever was speaking, if he recognized their voice and tell them that he was Rohan and that he would give the phone to Mr.Righteous.

Today was the opposite.

"Uncle uncle, actually I want to speak to you only," the caller said.

I wonder what Mr.Righteous might have thought then, as if he was being flirted with.

"You know uncle? I love your son Rohan?"

"Ok!"

"And I want to marry Rohan."

"Ok!

"I really really really love Rohan."

"Girl how old are you?'

"12yrs"

"And you want to marry Rohan?"

"Yes I want to marry Rohan."

"Which class are you in?"

"6th"

"And you want to marry Rohan?"

"Yes uncle, I want to marry Rohan."

"Do you know child marriages are banned?"

This was Mr.Righteous at his best, who knew to play his cards even with a twelve year old. An ace for an ace.

"Yes uncle, but I love him so much that child or no child, I still want to marry him."

"Ok!"

"And I want to have his children."

"Even though child marriages are banned ?"

"Yes uncle!"

ADHOCACY

"Go ahead girl, Rohan is all yours, he will be available in an hour, call him then and marry him on the phone, ok little girl, bye."

What was Rohan to do, broadcast on Facebook or Twitter or on a blog site that Mr.Righteous's and his voice were similar,

"When you girls want to call, even though I don't know who you are, note my dad's voice and mine are similar."

There was no internet, forget Facebook and Twitter. The only Twitting Rohan knew was his number given by some bee, which gave it to the birds in the trees, who gave it to the Tweetie bird who went about Twitting his number.

There was anything to be expected.

"The depiction of the scene is very important. It is here in this scene that Titania has had a love juice and enters the stage. The love juice is a love portion, which Titania has drank and stands in a stand to be vulnerable to fall in love, with the next man that comes in front of her. Just then a clown enters the scene and there is an instant reaction from Titania, pledging her love for the clown and begging him not to leave," said Professor Joe Sheth Rohan's English teacher, trying to explain to the students a particular scene of the play Midsummer Nights Dream. Which is a comedy. One of the many plays written by Shakespeare, though in an abridged version, being the 8th standard. Abridged or not, plays written by Shakespeare is like climbing a mountain, whichever side you try to climb, it is still a mountain to climb.

There was a simple depiction, which Sir Joe Sheth was trying to get across to the class about the scene.

"Have you got the atmosphere of the scene?"

The whole class was numb and Sir Sheth was finding it difficult to explain the scene.

"Usually it is a boy who proposes to a girl. But here it is a girl, proposing to a boy undying love. It is the opposite. Are you now able to grasp the atmosphere of the scene?" asked Professor Joe Sheth to the class, except then his prefix was sir.

This was Sir Sheth trying to explain the scene again. But the class was still numb and looked at Sir Sheth blankly. Which made him frustrated.

It was then that he said, "If you don't understand the scene that it is a boy who proposes to a girl and here it is a girl pledging undying love to a boy and if you don't understand ask Rohan and he will tell you that it is a boy who proposes to a girl and here it is a girl pledging undying love to a boy."

All eyes were on Rohan. This was an acknowledgement of the noted English teacher Sir Joe Sheth of a Casanova status of Rohan.

A realisation of the term Casanova took place that it is not what you term yourself. But what you are termed by others. Rohan just went on to protect his status. Since he had a reputation to protect that of being a Casanova. The number rose to forty two at one point of time and each not knowing anything about the other. Something he would never attempt today. Since everything is open with the internet.

What would his status on Facebook be, its very complicated, multiplied by the word complicated, by forty two times. Rohan must be surely outdated.

There was not just one occasion, when Rohan was friendly with two girls both twins and both sleeping in the same bed.

ADHOCACY

On one occasion, it was where there was, two twins a neighbour and a cousin of the twins who he was friendly with. After all Sir Joe Sheth had acknowledged the status that of being a Casanova and Rohan had a reputation to protect.

Government Law College

A tour of GLC would make the tour start with an entrance of the building on the ground floor, on either side you will be engulfed by the sweet smell of the greatest fertilizer, catalysts ever made or being and will be made, varsati. At least that was how Rohan saw it when he entered GLC for the first time. From here some of the greatest advocates sprung and so did Rohan's mentor Sir Nani A. Palkivala.

"Which year are you in?" a question Rohan was asked by someone, who was going to be his senior, George A. Rebello, Advocate High Court.

"Final," was Rohan's reply. Rohan was in his final year, majoring in Political Science.

"What are you planning to do, after you graduate?" was his next question.

"I want to do law," what people say in conversations can be really hilarious when it's put on paper. But in conversations it doesn't. Rohan had always wanted to do two things, either journalism or law. Journalism had already taken a backseat.

"Then you join me. After graduating, join Government Law College and come and see me. This is my card," was George's reply.

This is how Rohan got an invitation to join the chambers of George A. Rebello Advocate High Court, someone he has always adored before his stint as a junior and loved and will and still.

Rohan had always heard of juniors scouting, to get a senior. Here he had a senior, even before joining Government Law College. When opportunity knocks, the words knock knock, who is there, is not how opportunity knocks. Every time opportunity knocks the sound is different and so the knock is unique. Unfortunately it is always perceived that opportunity always knocks the same way every time and many miss the opportunity.

The final year of college, did not have any untoward, notorious scenes. In fact Rohan abandoned the idea of using any inventions and passed the exam in six papers of Political Science, keeping law in mind. Even though most aspiring advocates, take literature as a major.

But there were other things, which were planned by the planner. Rohan was supposed to be only the executor of the plan, the will.

Rohan had decided he was not going to be the last bencher, as he was in school. Rohan was, is and will always be, very serious about the profession of law.

"The profession of law teaches you when to speak and when not to, when to act and when not to," was what Aspi Chinoy Senior Advocate who Rohan reveres, told him in Court Room No.36 after the Honourable Mr. Justice S.N.Variava had just arisen at 2 o'clock, one fine afternoon.

The profession of law actually does.

With the first lecture starting at 6.45 am. It was an impossibility for many students to actually attend the first lecture and invariably the class would be empty. But Rohan was always there on the first bench, taking down notes. Which were practically, verbatim of what the professor said. In a class of 150 students only an average of 5 to 25 attending the first lecture, was miserable. It was even worst than the turn out for elections at least taking into consideration the turn out of Rohan's Colaba constituency. The other students were zapped and he was called amazing. What a change from school, where the corridors Rohan always remembers as his best buddies.

The professor Ashok Kotangle taught Law of Torts. The meaning of tort a civil wrong, was the lesson to be learnt in that stream. Rohan always had a habit of going the extra mile.

"You don't have to explain, I know the meaning," is the reply Rohan would receive for going the extra mile.

But Rohan once asked an advocate Mr. Wanekar from a town called Mangoan in Maharashtra.

"What is the meaning of a tort?"

"Tart tart, yeh tart kya hai?" was his answer.

Ashok Kotangle put up a proposal to the students that who would want to give a lecture on the next chapter and the chapter can be chosen by the student. Another professor Mrs. Chugani teaching Contract Law put up the same proposal. The professor teaching Constitutional Law professor Mathew didn't nor did the professor teaching Mohamedan Law or Criminal law being Indian Penal code.

Rohan had opted for the Law of Torts and Contract law. Rohan had never landed being a professor. Though he had already taught and Sheena landed up, topping the charts. Rohan had done many things before time, but this seemed exciting to him and scarry. Moving up from the last bencher to the teacher, the professor, the lecturer, gave Rohan shivers down his spine.

The topic which Rohan took was section 27 of the Indian contract Act 1872 'Restraint of Trade.'

The chapter, "Agreement in restraint of trade void," section 27, it never occurred, the importance of this section would play in his life and that of every advocate, anyone who has and will have an L.L.B degree and every citizen of India.

The section seems a straight one but the exception to it, is what explains a term reasonable restriction.

"Every agreement by which anyone is restrained from exercising a lawful profession, trade or business of any kind, is to that extent void," is what the section says.

"One who sells the goodwill of a business, may agree with the buyers to refrain from carrying on a similar business, within a specified local limit, so long as the buyer, or any other person deriving title to the goodwill from him, carries on a like business therein. Provided that such limits appear to the Court as reasonable, regard being had to the nature of business," is what is, the explanation to the section.

Section 27 turned out to be an important section in Rohan's life and others. He was the first of the other three students, who decided to give lectures. Since Rohan was the first, the turnout of the students was a near full house with 149 students attending, out of a class of 150. Rohan had never seen such a good turn out, even when the professors, who the students liked was teaching. Rohan was like the piped piper who pulled the students.

Usually there is always a fear, when one goes up on a platform to speak. But having already done a public speaking course, stage fright was not a friend of his, unless he did not have any post cards ready.

Rohan standing up in front of 149 students began his lecture, with reading the section 27 and carried on.

"It is difficult to imagine that when the goodwill and trend of a retail shop were sold, the vendor might the next day set up a shop within a few doors and draw off all customers. Therefore some restriction is the only means by which a saleable value is given to the goodwill of the business. Far from being adverse to public interest, the restriction, by giving a real marketable value to the goodwill of a business, operates as an additional inducement to individuals to employ their skills and capital in trade and this tend to the advantage of public interest," is what Rohan read from his points and explained.

The class was in awe and he went on.

"The meaning of goodwill is that there should be real goodwill to be sold. Goodwill being an abstract property, is not easy to define. The goodwill which has been the subject of sale is nothing more than the probability that the old customers will resort to an old place. Often it happens that goodwill is the very sap and life of the business, without which the business would yield little or no profits. It is the whole advantage, whatever it may be, of the reputation and connection of the firm, the business, which may have been built up by years of honest work or gained by lavish expenditure of money," Rohan explained the meaning of goodwill and carried on further.

"The agreement has to specify the local limits of the restraint. The seller can be restrained within certain territorial or geographical limits and the limits must be reasonable. Reasonableness of restrictions will depend upon many factors, for example, the area in which goodwill is effectively enjoyed and the price paid for it," Rohan explained the limits of restraint and carried on.

"There are four provisions in the Partnership Act which validate agreements in restraint of trade. Section II enables partners during the continuance of the firm, to restrict their mutual liberty, by agreeing that none of them shall carry on any business, other than that of the firm. Section 36 enables them to restrain an outgoing partner, from carrying on a similar business, within a specified period or within specified local limits. Such restrictions shall be void, if the restrictions imposed are unreasonable. A similar agreement may be made by partners upon or in anticipation or dissolution by which they may restrain each other from carrying on a business similar to that firm," Rohan explained the Partnership Act as far as restraint of trade is concerned.

Giving the lecture was like getting a high for Rohan. A try is always made everyday, for people to do, the act of listening. Here Rohan had 149 students exactly his age, listening to him with open ears. He knew ears don't close, but here, it felt that their ears were actually popping out of their sockets to pick what

Rohan was saying as mikes. For the first time Rohan did not find any of his own fellow students chit chatting.

"An agreement between two companies that one would not employ the former employees of the other has been held to be void by generality."

"Where a manufacturer or supplier, after meeting all the requirements of a buyer, has surplus to sell to others, he cannot be restrained from doing so. The buyers cannot restrain the seller, from dealing with others unless he can acquire the whole stock during the period of the agreement."

"A seller of combs entered into an agreement, with all the manufacturers of combs in the city of Patna whereby the latter undertook during their lifetime to sell all their products to R. S. and to his heirs and not to sell the same to any one else. The agreement was held as void by the Court under section 27 and said that it bound the manufacturers from generation to generation, it was unrestricted both as to time and place, it was oppressive, it was intended to create a monopoly."

"The House of lords has held that twenty one years of exclusive dealing would be a long period to restrain. The doctrine does not apply to ordinary commercial contracts for the regulation and promotion of trade during the existence of the contract. Provided that any prevention of work, outside the contract is viewed as a whole, is directed towards absorption of the party's services and not sterilization. Sole agencies are a normal and necessary incident of commerce, and those who desire the benefit of a sole agency, must deprive themselves the opportunities of other agencies."

"Where a contract is reasonable and fair at the beginning, but circumstances have arisen, which show that it is being enforced by one party in a manner which is prejudiced to the interest of the other, the Courts will hold the agreement to be unenforceable though not void or invalid."

"A stipulation in a contract, which is intended for advancement of trade, shall not be regarded as being in restraint of trade. There is a growing trend to regulate distribution of goods and services, through franchisee agreements, providing for grant of franchisee by the franchiser, on certain terms and conditions to the franchisee. Such agreements often incorporate a condition that the franchisee shall not deal with competing goods. Such a condition restricting the right of the franchisee to deal with competing goods is for facilitating the distribution of the goods of the franchisee and it cannot be regarded as in restraint of trade."

This was Rohan's lecture in a nutshell. The lecture was to become the lecture of his life. Except, Rohan in consonance of the happenings would change the wording of the section, instead of trade in the whole lecture, "Agreements in restraint of profession, void."

Shalini Sen

It was a Saturday, one when the High Court was closed. It was not that advocates and court clerks do not come to the High Court on Saturdays, when courts are closed. But today the place was exceptionally deserted. Rohan had to come to the High Court to get a certified true copy of an order recently passed in Court Room No 3 in its Admiralty Jurisdiction being taken up by the Honourable Mr. Justice M. S. Ratnade, which was with Shankar, one of the many peons, who would go out of his way to get things done, albeit for remuneration. A year had actually passed as an assistant. The High Court had become so familiar, that it was like a second home to Rohan. One lands up discovering things he likes at his own home, in nooks and corners.

"Hi Rohan!"

Rohan had just come from the testamentary department, though closed being a holiday and was at the gate, when Shalini did the bump into him.

"Hi Shalini! What you doing here? You look beautiful as ever in this white kurti and whatever you wearing below," said Rohan.

Rohan had to reply to Shalini with what came to him naturally. The saying, once a thief always a thief. That hat fit Rohan well. Except not where the thief part is concerned, but the charm doing. She was wearing something which wasn't a salwar nor a pant. Rohan didn't know what to call it.

"What do you mean? What I am wearing below? What are you insinuating advocate Rohan? Anyway I am not bothered about your insinuations. I love when you say I look beautiful as ever. Do you really mean I look beautiful?" asked Shalini exasperated at what Rohan said first, but making a change of gear immediately in consonance.

Shailini had to probe, like most girls. Girls don't gossip, they probe. From probing, you get the outcome called gossip. It was difficult for Shalini to believe when a guy like Rohan, an aspirant to be an advocate, saying she is beautiful. When Rohan did Shalini would probe with questions.

"How beautiful? Do you really mean it?"

The most gorgeous, the most beautiful and we all know, beauty is a perception created in the mind of an individual, through ideas and conflicting ideas between the conscious and the subconscious, will always probe whether they are really beautiful. Why because the concept of beauty will always be different. Since the analysis process between the conscious and the subconscious never stops.

"Yes I really mean you look beautiful and whatever you wearing below is your salwar. Except it doesn't look like a salwar nor a cullotte nor a pant, counsel Shalini," was Rohan's diplomatic reply.

Shalini worked for Sen & Sen & Co. A law firm dating back to 1873 and was basically a solicitor firm. Which brought the calling of counsel of Shalini and since Rohan was attached to an advocate firm, Shalini called Rohan advocate.

The Sen family obviously hailed from Kolkata. Mr. Sonen Sen Shalini's father being a senior advocate at Supreme Court obviously had to be settled in Delhi.

"Oh, so I only wear a salwar below," said Shalini. She was a wizard with words, a word player. Though Rohan had innocently said, "Whatever you wearing below," she had the word playing power.

"At least that is what I can see," said Rohan.

'Since she did have the word playing power, why not win at her own game,' thought Rohan.

"Rohan?"

"Yes thy ladyship Miss. Justice Shalini Sen."

Shalini was studying with Rohan at Govenrment Law College. She was from Delhi, since her folks were settled in Delhi. But was in Mumbai because of Government Law College. She didn't have to come to Mumbai to study law. But Mr. Sen better known as Hitler, had ordered that she do, since he did too. Like father, like daughter was his motto. To Rohan it was a good motto. Had he not had this motto, Shalini and Rohan wouldn't have met.

Sen & Sen & Co was owned by Mr. Sonen Sen even though he had partners who were practically sleeping.

"Please I do not want to be Miss Justice Shalini Sen."

"Why, because your pop and you will wear the same flaps. Ethically and under conflict of interest, you cannot hear cases if you were Miss Justice Shalini Sen and Mr. Sen Senior Advocate Supreme Court appearing for defendant or Plaintiff."

"No Rohan. How can I be Miss Justice Shalini Sen? How about making me Mrs. Justice Shalini Sen Joseph?" Shalini asked and put Rohan in a dilemma since it's always been the guys proposing to a girl. But here it was Shalini. This wasn't the first occurrence, number of times Rohan has never kept count of.

So why was Rohan in a dilemma?

Why because that is how life is, just like eating a Karvanda outside school and every time he did, it gave Rohan shivers.

Shalini had these beautiful eyes, you could look into and drown and in the state of drowning, dream as if you were in wonderland. Except Rohan would call it brownie land, the land receiving its name from the colour of the owner's eyes. Whenever Rohan looked into them, Rohan felt as if he was looking in a Kaliedosccope.

Kaliedoscopes are fun, but when looking into Shalini's eyes, the picture was never the same. It made him want to look in her eyes again and again and again. An addiction of a video game would give the same feeling. Except here it wasn't a video Game, but Shalini.

She had long hair, brown in colour, with flicks at the side. The flicks made her look, as if she was just out of school. The beauty of any girl is having the looks of, as if just out of school and a figure of a sex bomb. To Rohan, that was exactly how Shalini looked.

"Shalini?" Rohan said her name above normal decibel levels that they were using.

This was their standard procedure adopted, of using her name at a tone higher than normal by Rohan, when Shalini said something obnoxious and the same by Shalini, when Rohan said something obnoxious.

"Ok lets take a walk of the corridors," said Shalini, trying to persuade Rohan not to go back to office straight away and changing the topic. Girls always get a high, if they make the guys do something, which the guy did not want to do, but land up doing.

Why do, girls like to take walks has always been a mystery to Rohan? He never learnt the art of walking. Being an interschool footballer, walking was never allowed. He had to jog at football practice. If anyone was caught walking at the drill, he was sure to be twelfth or thirteenth man. A ninety minute game, where a ball goes from one end to another, in some hundreds of times, how can a player walk and chase the ball, was the explanations of the coach. Every time he gave his explanation, all of Rohan's team mates would burst into internal laughter and would smile at the goalee.

"How can the goalee go chasing the ball?" was what made all Rohan's team mates burst into internal laughter, being the standard joke.

Walks were not meant for footballers like Rohan.

"They slow me down," is what Rohan's idea of walks was.

"I take walks off these corridors every day. You have a court clerk in your office who calls you madam. I do all the work of those court clerks."

"Yes advocate Rohan I know. Lets at least have coffee. Nescafe from the machine on the third floor tastes better than the coffee on the ground floor."

The Nescafe vending machine on the third floor was always a better decision for coffee, than having to wait for the coffee to be made and brought.

"I am not a coffee freak like you, I love my chai," Rohan said trying to dissuade Shalini.

"Ok you have your chai, but let's go to the third floor."
"I have to go back to office."
"Today is Sat-ur-day. Which means to sit and relax."
"That is Sunday."
"Sunday is to be in the Sun and relax."

Shalini was definitely going to get her way. She was good at it and if she was, then why prolong the getting of it. Though it made her feel important.

"Ok lets have your coffee."

"What?" asked Shalini loud enough, to make it feel like a bark. It didn't make any difference, even though what was said loud enough for others to hear, with others who were around at the bottom of the spiral staircase at the original side.

Rohan knew what Shalini's reply would be. They were good at their innuendos. After all the legal profession, was all about reading between the lines. What is said is important. What is not said but implied, is as important, as what is said.

"I mean you have your coffee and I will have my chai."

A fact apparent and known to both of them that Shalini being a coffee freak and Rohan a chai freak, were worlds apart. They had nothing in common, except that they were studying to be enrolled to the Bar.

"Those couples with one a freak of coffee and the other a freak of tea, they will always be worlds apart from each other, in characters," something Rohan read in the book Psychoanalysis through Sun Signs.

But opposites attract, minus and minus and plus and plus just lie at the side of each other.

They were walking up the spiral steps when Shalini pulls his left hand and said, "You know what, I would love to be Mrs. Shalini Sen Joseph and have you appearing in Court before me and I did rip you apart instead of you pleading a Notice of Motion. I will make you have motions."

Where did that come from, Rohan had no idea. But he couldn't be a lame duck and not reply. Silence amounts to acquiescence.

"You think you have such an ability?" Rohan retorted.

"All I have to do advocate Rohan, is look into your eyes and I know you will melt."

"I won't look at you."

"Counsel you are insulting the bench, you are looking elsewhere and not at the bench."

"My apologies thy ladyship, I am only focusing on the case, since I have benchophobia."

Rohan didn't have to explain the meaning of benchophobia to Shalini, she already knew it was bench fright. A term they would use for all judges, who made the biggest counsels shudder.

"Counsel you will not insult the Court by looking elsewhere, but at the bench."

"Shalini . . . . !"

"How dare you address the bench, with her first name."

"You are debarred from appearing in any Court of law for 5 years, due to contempt of Court in the territory of India under The Contempt of Courts Act 1971."

"Shalini Shut up," Rohan said in a standard tone appropriated for the words.

"See I got you motioning me, ain't I good?" said Shalini.

Yes she was good and she knew how to motion Rohan.

"Yes thy ladyship."

"No say, thy ladyship Mrs. Justice Shalini Sen Joseph."

"No thy ladyship Mrs. Shalini Sen Joseph and yes thy ladyship Miss Shalini Sen."

They were on the third floor balcony area of the High Court. The view of Mumbai from there is spectacular. In front the lush green gound the Oval and beyond.

"What a view this place has, na?" observed Shalini.

"You wanna see this view in a 70mm screen?"

"Yes yes . . . !" Rohan knew Shalini would say yes. But she began jumping.

"Why are you jumping, this is the High Court not a cinema hall."

"Shut up and show the 70mm screen, remember I am Mrs. Justice Shalini Sen Joseph."

"Yes thy ladyship let me finish the tea."

Just then Shalini said one of the most standard lines couples ever said to each other, at least then.

"Advocate Rohan coffee tea or me?"

"You Shalini," was Rohan's reply. He didn't feel like saying thy ladyship. He wanted to show his reply as personal, not legally personal. Besides what other reply could he have given. But he didn't know, what was in store for him. Had he, his reply might have been different.

Shalini at that very moment took Rohan's plastic tea cup, which had half a cup of tea remaining in it and threw it down at the side, on the floor. No one was there, since it was a Saturday. But never the less, tea and coffee cups are not thrown down on the floor, but in the waste bin. Rohan was burning with anger.

"Fuck Shalini what are you doing?" Rohan blurted and wondering what else she had up her sleeve.

"I have got Counsel for Tea agitated."

"What?"

"Counsel the issue of estoppel shall lie against you and under section 115 of the Indian Evidence Act you are estopped from making a different statement and advocating for tea, when you have categorically stated when asked coffee tea or me, you stated me, so no tea for you counsel."

It was the tea which was thrown down by Shalini, which got Rohan agitated. But Shalini was good. Rohan was check mated.

The High Court building has a spiral staircase to the top, the terrace from the third floor. The view from the terrace is awesome.

"Rohan where are we going and why are we climbing this spiral staircase? I have always seen this staircase locked."

"Why you scared of coming with me?"

"No I will go anywhere with you."

"Even to no mans land?"

"Yes!"

"Yes!"

"Then shut up and follow me and remember you are not suppose to come here and you will always find this gate locked."

"Then how did you get the key and why have you locked the gate again."

"One you ask too many questions, two like you can't pass through the judges corridors, three you can't pass through that gate we have just passed. Four if you want to know why I have locked the gate, I have already answered it with point number two, but thy ladyship always wants an explanation, so I shall give you one. No one is suppose to pass through that gate unless authorised to do so. You and me are not authorized to do so. Therefore thy ladyship, the door should be locked, so that no one gets suspicious and comes and finds out we are here," was Rohan's explanation going the extra mile for Shalini.

They had already reached the top, at the end of Rohan's explanation and the moment Shalini saw the view, She ran from one steeple to another.

"Yes sire," was Shalini's beckoning.

"What?"

"This is a 70 mm screen. Standing here it feels like I am a queen and you are my sire, my king."

"From advocate I am now your sire. How cool, you change as and when you please."

"Shut up Rohan and give me a hug," said Shalini.

For Rohan it was dreamy to be holding Shalini in his arms. She felt so warm and made Rohan feel wanted. Rohan would apologize to that statement, why because Rohan felt like a king, in his queens arms. There was definitely a clause in the act of God making women. The clause of giving a man warmth in holding her.

"Talk to me Rohan."

Rohan :Thee is thy most beautiful soul and me a simple fragment.

Shalini: No sire. Thou art my sire and I your fragrance, thy shadow and I shall follow sire, as a flower follows the rays of the gleaming sun.

Rohan: Thee is my flower, but I shall carry you around with me.

Shalini : Why what you will?

Rohan: I will discharge you to the ends of the earth, here and now. And if thee be my fragrance then let not the hand of the chime, loose its breath in striking the hour and thy fragrance lay lost. You have aggravated me and I will roar thee as gently as any sucking dove. I will roar thee, ain't were any nightingale.

Shalini : Come then sire, let us not scurry the clock which belows us at our side. Let your roar be demanding as the light of dawn on me. Let your arms hold me soaking our villagery and alongwith the pour of our gods and fill our souls and the villagery and me be dicharged with you. I no longer want to be captive, waiting for your roar. Let the bondages of my cloths meet distance.

Rohan: Here my fairy queen. I have opened the gates. It is honour. For thy meadows are moistened with dew drops. Is it the work of the Gods or it is the work of the elves.

Shalini: The work of my sire, it is not the elves. My sire doth keep his revels in me, for you are the head of the villagery and the head of my villagery too.

Rohan: Are you that shrewed and knaivish sprite. Have I mistaken you shape and making sprite and misled this afternoon wanderer and laugh at my baam.

Shalini: Sire you are my sire and the villagery is our kingdom. Make me filled with your drink. My cup with your life, to bear the fruit of luck to all the villagery.

Rohan: Thee shall speakest no more.

Shalini: Why what you will?

ADHOCACY

Rohan: For here comes the pour. The pour of my drink my fairy queen.

"What a scintillating performance that was Rohan" said Shalini.

"Was it? I would never be able to act a Shakespearan character without you Shalini, you bring out the best in me," was Rohan's reply whether in sincerity or flattery, even Rohan would not be able to answer.

Having learnt Shakespeare plays at school Shalini and Rohan decided to act a scene of Artemis and Cecilia in the rain in the balcony of their castle, with verbal jugulary, was a scene Rohan will never forget.

Shalini and Rohan never landed up being together, for the rest of their lives. He had failed the first year L.L.B. exam and next Mr.Righteous got sick. Shalini went back to Delhi and Mr. Sen didn't allow her to have anything to do with Rohan.

A plot was played by Mr. Sen. He got a girl to say she was Rohan's girlfriend, Sundari. He knew Sundari and she was a friend of Rohan's, on an acquaintance level. But he never knew she had feelings for him. How Mr. Sen got in touch with Sundari, ploughed the plot into her, has not come to light till today.

Shalini broke down but accepted the corroborated evidence given by Sundari, brilliantly worked out by Mr. Sen. Rohan tried contacting Shalini but of no avail. Went to Delhi and tried to meet Shalini. Mr. Sen came to know of his standing outside his Bungalow near Akbara Road waiting for some sign of either Shalini coming out of the Bungalow or looking out of the window. Weird thoughts went through Rohan's mind. Standing outside her Bungalow. A scene from the movie Betaab crossed his mind and he began to hear the tune of, "Parbotoh seh aaj mein takara gaya, tumne di awaz, loh mein aa gaya."

Unfortunately the, 'loh mein aah gaya,' was the cops who came to pick Rohan up and pick Rohan they did. He had to catch the next flight back to Mumbai, if not he might see some act of MOCCA put on him not that the cops said they would.

"But isn't there enough sections of the Indian Penal Code to charge me with?" is what Rohan knew.

Shailini is married today. Not a senior advocate, nor is she Mrs. Justice Shalini Sen Whatever. But a housewife in the U.K. with a beautiful baby boy. Who seems to be growing up to have choclaty looks.

Life goes on.

George A Rebello Advocate High Court

&

The High Court of Judicature at Bombay.

Rohan's first day at his Senior's office at Nariman Point, Rohan had put the best tie he could, to stay as part of a respected advocate's office. Not that he had a huge hangar full of ties. Though later, as the remuneration came in, he did and came to be known at the High Court for wearing ties with tweeties and genies when everyone else, wore sombre ones. Rohan thought, it would be great for tweetie and genie to see the High Court and its proceedings once in a while and they to bring some colour through his ties.

Rohan had just rushed from GLC to Nariman Point and greeted George good morning. He didn't take the liberty of calling his senior George, George gave. Rohan loved his senior's sense of dressing, never did his white shirts, ever have a crinkle, nor did his Geneva bands. In Court the colour is black and white, but at office, George's suits gave one working at his office a sense of regality.

"George had white strands of hair and the look was that of Richard Gere. Everytime I would look at him, it felt like, I was in a real life film, being enacted and I was one of the actors being assistant of Richard Gere, George A. Rebello. The name of the film my life," is what Rohan would say.

"Go with Rubin," was George's first order. Rubin was George's first assistant when George began his solo practice. Having been given the order Rohan just followed Rubin.

They landed at the High Court of Judicature at Bombay, fighting for a taxicab outside Mantralay's corner, with other fighters. The High Court then and the High Court today is the same, except at the entrance is found the army charade. Entry is governed by the modus operandi of initialization of taking a flight, being The High Court of Judicature at Bombay, flight number being, the date of the day multiplied by the times arrived and departed. The chai stall at the entrance stands vacated. The last time Rohan saw such a scenario, was the USIS building at Marine Lines and Miami at Breach Candy. No other building had the charade but the USIS building and Miami. It seemed, only the USIS building was at war with Miami. Today even the High Court of Judicature at Bombay is. Rubin was and is and if my good foresight doesn't forsake me, shall be of the high built types. Obviously he had already had his go at The Mr.Maharashtra, being part of the gossip. Some gossip you never question, why if reality gives you some resemblance to it, you accept it. So Rohan wouldn't put it as gossip, since Rubin was the high built man, who he often called George's bodyguard.

ADHOCACY

We had entered the High Court, without the flight initialization.

"You want to see how the Court functions?" Rubin posed the most interesting question of the time.

Obviously Rohan's answer was going to be, "Yes."

Rubin just pushed the doctors examining doors of Court Room No. 6 and Rohan followed him. The first thing which stunned Rohan was, no space between the podium of the judge and the table on which the lectern was, from where the advocate who was advocating from, was speaking. It was then, that Rohan realized court rooms are not like what the Hindi movie depicts a huge area from the lectern, from where the advocate addresses the Court from, the podium from where the judges sit. There is no jalwa, as was depicted by Anil Kapoor in 'Meri Jung.'

"Rubin, why is the advocate who is speaking wearing a different cloak from the other advocates," something Rohan thought was prudent to ask after taking the ceremonial bow. The ceremonial bow seems to be forgotten by many or never taught to them. Visits to various Magistrate Courts, it was found by Rohan that advocates do not do the bow and with Rohan always adhering, every one else would look at him, as if Rohan was an alien. If its so difficult to do the bow, India should make the Namaste action mandatory. But just as the names of the High Court of Calcutta and Madras cannot be changed unless done by due process of law. The bringing about of Namaste, doesn't seem to be one which may happen. But it is imperative that an advocate does greet the lord of the conscious the judge. Just as everyone does greet the gods of the subconscious at the Mandir, the Gurudwara, the Mosque, the Fire Temple, the Synagogue, the Church.

"He is not wearing a cloak, it is a gown and he is not speaking, he is addressing the Court, you idiot," was a verbal slap Rohan received from Rubin. Rohan had no idea that speaking was known as, 'addressing the Court.' *'But attendance of the first day at office, one has to be ready for receipt of a few verbal slaps, which is acceptable, since sticks and kicks and stones shall break my bones but words will never hurt,'* is what Rohan said to himself. A lesson he had to learn the hard way.

"And you know who he is. He is Fali Nariman Senior Advocate Supreme Court, from Delhi. Which ever the case he is arguing, his clients would have flown him down from Delhi for this case. See his gown, it is the same as that of the judge," Rubin went on.

How was Rohan to see the gown of the judge? All he could see was the judge's face with his black gown on his shoulders. He wanted to see the back of the judge and compare the gown with that of Senior Advocate Fali S. Nariman, since that is what Rubin expected Rohan to do. It seemed as if Rubin expected Rohan to have more than X-ray eyes, but to have the power and an ability to put a mirror behind the Honourable Mr. Justice S.H.Kapadia, who was the presiding judge at that particular time of that particular case on the 28th day of August 1996. It would have been a calling of death, for such an act to have been carried out in the Honourable Mr. Justice S.H.Kapadia's Court. Oh! In any Judge or Magistrate's Court. It just took Rohan, passage of days to crack the riddle instead of putting a mirror.

ADHOCACY

Rohan's next court outing of the day was to the City Civil Court, which housed the NDPS Court, being following Vernon Da Gama Advocate High Court and at that time was a Government Pleader. The word pleader sounded so begging, it simply meant advocate for the government. But it was a term given a century past. If we go five centuries earlier, from today and was to say the word naughty, it would have the effect of being called by another an illegitimate child.

Vernon as Rohan was allowed to call him, had briefed Rohan in short about the case.

Rohan tried guessing the meaning of NDPS.

His guess was, "National Defence Protection Sessions Court."

"Ha Ha Ha," was Vernon's laughter. Rohan had only heard that laughter at kiddies Christmas Tree parties. Vernon anyway looked like Santa Claus, except his gown was black, instead of red and his laughter did not have the ho, ho, ho though.

"I don't know the meaning of NDPS," was Rohan's answer.

"It is Narcotics, Disruptive and Psychotropic Substances Court," was his answer and in a lakh guesses of Rohan that would never have been the outcome.

Rohan just followed him to the 28th Court as it was known. They entered and since Vernon bowed, Rohan did too. Their case was not yet called and so Rohan sat at the back, on the benches. On the left of the judge, was where the witness box was. Arguments were going on of a particular case and since the Court was the NDPS Court, Rohan presumed it would be a case concerning narcotics, well easier to understand in colloquial terms, hash or grass. The advocate for the accused, was pleading with the judge for mercy. In the witness box was a dark skinned African, outside the witness box was his wife. The judge then went on to pronounce his verdict.

"By the powers given to me, you are hereby sentenced to twenty years imprisonment for possession of Narcotic and Contraband substances under the NDPS Act," was the order, the Magistrate had just delivered in open Court.

The dark skinned African said nothing, his wife pleaded that the accused and she had children and to please have mercy.

It was then that the dark skinned African disappeared in a jiffy.

Everyone in the Court began to wonder where he could have gone.

There was pin drop silence.

Thoughts of the dark skinned African, being a friend of Captain Kirk or Spock went through as a wave in everyones nerve endings, in their heads, except Rohan.

The suspense was killing.

Till the constable brought water and began to splash it on the dark skinned African who had just collapsed and fainted. Who wouldn't, twenty years is an odyesey. Those present in Court began to come to their senses. The dark skinned African was literally dragged out from the witness box and the Court room.

Rohan didn't expect his first day in Court to witness the dark skinned African disappearing, only to be found at the bottom of the witness box after fainting. This was more than a Bollywood flick. Their case was called out after the episode. They were appearing for the vessel M.V. IBN Khallikan, a vessel owned by United Arab Shipping Company better known as UASC.

ADHOCACY

Though Rohan was't in actuality, but assisting Vernon. Narcotics better known as drugs, was caught on the vessel and the vessel was anchored at the Mumbai Port anchorage and the ship was arrested. For Rohan, the word arrested, he thought only applied to people. Arguments were put forth by Vernon that the narcotics found on the vessel had nothing to do with regards to the plying of the vessel and the captain and the crew, were ignorant of the fact that there were narcotics on the vessel. In such cases, a judge can be lenient or tough. But for everyday a vessel lies arrested, the owners or charterers loose an amount of ten thousand dollars in costs and demurrage charges. A presumption, that inflation does exist.

M.V.IBN Khallikan was now arrested for two months. The judge after hearing Vernon's arguments, accepted to give a release order, on furnishing a bank guarantee of 84 crores, which was anyway put forward, as the offering for release of the vessel.

Rohan left to go back to Nariman Point at 4.40 p.m. that day. He was under the impression that the day was coming to an end. Only to find, that he was summoned to George's cabin and advocate the case of M.V.IBN Khallikan. Rohan was zapped for a moment. But he is a note take outer, which is nearly in verbatim, which normally one would do, if they knew short hand. Rohan was a long hand, doing what short hand does. He began his appearance for M.V.IBN Khallikan except the judge hearing the case was George A. Rebello his senior.

They had a peon in the office, but all the filing of cases were done by Rubin and later Rubin alongwith Rohan. Every advocate's office had and have what is called a 'court clerk' or a 'filing clerk' at least an office as The Georges's, as what the

Reoferron Martin

Chambers of George A Rebello Advocate High Court came to be called. Advocates themselves do filing, but it is for saving of the money of keeping a court clerk and obviously they do not have a roaring practice and some just have, the do it themselves attitude. George could afford umpteen court clerks but Rubin and Rohan had to do all the filing of all the cases of George's office.

It was around one month later of joining George, that Rohan was summoned to his cabin.

"Why I make Rubin and you do the filing of the cases, when all the other law firms and advocates do it through court clerks, is because there are two aspects of law, one is law by itself and that being arguments. But there is another important aspect and that is procedure. It is through filing of the cases yourself, which is done by court clerks, that you understand procedural law, which is not taught at college. A good advocate is one, who knows to plead and knows procedural law too. Tomorrow your own court clerk or junior will not be able to lie and tell you that a particular department was closed, since you would know yourself," said George and it opened up a whole Pandora's Box with regards to this whole concept called procedure. But little did Rohan know, George's last words could be used on Rohan, one fine day and that one fine day, was only to take place three months from the date of joining the chambers of George. But before that came another trying incident.

Rohan was again summoned to George's cabin.

"Here are the details of my liftman he is a Muslim, make a will."

"Yes George," is all that Rohan could say to Geroge's order.

Rohan didn't say anything then besides, 'Yes George.' He came back to the junior's cabin and sat in front of Rubin and the others in despair, not knowing what to do. Muslims do not make wills, so how was Rohan supposed to make a will, since the Holy Quran has already made a will for all Muslims. Rohan was studying Mohammedan law at that time, so he knew that Muslims do not make wills. Rohan was left with no choice. He went like a rat and knocked on the door, got the entry signal and stood in front of his judge, his senior.

"George a will cannot be made by Muslims."

"Why?"

"Because the divisions have already been made by the Holy Quran," is what Rohan said like a rat because it meant challenging George's intelligence.

"How do you know?" was his question.

"I have learnt it in Mohammedan Law, in college."

"I am impressed, good, give me the papers which I gave you, with the details," was his answer. Getting the boss impressed makes the world turn another place. Except George wasn't Rohan's boss he was Rohan's senior and impressing George was like moving a mountain. It wasn't that you couldn't impress George except the rules were laid and they had to be followed.

After a hard days work which was a full day at the High Court, hearing the arguments of Senior Advocate Khattu Cooper, put forward a writing, what he said in verbatim which would be accepted as next to totality, but in Rohan's shorthand, Rohan was summoned to George's cabin.

"You took down notes today at Court," was George's question.

Rohan thought he had done something wrong by taking down notes.

But how would taking notes be wrong?

"Yes George."

"Where are they, get them?" was his order.

The question which kept popping up in Rohan's head was," *How could taking down of notes be wrong?"*

Rohan rushed out from George's cabin, to the juniors cabin to pick his notes which was 25 pages in Rohan's gibberish short hand, it would be 40 when the same would be changed to decipherable English.

"George these are the notes but you won't be able to read it, as they have my codes. I will write the whole thing in fair and give it to you."

"When will you finish it, Senior Advocate Aryamma Sundaram wants these notes," was what George said.

Rohan was sitting in front of George and didn't know what to say. Senior Advocate Aryamma Sundaram was appearing for the owners of the vessel M.V.Ya Mawlaya and The George's was appearing for the crew of the vessel.

"I will rewrite the notes in the night and give it to you in the morning,"

"Take the fair notes and go to the Taj where Sundaram is staying and give him the notes by 9 o clock in the morning." was George's order.

George knew that the last lecture would be missed by Rohan.

Rohan had taken all the pains sitting up the whole night and writing the arguments in fair, which amounted to 56 pages in

ADHOCACY

decipherable English. In the night again, another 56 pages was unfair. Even in an examination Rohan had never written so much. But examinations are only a practice, a dummy of life. It is like playing flight simulator. Not flying an aircraft in reality, like Tom cruise in Top Gun.

"Sir you asked for these notes," Rohan was outside Senior Advocate's Aryamma Sundaram's room at the Taj and Rohan felt like a bell boy, since Senior Advocate Aryamma Sundaram had just showered, which is what Rohan felt, since he was wrapped around in his bathrobe.

"Yes thank you," was what Senior Advocate Aryamma Sundaram said.

Law is a weird profession, its all about digs. When the incident was narrated to his colleagues at the office, Rohan was called the bell boy of Senior Advocate Aryamma Sundaram. A case in question for which Rohan's notes were asked was a landmark case, being that of a collision which took place off the coast of Portugal between two vessels M.T.New World and M.V.YA Mawlaya. The names of both vessels are so striking, one took you to the new world, the other to god. The question was whether a limitation of liability could be set up in India since the crew of M.V.YA Mawlaya was supplied by an Indian company. When the collision took place in the high seas in December 2004 a suit was filed in the Admiralty Court in Lisbon. The suit was dismissed on the ground of jurisdiction. An action was filed in the District Court of Louisiana in the U.S. from where M.V. Ya Mawlaya had sailed from, with Soya beans. The District Court of Louisiana held, it had no jurisdiction. A suit was filed in Hong Kong, since M.T.New World was flying the flag of Hong Kong, at the time when the collision took place. But here too, the Court held it had no jurisdiction. Arbitration proceedings were filed too at a certain stage by the Protection and Indeminty Company of M.T. New World. It was in these circumstances that a suit was filed in the High Court of Judicature at Bombay for setting up a Limitation of Liability.

The case had already come up for hearing earlier, and was now kept for arguments on the preliminary issue of jurisdiction falling under section 9 of the Civil Procedure Code. The case was argued by Senior Advocate Khattu Cooper for 4 and half days for M.T.New World, though not in totality only by him. For the owners of the vessel, Senior Advocate Aryamma Sundaram and Senior Advocate Aspi Chinoy for the crew of the vessel M.V. Ya Mawlaya was in reply. The Honourable Mrs. Justice K.K. Baam passed an equitable order, which was going to be appealed to. Though it cannot be said equitable as comments should not be made, but if comments are'nt, then it would amount to silence, which would amount to inaction, which in entirety would be unrealistic. The case was going to be appealed with an SLP right to Supreme Court and to the extent of a Revision Petition.

The Honourable Mrs. Justice K.K. Baam had passed her judgment by reading the operative part of the order in open Court. The copy of the order had to be obtained, which takes some days before it is given, which happens only after the order is signed by the judge. George put Rohan as a watch dog, one of the days in the evening, to check whether the order was signed. Rohan asked the personal assistant of Mrs. Justice K. K. Baam, whether the judgment was signed. Who answered in the negative.

ADHOCACY

Taking his word he went back to Nariman Point and the moment he reached the office he was summoned by George.

"Is the order signed by justice Baam?" obviously no one in conversation is going to say the Honourable Mrs. Justice K.K. Baam not even, the ever articulate George.

"No George."

"Did justice Baam leave?"

"I don't know."

"Then why did . . . . . . you . . . have come back?" asked George shooting Rohan with verbal bullets and Rohan had his tail between his legs. He didn't know what to do, the same thing which George had said, why he made Rohan alongwith Rubin do the filing and not by court clerks was a slap on Rohan's face.

"What if justice Baam has signed the judgment and the other side has already received a copy. You were told to wait till justice Baam leaves her chambers only then come back," George carried on the reprimand of the innocent lamb.

Rohan had no malice in returning to office. Had he to, he would have told George that Mrs. Justice Baam had left her chambers.

"What you standing in front of me, go back and check whether the judgment has been signed and only come back, after she has left. Even if she stays till night or the whole night at her chambers, you stay there till she leaves."

Rohan wasn't told earlier to wait till the Honourable Mrs. Justice K. K. Baam leaves her chambers. Rohan was only told to go to her chamber and check whether the judgment has been signed and if so, to get a copy. Rohan went back to the chambers of the Honourable Mrs. Justice K. K. Baam but she had already left. The only thing that he could do, was patronize the Malbari chai guy, at the other end of the High Court being at the Original Side, since the Honourable Mrs. Justice K. K. Baam's chambers was towards the Appellate side.

George A. Rebello's chamber specialized in the stream of Admiralty law. A field of law Rohan has been grateful to have been associated with to this day and has his senior to thank.

George's senior was Senior Advocate S. Venkateswaran for whom he had the greatest regards for, just like Rohan has for George. In guesses it's a junior, senior thingy. Rohan will never forget the day George came to the juniors cabin and said, "Venky's brains need to be preserved in a bottle even after he dies." Venky is short for Venkateswaran. Rohan as junior of George would like to have George's brains kept in a bottle preserved too. Wants are and will always remain an unrealistic, phenomena of the platform, the plethora of discussions, that take place between the conscious and subconscious.

Maritime Law stems from The Admiralty Act 1890 and Merchant Shipping Act 1958. Unlike the U K India has only one Act on shipping The Merchant Shipping Act 1958 with an amendment made in the 70s. While the U K has a 1995 Act.

One of the reasons, Rohan loved working at the chambers of George A. Rebello because of Maritime Law. Justice delayed is justice denied, but here in Admiralty, there was no justice delay or denial, only reality. In no other Act does urgency require what Maritime law does, at least where civil law is concerned. Maritime Law being all about shipping law is basically about vessels. Vessels are arrested at ports by a claimant by filing an

Admiralty Suit under the Admiralty Jurisdiction of the High Court. A vessel can be arrested in India, only when it comes within the jurisdiction of India being twelve nautical miles of the coast, be it anywhere. If the vessel leaves port and an order of arrest is not obtained, a trawler cannot be sent in the high seas to arrest the vessel. The trawler would be termed as an Indian Government pirate and it would be against International Maritime Laws to do so. It is this urgency, which gives advocates the liberty to obtain an order of arrest from even the judge's bungalow and petitioning of vacation judges, when the courts are closed for vacations.

Suits for arrests are drafted in a span of hours, if need be and practically 90% of the clients are based overseas. The only point which The George's had to wait for was the transfer of the advocate's fees, which had to come from overseas, since court fees had to be paid and practically 95% of the time the amount would be the maximum court fees. An arrest order was received, by making an application at 2.45 p.m. in the afternoon, when the court resumes after a lunch recess. Normally no court order can be acted upon, unless it is a certified true copy. However leave is obtained from the judge hearing Admiralty suits to direct the Sheriff of Mumbai to act on the ordinary signed copy of the order. Urgency in the matter, allows for the leave to be granted.

Papers of the arrest warrant to be slapped on the vessel, even before an order of arrest was obtained, were always typed before the arrest order was passed. Slapping of the arrest warrant, doesn't literally mean the slapping of a ship. If the bailiff did, he would receive a slap himself, a boomerang. In a rare case, where an order of arrest was not obtained, one might say that it was wrong to have kept all papers of the arrest warrant typed in advance. But the concept is the same as that of an operation theatre staff, keeping the operation theatre ready due to urgency with regards to a patient. However a case may arise that even though the operation theatre was kept ready, the doctor who is suppose to perform an operation may not feel it feasible to carry the operation. To Rohan it was an act of being prudent.

The bailiff of the Sheriff's office would go to whichever port in India and arrest the vessel. It is a simple act of the port authorities, with whom the papers of the vessel stands handed over to, at the time of docking at a port, which are not returned to the captain of the vessel, till the release order is received from the Court. There is no physical arrest that takes place.

What is even more interesting of Admiralty Law that after the vessel gets arrested the owners of the vessel, within a span of twenty four hours, appoints an advocate and an application for release of the vessel is made, within a maximum period of five days, from the date of arrest by furnishing a bank guarantee. Since every night a vessel stands arrested, a loss of ten thousand dollars stands incurred. Most of the arrests take place for necessaries supplied to the vessel. Necessaries are those as per the Admiralty Act, which are needed for plying of the vessel, such as bunkers. Bunkers doesn't mean holes made into the ground, bottom of the vessel but it is a word used for oil, as far as vessels are concerned. Around 70% of Admiralty suits are settled through an out of court settlement. If only all other courts function with such urgency, the backlog of cases which are pending, would stand adjudicated and disposed off, just like

ADHOCACY

Admiralty suits and there would be no justice delayed or justice denied.

"Ignorantia Juris Non Excusat"
                                         Legal Maxim
Ignorance of the Law is no Excuse.

L.L.B. Degree

Once upon a time, the L.L.B. degree, an attachment to ones business card, would bring about the statement, Rohan is an L.L.B.

This was when, Masters of Business Administration had not made the statement, "He is an MBA." There will be a day, when another degree will take over the MBA degree and that is how life evolves.

On an analization of the MBA degree. It has brought about the dissimilation of the myth, that businessmen are shrewed and calculative people. Do it the right way, an earn profit is the MBA mantra. Profit is nothing but remuneration earned for the work done, as an employee would get wages for work done. However as an employer, the psychological trauma has to be endured.

Rohan had joined Government law College in 1996. The road ahead was an upheaval one. After reading the book Psychoanalysis through Sun Signs, Rohan thought that he should change his sun sign from Aquarius to some other sun sign or a new sign. Two of the biggest Aquarians he knew, had not gone through elementary schooling. The first, was thought to be one, who lacked basic human ability to learn and was taken out of school and taught by his mother. The second, did his education by himself in a log cabin. The first, has lit the world. The second, stitched the north and south of USA. How was Rohan to fit in the world, having failed the first L.L.B. exam the parable of the two biggest Aquarians Rohan knew, would ring in his head, as it had done a billion times before.

There was a lacunae in Rohan's acts after the first L.L.B. exam. Along with others, Rohan filed a Writ Petition against the University of Mumbai for correction of answer sheets again. Everyday the University of Mumbai was in the newspapers, with regards to the law exams, at that point of time. The petition was filed by Rohan's professor teaching him the Law of Torts. The petition came up for hearing for admission before a division bench, headed by the Honourable Mr. Justice V.P. Tipnis and Mrs. Justice Ranjana Desai. The petition was dismissed at the admission stage itself, on the ground of, prima facie the petition having no locus standi, for it to be admitted.

The year was 1997. ATKTs (allowed to keep terms) were allowed. Rohan started his journey of the Contract Law, in which he scored the highest marks at college in the first year, kept him hounding.

What dawned on Rohan was that the answer sheets of the exam papers did not need answers, which had any relevance of the present day. He had written his answers with explanation of cases, which were adjudicated in the High Court at that present time, having knowledge of the same, being in the High Court nearly every single day, filing plaints, affidavits, written statements, lodging suits, dispensing of objections raised by Associates and various other acts. But that was not what was expected, as answers to be given. The answers, which were expected, were set answers.

In 1999 all six papers of the second year were passed. But the hounding of the Contract Law, still pounded Rohan. The hurdle was still to be passed, before he went to the next year.

In the meanwhile, as a confirmation of his legal acumen to himself, he took up a case filed in the City Civil Court against the husband of Pragati Kamat. Pragati and Rohan had done a public speaking course together. She knowing that Rohan was studying law and was working as an assistant to an advocate, she asked for help. Pragati and her husband were taking care of an old man, in whose house they were staying. Before the old man died, he had made a nomination in the prescibed format, to the society of the building, in the name of Pragati's husband. After the death of the old man, the old man's brother gets up from Bangalore and says the transfer of the flat was done fraudulently and files a case in the City Civil Court for reliefs, that the transfer needs to be revoked and since he is the only legal heir, the suit premises should be transferred in his name.

A Notice of Motion was filed for ad interim reliefs. If the case went against Pragati's favour, she could loose her house and Rohan would be in trouble. It is like an intern who is not a doctor, decides to operate on a patient. If the patient dies, the intern would have to live with the trauma that he killed the patient. But an intern has to operate someday.

Rohan drafted the reply to the notice of motion and asked Pragati to appear in the case and stand in the witness box and submit the affidavit in reply to the notice of motion. If he was advocating for the case, then he would have been arguing the case in person. Since he wasn't, all his arguments were put in the reply with the heading, 'For Arguendo.' The notice of motion was dismissed in Pragati's favour. The right term would be in Pragati's husband's favour.

The same act was done, for the reply to the plaint of the suit, the Written Statement. Pragati again gave the written statement to the judge and the suit was dismissed in Pragati's favour.

Pragati who had appointed an advocate earlier, was asked an amount of Rs.70000 for the suit and notice of motion in 1998. She saved that amount and her house.

Unfortunately or fortunately it was only in 2005 January that Rohan received the passed mark sheet of the L.L.B. exam. A long journey started in July 1996 only to be thwarted further by the impugned rule of the Bar Council of Maharashtra and Goa.

>Things done cannot be undone
>Things hardly attained are longer retained
>Things past cannot be recalled
>Things present are judged by things past
>
>   16th Century

The Filing Of The Case

In every case, there is usually one such case, which has already been decided as a precedent. That precedent was the Dr. Haniraj L. Chulani's case.

The case was decided in 1996 by then Chief Justice of the Supreme Court The Honourable Mr. Jusice A.M.Ahmadi, Mr. Justice S.B. Majumdar and Mrs. Justice Sujata V. Manohar J.J.J.

The question which was decided had all the relevance to the present case. Dr. Haniraj L. Chulani was a colorectal surgeon and was a practicing medical practitioner and a resident of Mumbai, just as Rohan. He had finished his L.L.B. course and obtained his Degree of Bachelor of laws on 4.3.1991. He applied to be enrolled as an advocate, even though he is a medical practitioner and stated that he is entitled to carry on simultaneously both professions.

His request was rejected by the enrolment committee of the State Bar Council. He was informed of the rejection on 16.11.1992 alongwith a copy of his rejection. He then filed a Writ Petition being Writ Petition No. 2584 of 1992 in the High Court at Bombay. His petition was dismissed on 14.12.1992.

The short description, which was stated as the question to be decided was

"Whether the Bar Council of Maharashtra & Goa was justified in refusing enrolment of the Appellant as an advocate under the Advocates Act 1961 being a medical practitioner who does not want to give up his medical practice but wants to simultaneously practice law?"

Why did such a case come up?

The very polity of Indian society is embedded with the multi lingual, multi religious and multi cultural society. A pluralistic society in nature. Obviously the same pluralism shall lie to the species of the genus being profession. Since in our education system and our daily life, we have to learn three different languages. It is this pluralism which is distinct from any country in the world.

Here counsel appearing for Dr. Chulani had submitted, that the rule 2 under section 28 of the Advocates Act prohibiting a person who is otherwise qualified to be admitted as an advocate, from enrolling as an advocate, if he is carrying on any profession like the medical profession as far as Dr. Chulani is concerned, was wrong under the Constitution of India stating that it amounts to extra power granted by the Parliament. She further stated that the same rule is wrong and violative of the Constitution of the Article Right to work even though the article has clauses and stated the Constitution of India gives the Right to Equality and therefore it being wrong, violative under these articles of the Constitution.

Rohan agreed with her, that there is nothing obnoxious or illegal in a practicing doctor, insisting on being enrolled as an advocate and in practicing both as a medical practitioner, as well as an advocate in his arguments. The only difference here was that he was a businessman, not a doctor, not a surgeon, when compared to Dr. Haniraj L. Chulani.

The first point put forward to the Chief Justice of Bombay Mr. Justice R Bharuch and Mrs. Justice Shalinee Mathur J. J. when Rohan's Writ Petition came up for hearing at the admission stage at 2.45 p.m. was Chief Justice R. Bharuch's dismissal order of the petition, "The Petition stands dismissed as the matter stands decided by the Supreme Court in favour of the Respondents in the matter of Dr. Haniraj L Chulani's case. The Appellants are at liberty to file an appeal to this order in the Apex Court. No order as to cost."

Chief Justice R. Bharuch of The High Court at Bombay knew exactly where Rohan was coming from. His father Mr. Justice J. Bharuch had been the the Chief Justice of India and he knew Rohan as an advocate's assistant. Then he was a practicing advocate. No one is going to file a Writ when the matter in question has already been decided in another case by the Supreme Court. But he knew the facts and circumstances and that Rohan would have definitely done his homework.

He came forward shut the mike and said in open Court. Something which is never done by a High Court judge, Mr. Justice R. Bharuch was the Chief Justice of the Bombay High Court.

"Son," he was obviously nearly double Rohan's age and so took the liberty of calling him son, another act not done by a Judge.

"This is a long drawn road. You want to travel it, you got to go in appeal to my order. I can't help you sitting in a division bench."

Little did Rohan know that this statement of Chief Justice R. Bharuch was like a prediction and a sound advice. He just didn't want Rohan to waste time. He knew his hands were bound by an order of the Supreme Court and by Rohan putting his submission his order was not going to change. Chief Justice R. Bharuch definitely conferred with Rohan's arguments even without any arguments made by Rohan, that was the current running of the rumour mill. Many times in Court a situation arises, when the judge's hands are tied, there already being a settled law and a lower Court cannot override a judgment.

Dr. H. L. Chulani's case had sprung from Mumbai itself and the case was first dismissed by the High Court at Bombay. Bombay High Court was not going to override itself, nor could it, under the law as settled that only a higher court can override a lower court judgement. Rohan had to begin walking to the Apex Court, The Supreme Court of India.

A dreamer is one who can only find his way by moonlight, and his punishment is that he sees the dawn before the rest of the world

Oscar Wilde

The Family Business

Mr.Righteous was always an entrepreneur. His selling of coconuts at the Onam festival, resembles Mr.Krishnan Iyer M.A. who made India, if not the world, knowledgeable of the status, of what a coconut man is. Except Mr.Krishnan Iyer M.A. Mithun Chakraborty, got to marry the beautiful Neelam Kothari. After all Rohan did have a tete a tete with Neelam at the Santacruz airport, when she was going to Sholapur with Rishi Kapoor for a shoot to Sholapur in May 1990.

"The only place I know, where actors and actresses are given some decent behaviour, is at the airport just at the boarding lounge," is what Rohan would say after the incident. Since that is what happened. If it was another area, Rohan definitely would not have got a chance to have a tete a tete. It is only fair, for his jealousy and kept thinking of Neelams' signature line, 'Cho Shweet.'

Mr.Righteous had burned his fingers with many a business. The prominent ones Rohan knows about is that of 'Cafela' the cold drink and 'Dragon' the noodles. It was in 1977 when the Janata Dal came to power, with Coke being asked to reveal its formula to the government and reduce its stake under FERA. There was no formidable cola available then and the playground was open. 'Cafela' had a bottling plant at Mahim. Mr.Righteous would supply the whole of Mumbai and neighbouring parts and had made in roads into Gujarat. All it took was one tempo in Mumbai. In those days, the greatest transport of these bottled

ADHOCACY

drinks were handcarts. Just how the dabbahwallahs cart their produce, for which even the not yet king, Prince Charles of the United Kingdom, made time to meet the wallahs.

Mr.Righteous always believed in the Chinese proverb 'Calamity brings in opportunity'. In the manner in which Coke going out from India, which gave Mr.Righteous the opportunity to distribute Cafela, in the same manner the calamity was faced by 'Thumps up' manufactured by Parle, which is an interpretation, otherwise why would one sell the most trusted brand in India Thumps up. After all Thumps Up has always been Rohan's favourite drink. Its an age old concept. The big sharks eat the smaller ones and Coke bought the brands of Thumps up, Limca, Citra, Maaza and Gold Spot. However the two drinks which got eaten up are Citra and Gold Spot. It is unforgetable the furore with which people drank Gold Spot because of 'Mooglee', who came jumping out, from the book of the Jungle.

Cafela was being sold with no freebies to the vendors. It was being sold on a hand to mouth basis. Parle began supplying ice boxes to the vendors. Something which the vendors could not afford and Mr.Righteous could not afford either. When a shark comes to eat you, a fish, it is impossible to run. It is better to surrender and make peace. Most of the times, the act of being eaten might not happen. Mr.Righteous did exactly that, he cut his losses and the business down.

One thing definitely helped, was the giving of the tempo to a friend, who needed it for starting his career in politics and needed to go around canvassing in it. The friend remained a loyal friend of Mr.Righteous and Rohan.

In the early 90s India began to open some doors. Whereby Pepsi came into India. Wow was the scene with Lehar Pepsi. Wherever Pepsi went Coke wants to follow and vice versa. With Pepsi in, Coke followed in India. By then Pepsi had already began supplying small refrigerators to vendors. What ice boxes and refrigerators can do?

'Dragon' noodles was being manufactured and being sold in Bangalore. Bangalore has one of the highest consumptions of noodles in India. Mr.Righteous took the agency and began marketing it along with a relative in Mumbai. Business flourished in Mumbai and Mr.Righteous began marketing Dragon noodles out of Mumbai and Maharashtra. When pop came the giant as a weasel. Maggi ate the fish, though its name was Dragon. However Maggi stole a million hearts and Rohan's, since Rohan had and still has a habit of eating Maggi from the packet itself, just like the Maggi cube. Then one had to be a scavenger on the goods, on anyone, being a Gulf return, for Maggi cubes.

In the late 70s Cafela passed, in the early 80s Dragon passed. Now came the late 80s. Mr.Righteous must have been a spectator of Bruce the King with that episode of the spider in his earlier life. In October 1987 Mr.Righteous started 'International Business Travellers' Club' better known as IBTC with an office address in Mumbai and an office address in the U.K. With a contract to market IBTC with India Book House, memberships forms began to trickle, then pour.

In 1990 a contract was signed with Citibank credit cards, whereby all Citibank Diners Club members would automatically receive an IBTC membership and the same extended to Citibank

ADHOCACY

Master /Visa credit cards. A similar contract with Bobcards of Bank of Baroda was signed in 1991. The IBTC membership gave an IBTC member an upto 50% discount in 1500 hotels worldwide, besides giving the member, VIP treatment in 1987.

With no internet to make a reservation. A fax to an International destination costing Rs. 125 per page and more, telephone calls being equally high. The IBTC card made a lot of sense, whereby one could get an upto 50% discount in 5000 hotels worldwide.

With the internet coming in the 2000s the cost of International calls came down. Email had already hit the market, websites began to pop up and everyone thought that everything would happen through the internet, even getting married and procreation or that a website would feed them their lunch or dinner physically. The advent of applications, instant hotel reservations and airline bookings became a part and parcel of everyday life, on the mode of do it yourself. In the early 90s one had to learn the Disk Operating System, where computers are concerned. Today all those commands are done by the computer itself. Windows have been gratuitous to us and on us. With the passage of time, new products had to be inducted in the offering of the IBTC membership.

Today an IBTC Bluecard member can make an instant reservation in 95000 hotels worldwide in 190 countries and receive an upto 90% discount and a guaranteed 50% discount on car rentals in India.

A product which is not offered by any organization or club in the world is now offered by IBTC. A guaranteed 50% discount in 3000 star restaurants worldwide in 60 countries. Just like medical insurance where a hospital doesn't give any discount to the patient. The restaurant may or may not give a discount. However the 50% discount is guaranteed by IBTC to its Silvercard holders, through direct credit or cash back.

Obviously to get an IBTC Silvercard the IBTC Bluecard holder needs to make a certain number of hotel or car rental bookings and accumulate 10000 IBTC points or IBTC Add On points through bookings of hotel rooms of family friends and relatives or transferring of their credit card points to eat free faster. The same points can be earned and transferred to a frequent flieraccount i.e. Air India.

How IBTC gives a guaranteed 50% discount in 3000 restaurants worldwide in 60 countries, which with time will rise to 95000 in 190 countries like hotels, or a 150% discount in hotels, is not a very big trade secret or rocket science. It is section 27 of the Indian Contract Act. Being the first card of its kind in India. Having started operations in 1987 and contracts signed then, 'Goodwill'. www.ibtc.me

The Loans

'The verb loan is one of the words English settlers brought to America and continued to use after it had dried off in Britain. Its use was soon noticed by British visitors and somewhat later by the New England literati, who considered it a bit provincial. It was flatly declared wrong in 1870 by a popular commentator, who based his objection on etymology. A later scholar showed that the commentator was ignorant of old English and thus unsound in his objection, but by then it was too late, as the condemnation was picked up by many other commentators. Although a surprising number of critics still voice objections, loan is entirely standard as a verb. You should note that it is used only literally, lend is the verb for figurative expression such as lending a hand or lending enhancement.'

Meriam Webster's Dictionary

The question of loans began because of buying a new office, where the family business was concerned. Every businessman takes loans. You can state, you don't take loans. But if you buy goods on credit, that too amounts to a loan.

A loan was already taken, with a mortgage on the family house of Rs. 52 lakhs from a Rabitat Loan Company. Besides the home loan various personal loans were taken. One could say a personal loan from every major private sector bank or multinational bank. The first loan was a personal loan taken on Mrs.Sonal Modi Joseph's name of Rs. 1.75 lakhs from the Rabitat Loan Company. In late 2005 having decided to try and purchase a bigger office, for the business, a loan had to be procured. It so happened that there being two joint secretaries to the building, one wanted to buy the same shop, which Rohan wanted to purchase and was to be used as an office. The premise was already rented out to a Pune bank. The normal practice goes that the builder receives one consolidated share certificate, for each of the properties owned, by him and doesn't receive individual share certificates for each. The shop was owned by the builder, from the time of the construction of the building and was later sold to Mr. Sawarkar. Mr.Righteous had given the tempo, used for the distribution of Cafela to Mr. Savarkar, who had used the tempo for his political campaigning.

The question which arose by the banks, for granting of a loan being, why didn't the first owner, the builder not have a share certificate. The secretaries of the building did not explain the acts, which were committed by their predecessors for two years. Rohan had to raise the funds from some fictitious place. Selling the office from where Mrs.Sonal Modi Joseph and Rohan were operating was not an option, as they had to operate from some place and obviously possession of the new office would take some time.

In the meantime, payment had to be made to Mr. Savarkar. Rohan had to swipe Mrs.Sonal Modi Joseph's and his own credit cards on various EDC terminals for others who did not have credit cards and who gave him cash in return for payment by his credit cards. The total amount of credit cards of Mrs.Sonal Modi Joseph and Rohan were twenty six then.

The ratio behind the act being, the moment the secretaries gave a proper explanation as to why, the first owner of the property did not have a share certificate, which was what the banks had asked, the loan would be granted and the amount swiped on the credit cards would be paid.

That act took 2 years.

The loan was disbursed in three days, from the moment the secretary of the building gave an explanation, as sought by the bank. The secretaries of the building could have given the explanation at the beginning itself, when sought. Had they to have done so, the personal loans would not have had to be taken for buying the new office at huge interest rates, such as 45% on the credit cards, since one has to add the service tax applicable and 24% on personal loans.

The total amount payable to the bankers had arisen because of non-receipt of the no objection certificate from the secretaries to Rs. 2,95,39,000. In the mean while, the Bar Council of Maharashtra and Goa had rejected Rohan's application for enrolment to the Bar on the grounds of being an active partner of the firm International Business Travellers Club. The company was not yet incorporated as Limited though an application was made to the Registrar of Companies for the name, "International Business Travellers Club Ltd." Which was rejected because of a company, with a similar name, International Business Travels Trade and Development Corporation Pvt. Ltd. in existence in Manipal. With Rohan's legal acumen and providence, he was not going to accept such blatant violation of the Companies Act, with a registered trade mark, 'IBTC.' The trade mark, being applicable since 1987 when the partnership was formed. A trademark supersedes any name already in existence and under the Copyright Patents and Trademarks Act 2000 the firm could ask International Business Travels Trade and Development Corporation Pvt. Ltd. to change their name. A forty five page legal notice was given to the Registrar by Rohan, which made a no choice situation, but for them to accept the name, 'International Business Travellers' Club Ltd.'

In the same year of, beginning the process of registration, of the limited company, Mrs.Sonal Modi Joseph and Rohan wanted to close the home loan, with the Rabitat Loan Company which was 62 lakhs. As collateral besides the house, they had a fixed deposit of Rs. 45 lakhs lying with the Rabitat Loan Company. Therefore the total amount lying with them was Rs.1.5 crores worth of property and an amount of Rs. 45 lakhs fixed deposit, on which a lien was marked. The total amount of security with the Rabitat Loan Company was Rs. 1.95 crores. A request was made to the Rabitat Loan Company to release the fixed deposit. A verbal communication was made by the Rabitat Loan Company stating that if Mrs.Sonal Modi Joseph and Rohan paid the amount pending as far as a top up loan of Rs. 20 lakhs, of which 18 lakhs was pending, the Rabitat Loan Company shall release the fixed deposit.

An amount of Rs. 16 lakhs was lying with Rohan. To gather the remaining amount, Rohan swiped his own credit card for Rs. 2 lakh. But the merchant acquiring bank, on whose EDC terminal Rohan had swiped his credit cards, did not credit his, the merchants account with the money, the merchant acquiring bank disputed the tranaction. Rohan informed the merchant acquiring bank that the transactions were totally legitimate. But they did not listen. If they listened or not was their prerogative, what became an issue was that they were not reversing the transactions. This seemed to be inexplainable. Reversing a transaction which has not been paid to the merchant is an action of 5 minutes. However this merchant acquiring bank took four months and kept an amount of Rs. 60,000 in lien and Rs. 45,000 in one of the credit cards in dispute for 3 years. An interest of 45% stands lost per year on Rs. 45,000 besides the interest on the other amounts which were not credited.

Rohan paid the amount to the Rabitat Loan Company and expected them to release the Fixed Deposit. But they were simply not doing so and didn't for 5 months. In those 5 months the amount which Rohan lost because the Rabitat Loan Company was 15 lakhs, since Rohan expected the Rabitat Loan Company to release the Fixed Deposit instantly by keeping their word. Which they didn't, for 5 months.

"But there was definitely more than what was visible," was what seemed to Rohan.

Having been rejected by the Bar Council, amounts were needed for the Writ Petition to be filed. An added expense. Though the application was party in person, amounts are needed for a petition to be filed.

At the same point of time, in the month of June, when the plea was made to the Rabitat Loan Company, to release the fixed deposit. Mrs.Sonal Modi Joseph and Rohan, each had personal loans with the same Rabitat Loan Company and who had not presented the EMI cheques for the month of June.

Why?

That answer only the Rabitat Loan Company can give.

Again in the month of July, the Rabitat Loan Company did not deposit the EMI cheque. But the Rabitat Loan Company sent their recovery goons. There had been no dishonour or bounce of any cheque issued by Mrs.Sonal Modi Joseph or Rohan's cheques to any bank or to anyone else. The once, when cheques were bounced was on July 10th 2006 when there was a bomb blast, which took place in the trains. Besides the bomb blast, Central Bank of India was on strike, whereby the amount needed for the cheques to be cleared, could not be deposited, since money could not be withdrawn from Central Bank of India. However the cheques which stood bounced on 10th June 2006, payment was made for the same subsequently in a matter of five days.

Rohan informed the thugs of the Rabitat Loan Company that they had not presented the cheques for clearance and that there was Rs. 5lakhs in Mrs.Sonal Modi Joseph's account and Rs. 5lakhs in Rohan's. For two and half months, Rohan was harassed by thugs from the Rabitat Loan Company, besides the Rabitat Loan Company sending their standard notice of default, for no fault of Mrs.Sonal Modi Joseph or Rohan's.

How does one counteract, the act of one not being a defaulter and being called a defaulter? Rohan asked the thugs to give the old cheques which the Rabitat Loan Company had not presented, since if Rohan did make payment to them, they could present the old cheques, which they had not presented, alongwith the cheques which Rohan might give them, then at that point of time.

They didn't, out of frustration Rohan gave them, two extra EMI cheques for Mrs.Sonal Modi's account and one EMI cheque for Rohan's. Exactly what Rohan feared happened. On 24th of July, they deposited the EMI cheques of both June and July, which was always presented on the 5th of the month, for both Mrs. Sonal Modi Joseph's account and Rohan's. All four cheques were honoured. Besides the two cheques given in Mrs.Sonal Modi Joseph's account and the one cheque given in Rohan's account. This could be done to some lakhs of customers.

"But this is again never done by banks or loan companies. There is definitely a reason behind all of this happenieng," thought Rohan.

Eventually the extra EMIs were paid after 5 months and after Mrs.Sonal Modi Joseph and Rohan had to keep asking Rabitat Loan Company to return the extra amount. What happened, was due to the Rabitat Loan Company not depositing the two EMI cheques of June and July of Mrs.Sonal Modi Joseph and Rohan, was that no further personal loans were granted by any bank or financial institution to Mrs.Sonal Modi Joseph. The reason, their track record was broken. For someone who has had 39 personal loans, two loans against property, plus 26 credit cards in totality, no default of payment, if suddenly is made to stop receiving financial oxygen, he is going to suffocate and die. Die, lets check whether it happened. The supply of financial oxygen was out, not because of an act of Mrs.Sonal Modi Joseph or Rohan's but because of an act by the Rabitat Loan Company. One such act which was of no fault of theirs became a death trap. However the realization and the impact happened later on.

In the meanwhile, while the Rabitat Loan Company commited such acts. The papers for transfer of the Loan Against

Property were given to three different banks and a Pecuniary Loan Company to be transferred. In October the Pecuniary Loan Company stated, they would sanction a loan of Rs. 80 lakhs. The loan against property from the Rabitat Loan Company of Rs. 62 lakhs was at 9% and which went to 10% on the basis of the floating rate. The Pecuniary Loan Company first paid the balance amount to the Rabitat Loan Company. The Rabitat Loan Company gave the share certificate and other documents pertaining to the house, which were then given to the Pecuniary Loan Company. However the Pecuniary Loan Company without even showing or taking a signature on the sanction letter, processed the loan for 56 lakhs only. Twenty four lakhs is what Mrs.Sonal Modi Joseph and Rohan should have had in hand. However they didn't and it seemed, wish got it. But Mrs.Sonal Modi Joseph was supposed to. This was in the month of November when the 26/11 attacks happened. The signing of the loan agreement was done fraudulently. Since if a sanction letter, was not issued and duly signed, the loan agreement would stand, null and void. However Rohan was told this was the loan agreement only in January after the first EMI was already deposited by the Pecuniary Loan Company, but by then there was little Mrs.Sonal Modi Joseph and Rohan could so, but accept.

"Banks and loan companies are regulated by the Banking Regualtion Act and Reserve Bank of India. This is again something which is never done by banks and loan companies."

ADHOCACY

In the midst, was Rohan, in the "Tempest" a battle in the High Court for enrolment to the Bar.

By giving the EMI cheques Mrs.Sonal Modi Joseph and Rohan had signed their death warrant. They had pleaded to the Pecuniary Loan Company to sanction the loan for 15 years, but the Pecuniary Loan Company wouldn't listen.

"Maybe, since they didn't know whether they would survive for 15 years," a thought that went through Rohan's head, when they rejected his plea for a 15 year tenure.

Once they had the house papers and the cheques, whatever they stated had to be done. Mrs Sonal Modi Joseph and Rohan had got themselves in a captive situation.

The amount of personal loans which were taken, were 34. There were those which were already paid in totality. The banks had already received an interest of upto 24% per annum on them, each being of a different rate, from 2003 till date, on the amount of loans taken. Not even one had a bounce of a cheque, for reason not just insufficient funds, but any other reason. Eligibility was out of the question. But receipt of loans happened, because of a track record. The standard concept, Rohan Joseph could not hurt anyone. Besides business, a petition of such a huge magnitude affecting each and every Magistrate Court, High Court and The Supreme Court, every advocate and aspiring advocate and those passed their L.L.B. exam, but not practicing needed finance. Rohan could not spend time fighting a petition of such a magnitude, which was going to change the face of advocacy and generate all the funds from the business. Loans had to be taken for fighting a petition of such a far reaching consequence, of changing the course of India. History was being written. To write history, money is needed, at least for such a cause.

When driving the Mumbai, Pune expressway, at kms ranging from 150 to 200 kms an hour if a block of 26/11 terrorist attack is met, quick decisions will have to be made to slow or divert.

An instance, when Rohan and his friends were on their way to Lonavla in a Maruti 800 and on a road at Chembur which has a span of four 4 lanes. But was being concreted, therefore three lanes was inoperational. There was only one road. Ahead was a turning. On the left, a trailer comes out. Rohan began to honk a 100 mts away. The trailer did not stop. Suddenly Rohan sees a 26/11 terrorist attack. The trailer blocks all four lanes. A back flip could not be done. Though Rohan has done back flips, not only with his back, but with cars. But here Rohan could not, not because the car was a Maruti 800, but because space is needed to do a back flip. Nor was this break dance. If the Maruti 800 had to do a break dance step, black flip, it needed space on the left hand side. All three lanes on the left, were filled with the act of concreting the road. In front was 26/11 terrorists, waiting for Rohan and his four friends in the car, in the form of a trailer blocking all four roads and was stationery.

"What do you do?"

"What does one do?"

"How to save ourselves?"

Questions rattled Rohan's head, but weren't acknowledged then.

"What?"

"When?"

"Where?"

"How?"

Were questions, which kept hovering in Rohan's mind, whether they did get registered, is history.

Three of his friends were sleeping, one was awake. Rohan could not brake his dinky friend. She was screeching, there was gravel from the concreting of the road, on the left and she was not willing to halt. No one would want to be in such a situation.

"Death was inevitable." thought Rohan

"Do I want to die so young. No. I will not die. ?"

"I am only 24 . . . . . then."

Thoughts which run faster, than the speed of sound ran in Rohan's head.

One friend of Rohan's was 20yrs. The girl a friend of his was 19. Life was not to be cut short.

In front was the trailer. They five, in a Maruti 800. On the left all three lanes of the road was being concreted. The road below with gravel. The car not stopping, the tyres were not gripping the road. No time to pray only time to act. In front was all metal of the trailer. Whatever they would do, it would be metal on metal, like a Hindi movie of yore.

"What do we do?"

The front of the trailer had turned a little. Rohan banged the car on the tyre of the trailer. The car became scrap. Rohan had a hairline fracture though minor. Another friend a nose fracture, for which a minor plastic surgery was needed. Another friend, a girl got a scar on her face. Another friend of Rohan's had to have a minor operation. The fifth friend the 20 year old, came out with nothing as a scar on him.

"*Time heals.*"

Rohan, even with a trailer in front, blocked and no escape, could save his life due to tyre rubber. But the 26/11 terrorists attacks?

The personal loan recovery men of banks had gone berserk. Mrs.Sonal Modi Joseph had a personal loan from 30th August 2005 for an amount of Rs.5lakhs from one Spontaneous Bank. The loan was topped in 6th September 2006 to Rs. 3,35,000. In 2007 Mrs.Sonal Modi Joseph had wanted to close the loan. However the Spontaneous Bank said they needed a notice of a month. *"How can such a rule prevail? If a person wants to close a loan, he should be able to walk in a bank and close the loan. Whether personal, home loan, auto, fibre glass, window pane, lane, cupboard loan, pen loan, toothbrush loan, toothpaste loan.Wasn't it beneficial for the bank to receive the loan amount,"* thought Rohan. Rohan just wanted to close whatever loans he had.

Within that period of one month, the bank who has access to all other bank loan details, which Mrs.Sonal Modi Joseph had taken and can create a scene whereby the other bank, can cause a prejudicial act, from where the party is going to make payment from. The problem being information is open to all banks of all loans and what the balance is, in any loan account. "*The consumer where loans are concerned is a "Nangaman" and if a bank can stipulate that the bank needs a month's notice before one can close a loan account then what can a "Nangaman" do or say,*" was Rohan's angry reaction to the situation. Anyone would react when connered in such a manner. For Mrs.Sonal Modi Joseph and Rohan the smoothness for closing of the loans were of utmost importance.

BUT?

It was in July 2007 that the Spontaneous bank whose loan would have been closed, had they not asked for a one month's notice period, offered an amount of Rs. 10lakhs to Mrs.Sonal Modi Joseph. In the month of March, two years later the first cheque of that loan bounced. But payment was made subsequently within that month. In June the EMI was dishonored but payment was made subsequently and the same happened in July. Every time one guy called Rincent from an agency of the bank landed up harassing Mrs.Sonal Modi Joseph and Rohan. All the possible pleas made to the bank to rework the loan, was thrown to the dumb and blind institution.

In the month of August came two black guys Randeep and Ruraj from the agency of the Spontaneous Bank to meet Rohan and another to meet Mrs.Sonal Modi Joseph. Mrs.Sonal Modi Joseph had fallen and had a knee fracture and dislocation. She was hospitalized for 8 days and was put on complete bed rest for two months. Rohan contracted Malaria, exactly from the day Mrs.Sonal Modi Joseph was discharged from the hospital. On the last day at the hospital, who was the patient, could have been asked, since Rohan was shivering and running a temperature of 105, while Mrs.Sonal Modi Joseph lay on the hospital bed looking at Rohan.

Radhika decided to take care of Mrs.Sonal Modi Joseph. It was the end of the month. Rohan wrote to the bank an email and called them and begged and pleaded and asked them 2 months sabbatical leave from the EMI but they did not listen. Rohan informed them that his mother is a senior citizen, besides being bed ridden. Rohan realized then having a track record makes no difference.

One Mr. Hirish from an agency of the bank goes to Radhika's house, while Ruraj and Randeep hold Rohan at Ransom. This Mr. Hirish kept Mrs.Sonal Modi Joseph on the bed that 29th day of August from 11 in the morning to 5 o clock in the evening. Wouldn't make a difference, since Mrs.Sonal Modi Joseph was supposed to be on the bed. But being held to Ransom and harassing her mentally, when she wanted to urinate is difficult to digest. Mr. Hirish did not allow her to move. Mrs.Sonal Modi Joseph cried. Whether in pain Rohan never came to know. This Mr. Hirish is a hefty guy, Mrs.Sonal Modi Joseph was hurt, but she could not do anything. All the crying did not matter to Hirish, ruthless was he and in comparison worst than a terrorist. If he could do that to Mrs.Sonal Modi Joseph, he could do that to anyones mother.

Rohan paid the EMI for that month. From that month onwards the three thugs Ruraj, Randeep and Mr. Hirsih kept harassing Rohan. Rohan thought he was supposed to be harassed by terrorist. These three thugs were worst than terrorist. They would come at odd hours and stick around and make Rohan completely paralyzed.

The proximity with this Spontaneous bank had happened, years ago, when Rohan had an accident with the vehicle, in which, the wife of one of the Directors of the bank were traveling. Rohan in the good old Premier Padmini and had to face the wrath of her, for not having a licence. He was made to write as punishment that he shall not drive without a licence a 100 times.

The punishment was ordered by her son, who was a little older than a toddler.

"Magar sir last month ka EMI bounce kiya, toh uska charges barna padega."

Even though the EMI was paid within the month, this was their readymade answer. The odd part was, when Rohan would tell them that their bank is the worst bank and has tortured Mrs. Sonal Modi Joseph and him the most. Randeep's reply would be, "Apna bank sabse worst hai, who kisse koh nahin chodte."

On diwali they, that is, Randeep and Ruraj land up at the house demanding the EMI. Since Rohan did not want these thugs to go to Radhika's house Rohan had to bear with them. Who would want their mother to be harassed by a thug as Mr. Hirish. For 5 hours Rohan was captured by Ruraj and Randeep and held captive on Diwali. The same is what Rohan had to do on Christmas day. This happened at least 15 days in a month. Randeep and Ruraj wasn't even from a bank agency and wasn't appointed by the Spontaneous bank but kept stating they were from a bank agency.

One day at a petrol pump a man says, "Rohan Sir."

Rohan began to walk away from his bike. It felt as if this guy was one of the bankers. Everywhere, whenever Rohan saw someone with a knapsack, or with a haversack, to him seemed as one of the bankers. On the causeway, knapsackers are found, one in every ten passerbys. Everytime ten people would pass and the tenth with a knapsack would pop up, Rohan would want to run. But where was Rohan to run?

"Rohan sir kai zala?" the man on the bike asked.

It was then that Rohan decided to check, at the back of his bike, the logo which read, "Mumbai Police."

Rohan felt relieved and began talking to him.

Everytime the house bell rang, it felt that it was either Ruraj or Randeep.

One Prateek Mistry from one of the banks came fighting stating the loan of Mrs.Sonal Modi Joseph cannot be settled for Rs. 30000. It has to be settled for Rs. 42000. Rohan's offer to him was Rs. 30000, not that Rohan didn't want to pay, the amount of Rs. 12000. He just didn't have Rs. 12000. Rohan had no choice but to agree with him. When he came again the next time, Rohan wasn't present. For an amount of Rs. 12000 this Prateek Mistry in a rage slapped Rohan's computer in anger. The CPU and the monitor stood as a stationary robot, who had his face and internal organs smashed. *"What a thug,"* thought Rohan. The loan Mrs. Sonal Modi Joseph has been paying regularly for the last 5 years and was topped up twice in that period. Never did even one EMI bounce earlier. Prateek Mistry was found later, not to be from an agency of the bank, nor from the bank.

Everytime such things took place, the words would ring in Rohan's ears, *'It doesn't pay to be honest'*. Somehow everyday, Mrs. Sonal Modi Joseph and Rohan right from 2003 had seen that the amount needed in the accounts were put and that at no point of time was there an EMI bounce. *"But it doesn't pay to be honest,"* would flash through in front of Rohan. But it does, if not the great Gurus such Dale Carnegie, Norman Vincent Peale, Robin

ADHOCACY

Sharma, Deepak Chopra, the ultimate number of Swamis and the list goes on, would be out of business, besides every religion. At school there was only one medal Rohan received proficiency in moral science and Religon. Rohan could go to the police, but going to the police was not going to stop anything.

One other bank, kept verbally stating that they would settle the pending amount at Rs. 210000 and after paying them 3 EMIs of Rs. 27682 they said, "Rohanji aapko patta nahin, bank kitne problem mein hain. Hum log yeh bhi patta nahin, khi apna job rahega khi nahin. Teen mahine pehle, joh bank mein the, who sab nikal gaye. Aapne ek EMI nahin diya, toh woh settlement void ho gaye. Waise bhi humne settlement letter issue nahin kiya."

"These thugs from the agencies had definitely gone to 'Liar School.' They have been trained to lie, in such a manner that, what is in front, if an apple, they will term it an orange. Definitely none of the banks employ them, unless they have gone to Liar School," thought Rohan

At least the banks which Mrs.Sonal Modi Joseph and Rohan had taken loans from definitely might have. At the end, Rohan had to accept the settlement for Rs.194000 and nothing less. They were suppose to be a bank which people could upgrade themselves from. Ideally the account should have been settled for Rs. 126954. A relationship was there, for 6 years and besides Rohan too had a loan with the same bank, which was fully paid up, made no brownie points.

There were two banks, where settlement amounts was entered into, with regards to Mrs.Sonal Modi Joseph and Rohan's account. Settlement cheques were given. The bank presents both the EMI cheque and the settlement cheques. When asked, they said they cannot stop the EMI cheque from being presented, it is presented by default. The EMI cheque seemed to be like a boulder, which the bank could not stop. As far as contract law, this would be a violation, as you can't have a settlement and a loan running concurrently. This would amount to 2 contracts.

Another bank a settlement was reached, where Rohan's credit card was concerned for suddenly deciding to reduce the credit limit, which caused an embarrassing situation at a store. The settlement which was reached, whereby the bank would settle the credit card dues for Rs. 30000 and the personal loan taken would be reworked, a proposal put forward, by them itself. They take the EMI cheques for the reworking, call and inform the loan has been reworked and inform the EMI amount. After a month, they simply send the cheques back. *"If the reworking of the loan could be done, why take the cheques and call and inform the reworked EMI amount. There definitely seems to be some bigger reason behind all these acts,"* thought Rohan.

Another financial company, where a personal loan was taken, on Mrs.Sonal Modi Joseph's name and Rohan in 2004 and was topped up in 2006. The tenor being for 36 months. The top up being exactly the same amount given in 2004. The EMI amount being the same. However they land up taking 3 EMIs extra for Mrs.Sonal Modi Joseph's account and 2 in Rohan's account. When they sent a cheque for the topped up amount, they simply sent a cheque for the topped up amount without sending any statement. Imagine if this is done to 100000 customers. But these extra EMIs were taken at the time when Rohan was already in the midst of the Writ Petition.

"Did all this have anything to do with filing of the Writ?" a question which Rohan kept pondering on.

But the greatest trauma suffered was with the Spontaneous bank one Mrs.Sonal Modi Joseph was already harassed by Mr. Hirish. Every month the EMI amount of Rs. 39000 was paid by begging and borrowing at 6% interest per month. In the month of March the next year, exactly a year from when Mrs.Sonal Modi Joseph had asked them, to rework the loan, they file a complaint under section 138 of the Negotiable Intruments Act 1881. Form 1 under section 61 of the Act was received by Rohan. Even though payment was made every month but the bank still files a complaint.

"If that was the situation, then one might as well not pay the Spontaneous bank the EMI amount," something which would pop in anyone's head thought Rohan.

But just as Randeep and Ruraj from the bank said their bank is the worst bank. When thugs from a bank, who come to thug you and say, their bank is the worst bank. They have to keep up to their reputation.

The complaint was filed in XIV Additional Chief Metropolitan Magistrates Court Mayo Hall Bangalore. The loan was taken and disbursed in Mumbai. The EMI cheques were presented in Mumbai. Where does the jurisdiction lie for a petition to be filed in Bangalore? When the cause of action took place in Mumbai, the cheques were presented in Mumbai and the disbursal happened in Mumbai?

Since going to Bangalore and when that Court doesn't have jurisdiction was ridiculous, when Rohan did not have money to eat a meal on 100 days out of 365. The prudent act for one, who doesn't have a pie to eat or normal meals and has to be happy eating a, 'Butta,' and going to sleep, was a Writ Petition seeking a Writ of Prohibition by Rohan.

"This Petition in the form of a letter is being sent to you for a Writ of Prohibition to be issued against the XIV Additional Chief Metropolitan Magistrate Court since that Court doesn't have jurisdiction and has usurped jurisdiction."

This was sent to the Chief Justice of the Bombay High Court, with all the details of the loan, right from the first disbursal in 2005, the top up in 2006 and the last disbursal in 2007. With the sanction letters and copies of all payments made till March. Citations with regards to ratios held in AIR 1934 Cal 725, AIR 2003 SC 3290 Tirupativ/s Thallappaka, AIR 1973 SC 1362 Raja Textile v/s IT officer Rampur were cited.

"With reference to your letter addressed to the Honourable, The Chief Justice, High Court, Bombay on the subject noted above. I am Directed to inform you that you may seek relief before the appropriate forum by appropriate proceedings."

This was the reply received from the section officer (P.G. Cell) High Court, Appellate side Bombay by Rohan to his Writ Petition.

It only meant that an L.L.B. degree could not save Rohan, even though he had one and when eating a, 'Butta,' a day and those employed for recovery by the banks are thugs. The appropriate proceedings for Rohan, was definitely committing suicide.

Though, all of this did take place. Rohan has the highest regards, for the Rabitat Loan Company and the Pecuniary Loan Compnay and the Sponaneous Bank and the various others. For it is they, who gave Mrs.Sonal Modi Joseph and Rohan financial oxygen, by granting the loans.

His assessment is when one does have a relationship of a husband and wife and if and when the road gets to the point of proceedings of divorce, then there definitely will be points for arguments. Whatever had taken place, between the banks and Mrs.Sonal Modi Joseph and Rohan, for Rohan is simple divorce proceedings to bring about an amicable settlement of the various loans. Which is, what exactly happened.

Nothing was done intentionally, for had the banks received the EMIs cheques, divorce proceedings for an amicable settlement, would never have arisen.

The loans were granted on the basis of the Rabitat Loan Company, the Pecuniary Loan Company, the Spontaneous Bank receiving their amounts as stipulated had they to have received it, there would have been no arguments.

But the question that arose and which was part of the Rumour mill and to Rohan was, "Was it the banks themselves or was there a third party or parties involved to stall Rohan from filing the Appeal in Supreme Court? The Special Leave Petition."

The answer was definitely in the affirmative. Since all the harassment which was endured by Mrs.Sonal Modi Joesph and Rohan was by hired agencies which were not hired by the Loan Companies or the banks but by some third party altogether.

The long drawn road had already been taken. If Rohan was to reach, the destination and carry the mantle, of the loans while travelling, to reach his destination. The acceptance of plurality of Indian Society. Then so be it.

All the harassment stopped suddenly. It was God's Providence that prevailed. An understanding God did with those harassing and they suddenly stopped harassing and peace harmony and tranquility prevailed permanently..

The Strike

It is a known fact that courts irrespective of hierarchy, tribunals and other functionaries, experience the phenomena called strikes. The Appendix II of The Advocates Act 1961 questions, whether these strikes by lawyers and here it is important and how it is said, in legal parlance, 'pertinent to note,' that the Act states Lawyers and not Advocates. Legal parlance or not, if Shashi Tharoor was to draft a plaint, he might "Twit" on Twitter with, 'imp,' and, 'pert.'

An apprehension can be, that on a reading, the understanding of, whenever read in any legal document, 'It is pertinent to note.'

The question arises, whether the strikes are on moral, ethical or a legal basis, apart from the cause or reason to strike. Various rulings have been passed by the High Court and the Supreme Court on strike calls by Bar Associations. But this strike, by all the Bar Associations of India, which started with the Lawyers of the City Civil Court in Mumbai and through out Mumbai with lawyers practicing in the Magistrate Courts and to towns such as Mangoan, Ratnagari and to cities such as Nagpur and Panaji. Later engulfing other cities of various states, Chennai and then the whole State of Tamil Nadu, Kochi and then the State of Kerala, Chandigarh and the whole state of Punjab and the others began to follow like 9 pins, except here there weren't 9 but 29 pins. With each and every Bar Association having lawyers on strike. The Judiciary was crippled. Which in turn, had crippled The Executive and The Legislature.

The people of India had realized that it is not the legislature, who made and sale laws to the people, but the people themselves. They had elected their representatives and these representatives were duty bound, when called upon to be answerable, to whom they were elected by. Without the electorate, the elected is a shepherd without sheep. Therefore the sheep need to simply decide, to move away from the shepherd and steer without a shepherd. This is what Rohan calls 'political consumerism.'

However in the 63 years of Indian Independence, never had such an issue propped up, whereby the whole country was brought to a stand still on one particular issue.

Before Independence, yes the country had come together, on one point and that being "Swaraj," "Independence." But it took 90 years for the country to gain independence from the revolt of 1857 to 1947. Here the entire country, right from Kashmir to Kanya Kumari, from the beaches of Mumbai to that of Kolkata. Every Indian, whether Hindu, Muslim, Sikh, Buddhist, Jain, Parsi, Christian was united on the issue. Even the issue of Independence, had not united the country to such an extent.

It was when the appeal was herd, by the Division Bench of the Chief Justice of the Bombay High Court Mr. Justice R Bharuch and Mrs. Justice Shalinee Mathur J.J. that caused the spark. Normally the case would have been referred to a full bench comprising of three judges.

The prayers of the Petition were

(a) To strike down section 24 of the Advocates Act 1961 as Ultra Vires of article 19(1)(g) and of article 14 and Article 29(1) and the Preamble of the of The Constitution of India being, Right to work and right to equality, right to preserve ones regional diversity. With reasonable restriction and not a blanket restriction, whereby law graduates should be allowed to be enrolled on the roll of advocates and be allowed to carry on such other profession, as the Bar Council shall deem fit, which would compliment their profession and accept the petitioner's application for enrolment, on the roll of advocates by the Bar Council of Maharashtra and Goa.

(b) To direct the Bar Council of Maharashtra and Goa to allow the advocates on roll, to carry out such other profession, which would compliment their law profession, after approval of such profession, by the Bar Council of Maharashtra and Goa and accept the Petitioner's application for enrolment, on the roll of advocates by the Bar Council of Maharashtra and Goa.

(C) In the event of prayer (a) or (b) not being granted, to direct all schools within the State of Maharashtra, to teach only one Language from the 1st Standard to the 10th.

(d) In the event, none of the above being granted, to direct the Bar Council of Maharashtra and Goa to accept the Petitioners application, for enrolment on the roll of advocates, after furnishing a bond, stating he shall resign as Managing director of International Business Travellers's Club Ltd. and shall only practice the profession of law.

(e) For orders which your lordships deems fit.

Prayer (d) was intended to be put, but was not. Having set on a path, keep walking was Rohan's motto. Prayer (d) is keeping the back door open. Which wasn't the intention of filing the petition.

Obviously the first and the second prayer, was not going to be granted, as the Advocates Act and various other judgments, like the Dr. Chulani's case was already a precedent. Therefore the petition was an open and shut case.

The third prayer (C) was never going to be granted, not by the Court, nor by the Parliament. The first Prime Minister Pandit Jawaharlal Nehru had wanted no linguistic division of states. But had acceded to, the first state being formed, on a linguistic basis, being Andhra Pradesh, due to a fast until death of Potti Sreeramulu. From then, one state after another, was divided on a linguistic basis. Prayer (c) was never, not in any degree, going to be granted.

However the third prayer was reported in the headlines of all leading newspapers and news channels and radio.

WRIT PETITION SEEKS SCHOOLS TO TEACH ONLY ONE LANGUAGE

This made all the political parties and various organizations, come fighting for the Marathi manoos, some for the Hindi cause and by surprise for the English cause. Rohan never expected any demonstrations for the English cause, but their contention was because of English, the call centers had propped up at Malad, Parel, Vashi, Pune, Bangalore, Hyderabad, Gurgoan and various parts of India. With various big companies such as 3G, J.P.Morgan, Intellinet, Convergys and hordes of others, who had set up shop. If the Chinese could speak English as Indians do, the business of call centers would have gone to the Chinese. If any other country, could speak English as India the U.S., U.K. Austrialia, Canada, would transfer the call centers to that country, obviously keeping in mind the cost of manpower. India is the only country which speaks English, without translating it into another language first. Even though, English is not the first language. But for the bureaucracy in India, it is easier setting up business in Manila, than setting up business in Mumbai.

Every newspaper and news channel and radio station, was informed about prayer (c) for the schools in Maharashtra to teach only one language from the 1st to the 10th standard. If they were not informed, they became informed, since others were. Rohan with a little help from his friends, in Public Relations, in various firms, this was achieved.

It was a joy, no boundary could bound, to see the headlines. Rohan never expected having worked for 'The Independent' newspaper of the Times Of India that one day headlines, would be created by him. He had seen Mr.Righteous's article with his photograph with his invention "a one peddle cycle." But that was Mr.Righteous, this was Rohan.

Headlines are headlines, whether good, bad or ugly. Everyday of life is a headline, whether good bad or ugly. People do not write a diary wherein everyday, they would be making their own headlines in their own newspaper, for instance 'The Rohan Diary.' Yes there is Facebook, Twitter which has made people do acts, which they have never done before, 'Typing their Diary.' Facebook and Twitter have made people do things, which the age of the Diary, couldn't.

The hearing was crammed with people and from all sections, besides the media. Since the case involved a Constitutional question and would have a mass effect. The petition would have been referred to a Full Bench, which would have to be convened by the Chief Justice of the Bombay High Court.

There was nothing to do for Rohan, as he had expected such a judgment. He was alone. Even though there were 3 others, who had joined him in the crusade, at the beginning. They backed out, since no advocate wanted to take up their brief, the cause. They had a family business and were running it themselves and had an L.L.B. degree, but could not practice because of the impugned rule of the Bar Council of Maharashtra and Goa. Just like the millions of Indians, who have an L.L.B. degree but cannot practice. Since it was already a decided question, that advocates should do nothing else but advocate, no one was willing to accept a loosing battle.

At this juncture, is when, the drama began. It was, after the headlines, in every newspaper, in every language, every news channel, covering the case and every radio station, mentioning about the case, after the first hearing that made advocates of all the Bar Associations of India realize what The Advocates Act 1961 had subjected them to. Those, who were successful, saw the petition, as a spade against their success and those who were not, saw it as a spade to success. But even those, who were successful, saw a silver lining that all those things, which they could not do, might see light, like run their family business. It was like a leach, present and one didn't know its presence, which was causing a hindrance, to the desire of living fulfilled lives. Since an advocate, who would like to run his own business cannot and one who has an L.L.B degree but runs his own business, cannot practice law.

The call for the strike took place, with the advocates from the City Civil Court boycotting proceedings and demanded prayer (a) to be granted in absolute. The advocates practicing in the City Civil Court were already well versed with boycotting court proceedings, through earlier strikes for the demand of the rule, that any case whose quantum of claim stands above the amount of Rs. 100,000, the claimant shall have to file an action in the High Court and the City Civil Court shall not have Pecuniary Jurisdiction, to try the suit.

The advocates of the City Civil Court were already aggrieved. Due to cases which would have been filed in the City Civil Court if the amount of Rs.100,000, stood increased and thereby receive more work. They were basically saying they wanted more work, whereby receiving higher remuneration and live better lives. Which, brings to the forefront that they were unhappy, with their standard of living and wanted more remuneration, yield from their profession, which is a matter of interpretation. But without the interpretation, whenever workmen for instance of a transport organization land up striking, it is mainly for higher wages. Advocates practicing in the City Civil Court jumped to the idea. It was a cause which they have been looking for in years, since the Rs. 100,000, had still not been increased.

The strike called by the advocates practicing in the City Civil Court was termed as unlawful, on the terms that it had no legal basis. The Chief Justice of the Bombay High Court cited the case of Rajinder Singh V/s Union of India [(1993-1) 103 Punj L. R. 562-563)]

The ratio being, the main reasoning of the case was an advocate of the Punjab and Haryana High Court did not wish to record his appearance in Court, since he was part of an ongoing strike. The recording of an appearance at Court is just how it is said, "present Miss or Maam," in school or college. The advocate, as in this case had to say, "I appear for the plaintiff, I appear for defendant 1,2 or 3 or defendant infinity."

The judge in this case had stated, "Shri Saini did not address the Court on account of Lawyers being on strike. When an advocate accepts the brief he is duty bound to appear in the case in Court. He becomes a privileged person who can address the Court under the provisions of the Advocates Act 1961. Under section 29 and 30 of the Advocates Act such an advocate engaged by the litigant has a right of audience in the Court in the cause. Lawyers engaged in the cases by intentionally and deliberately absenting from the Court, when cases are called are not serving the cause of litigants, their paymasters. Appearing in Court and not getting presence recorded and further not arguing the case is still worse and is unprofessional and unethical. Present is such a case where though Shri Saini has come to the Court but does not want to address the Court or to get his presence recorded. What legal sanction the Association of Lawyers has to give a call to the Lawyers to go on strike is beyond our comprehension. The fear in the Lawyers as is projected by Mr. Saini not to argue the case for being punished by the Association for his appearance in Court on account of the call by the Association to go on strike or in other words to abstain from appearing in the Court, has no legal basis."

But why was the first spark lit, by the advocates of the City Civil Court even though they were duty bound to appear in those briefs taken. They wanted a better life, freedom to do what they have been thought from childhood three languages Hindi, English, Marathi and thereby having the ability to carry out three professions at the same time.

"Under the provision of the Advocates Act 1961 he the advocate becomes a privileged person who can address the Court."

"But the fact is that when one doesn't have a steady income, on what basis should an advocate be privileged. The professions of doctors, chartered accountants and engineers and lawyers are always equated at par. However a doctor, always will receive a steady income, since every human on earth turns ill or is needed at the time of birth and the time of death to have a doctor mingle with him. Chartered accountants receive a steady income, with every citizen who earns a credible income, needs a chartered accountant and even those who do not. But there are those, who earn a credible income, visited doctors regularly, engaged a chartered accountant to file their returns, but might have had nothing to do with an advocate ever in their life," thought Rohan.

The first thing the air hostess demonstrates about life safety procedures at the time of take off, of an aircraft in emergency landing on water, is please wear your life jacket first, then help women and children. Rohan presumed the advocates of the City Civil Court had all traveled by flight in a Boeing737 or Airbus 320 just before the call of the strike and began to try and wear their life jacket, since they must have felt their flight 'life' was on water. Since when? Something only they could answer.

"Lawyers engaged in the cases by intentionally and are deliberately absenting from the Court when cases are being called are not serving the cause of the litigants."

"No one should blame the advocates of the City Civil Court. They, sure, had all, just arrived from the airport and the air hostess had reprimanded all of them, that they have to wear their life jacket first, before helping women and children. How could these advocates help the women and children who were the litigants, when they were reprimanded by the air hostess to wear their life jacket first? Obviously these advocates were going to wear their life jacket first, before bothering about the women and children, at the side of them being the litigants, even though these women and children might be their paymasters. Yes these women and children, the litigants might be their paymasters, for these advocates and since these advocates had to wear their life jacket first, which didn't seem to be happening, the women and children, the litigants were suffering at the side. But none, could be done or can be done since the Advocates Act was not allowing them to, whereby carry any other profession besides advocacy. Therefore the women and children were suffering, the litigants," thought Rohan.

What legal sanction the Association of Lawyers has to give a call to the Lawyers to go on strike will always be beyond the comprehension of all the Courts where this strike was concerned. Since the call for the strike was the grant of prayer (a) and (b) in absolute.

A similar situation had taken place in 2001 in the State of Uttar Pradesh. But that was just in one state.

In that case the Allahabad High Court condemning the strike said

ADHOCACY

"It has come to our notice that is in about half the District Courts in the State of U.P. the Lawyers are on strike for about a month and they are not permitting any judicial authority to work."

In the present situation the strike from the City Civil Court went to that of the Esplanade Court at C.S.T. the Chief Metropolitan Magistrates Court. It spread to the Bhoiwada Court at Parel.

"Some of the Courts need to join the fastidious clan. A Court is the temple of justice of the conscious, something Rohan read in Psychoanalysis through Sun Signs. In Court only 2+2 = 4 works. However the profession of advocacy is how you put 2+2=5=4. The Mandir, the Gurudwara, the Mosque, the Fire Temple, the Synagogue, the Church is the mandir of the subconscious where 2+2 = 5 works. The mandir of the subconscious is kept clean. But the mandir of the conscious defintely needs commonality with that of the subconscious. No one would want to admit themselves to a hospital which is filthy," were thoughts of Rohan.

From the Bhoiwada Court to the Magistrates Court at Andheri Station the Strike was spreading fast, like fire through the forest.

"This is deeply regrettable and highly objectionable. The Judiciary exists, for serving the people and not for the Lawyers and Judges. In our view the attitude of the Lawyers of the District Courts and Commissioner of U.P. who are on strike for the last about one month is most irresponsible. The act of the Lawyers will no longer be tolerated by this Court and nobody will be allowed to hold the Judiciary to ransom. A Division Bench of this Court in Manoj Kumar V/s Civil Judge, has held that if Lawyers go on strike even then Courts must sit and pass judicial orders even in absence of the Lawyers and if the functioning of the Court is disturbed by anybody police help must be taken by the District Judge or other presiding officer. The people of the state are fed up with Lawyers strikes and are suffering greatly. The Lawyers must understand that litigants, witnesses etc. come to Court from far off places, often at heavy expense but they find that the Courts are closed just because the Lawyers are on strike. This is most unfair to the litigants or their witnesses."

"We therefore, direct the judges of all District Courts, Commissioners, and other Presiding officers of the Courts or authorities where judicial or quasi-judicial work is being done that from tomorrow they must start sitting in Court and start hearing of the cases and pass orders even in the absence of the working of the Courts of the District Judge, Collector, Commissioner or the Presiding Officer of the Court concerned or authority and shall call the Police and prevent them from doing so. The Lawyers must know that enough is enough." is the latter part in a nutshell.

The situation was the same, except the Lawyers of the various states were on strike, not just in Uttar Pradesh but in every State. Maharashtra had broken the ice already and the agitation of the strike began to spread like wild fire, in the forest of India. Except here flames began to ignite in various states, even without the fire touching them from Maharashtra.

The Supreme Court in Raman Services Pvt. Ltd. had reviewed the entire law and laid down as far as strikes by Lawyers were concered. "When an advocate who was engaged by a party was on strike, there is no obligation on the part of the Court, either to wait or to adjourn the case on that account. Time and again this Court has said that an advocate has no right to stall the proceedings on the ground that advocates have decided to strike or to boycott the Courts or even boycott any particular Court." Here the Supreme Court made references as to earlier cases decided by them being U.P.Sales Tax Services Association V/s Taxation Bar Association Agra, K John Koshy V/s Tarkeshwar Prasad Shaw Mahim Prasad Singh V/s Jacks Aviation, Koluthumottil Razak V/s State of Kerela.

The Supreme Court has held that the advocates have no right to stall the Court or any Court. But the point in question prayer (a) and (b) had struck a cord. Even Mahatma Gandhi and the freedom fighters had no right to carry out any of the various acts and had no right to start the Swadeshi movement, but they did.

"Generally strikes are the antithesis of the progress, prosperity and development, strikes by the professionals including the advocates cannot be equated with strikes undertaken by the industrial workers in accordance with statutory provisions."

But the advocates had not bothered about thesis or antithesis or synthesis of progress, prosperity or development.

"The question of understanding Indian society, which is multi and pluralistic in nature, thereby becoming a multi professional society, is all that could be seen. In case of regional towns, there is only one language spoken, being the regional language. The language becomes the basis, from where ones profession stems. But with every regional language stems 3 dialects within the radius of a village or a town."

"With the holocaust of, always having the regional language and the National language and English and the 3 dialects. Each and every

citizen of India, lands up being able to practice 3 professions. Being able to practice 3 professions doesn't amount to making the Indian citizen junk of all trades and master of none. Unfortunately the meaning of master, can never apply. Since the only person, who used his brain to 6/10 of the brain level is Plato. Therefore no advocate, only allowed to practice the profession of law, becomes master of the profession of law. Indians having learned three languages in school have been trained to carry out three professions at the same time fairly well, without causing a hindrance to each other, just as they speak Marathi in a government office, English at their office and Hindi with their friends down the road while playing volleyball or cricket. Or Hindi at an office and English with their friends."

"This strike was definitely not an antithesis of progress, prosperity and development. But was the culmination of 50 years of subjugation of a section of an Act, which hindered progress. Prosperity of Lawyers all across India and those who obtained an L.L.B degree and the litigants. Since the advocates could not practice any other profession but law. The L.L.B. degree holder who were advocates and could not practice the profession of law since the profession of law doesn't guarantee a steady income, unlike a salaried job. Litigants suffered, since advocates had to keep their life jacket on," were Rohan's thoughts which he had written down with regards to the petition.

"The services rendered by the advocates to their clients are regulated by a contract between the two, besides statutory limitations, restrictions and guidelines incorporated in the Advocates Act. The rules made there under and Rules of Procedure adopted by the Supreme Court and the High Courts. Abstaining from the Courts by the advocates, by and large does not only affect the persons belonging to the legal profession but

ADHOCACY

also hampers the process of justice, sometimes urgently needed by the consumer of justice, the litigants. Legal profession is essentially a service oriented profession. The relationship between a Lawyer and his client is one of trust and confidence."

"But the advocates of every State of India who had gone on strike, was convinced that the restriction of not being able to practice any other profession, meant that they were not allowed to speak any other language, except Hindi, for instance when they have been taught the regional languages or English. The advocates were the consumers of justice and are entitled to benefit from the same just as the litigants," thought Rohan.

"The workers in furtherance of collective bargaining organize a strike as per the provisions of the Industrial Disputes Act as a last resort to compel the management to concede to their legitimate demands."

This is exactly what the strike meant, to compel the Supreme Court to Concede to their legitimate demands. Demonstrations were carried out at every High Court. Judges were sitting in Court, but they were practically empty. Cases were called out, but advocates for both sides stated, they do not want their appearance to be recorded. At Chennai, advocates at the Madras High Court had to fight their way, with the Police using lathis to wade off the agitating advocates. But that was a one off case, since it took place due to a misunderstanding, which blew out of proposition. Obviously advocates were learned people and were not going to resort to altercations.

There were two factions of advocates. One who believed that advocates shouldn't practice any other profession, but law and the other, being those who went on strike. The judges on the other hand, were all duty bound to be part of the first faction, because the Act laid down by Parliament and the precedent laid down by the Supreme Court in the Dr. Chulani's case.

The question now was whether the Supreme Court concedes or doesn't to the legitimate demands of the striking advocates.

The 26/11 Terrorists Attacks On Mumbai And The Security Threats

There are genes and they are everlasting. It was Radhika's turn, to prove the age old philosophy of genes. Like father, like daughter, like mother, like daughter.

Mr.Righteous was already dead and gone.

"I hope to heaven, which I am sure, without any blocks. Mine, I don't know, since my soul is half Christian, half Hindu."

If Rohan goes to heaven both Jesus and Ram will be fighting over his dead body. If Rohan goes to hell, Rohan would be kicked by both Jesus and Ram and if Rohan did not attain moksh, he will be kicked by the devil too. The mind can really wonder *was* what Rohan's notions were, about his journey after death which Rohan always said that thoughts which are inconceivable remain mind over matter.

At least it would be accepted and thought, that Mr.Righteous's soul received moksh, since he was Mr.Righteous.

"*Mine I will tell you in my next birth, don't forget to come and see me. Frankly don't, just connect with me on Facebook,*" were Rohan's thoughts.

Rohan loved is sister Radhika.

Keeping in mind the genes of Radhika, she married Ravi from Karad near Belgaum and was working in a security establishment, which landed having a connection with what took place at the Taj Mahal Palace and Towers. This was the year which had a two and two zeroes and an eight. The year which was going to change the lives of Indians and Rohan and make people take a flight rehearsal, while entering the High Court at Bombay with its charade in front except, for one dog who takes his nap on the steps of the High Court on a Saturday afternoon. He to might be on the roll of advocates, since he wears his gown, even while sleeping on the bottom of the spiral steps of the Original side. Nothing is written in the High Court on which side is the Original side or which side is the Appellate, at least to Rohan's knowledge but again its all about customs and usages.

Ten men enter Mumbai as amphibians and take India hostage, for three and a half days. The Mumbai Police is, again customs and usuages, known to be second to Scotland Yard after nabbing Charles Sobhraj at the famous restaurant outside Alto Povorim in Goa, 'O'Coqueiro.'

Were they sleeping?

"Lets not say that, since many died saving our lives. My life has been saved," was Rohan's answer to the question. But what actually took place is a question mark.

If the CIA being the sponge of knowledge, could not avert the September 11 attacks on the World Trade Center, lets not debate on the Mumbai Police. A guess and acceptance should be, that

Scotland Yard is a yardstick to be achieved by many, since they have definitely averted a September 11 and a 26/11.

Rohan is an ardent goer of the lane Choclate Gully. Why the lane is called Choclate Gully because in the late 80s, when Brown was the rampant drug, it was available there. A normal question would pop up, with regards to the accountability and verification and backing under the stipulations put down by the Indian Evidence Act. Its customs and usages which shall apply, or the gossip has not yet found the realms of statute law.

The attack happened on a Wednesday evening and with the practice which many a Christian, do not follow compared to the others at Mahim, have been a regular goer of the Novena at the Holy Name Cathedral at the back of the Olympia restaurant which is 90 degrees to the Leopold café.

On that fateful day, Rohan was attending the conference of the India Travel and Trade Distribution Summit 2008 at The Taj Lands End Bandra. Had Rohan not, Rohan would have been at the Choclately Gully. Rohan could have been saying, "Hai Ram."

Colaba is one place, which has never been affected by Force Majeure or Vis Majeure. But law of averages had to catch up. At the time of the activity of 6th Dec 1992 which led to the riots of 1993 every major part of Mumbai was burning and Rohan was playing cricket in the gullies of Colaba.

At the time of the flooding of the whole of Mumbai on 26/7 in the year 2005, Rohan was attacking frames of Snooker at a club called The Catholic Gymkhanna. Mr.Righteous always said to Rohan, "If you are not facing any problem on a daily basis at office, you are definitely going to face a big problem." Rohan wouldn't correlate the two, but 26/11 by far is India's biggest problem. It brought the whole of India to a standstill. But this dastardly act, by these ten men, was not something which could have been stopped even though it should have been, thwarted. To Rohan, Colaba seems to be the engine of Mumbai and India. Rohan might say the sky is red, when its blue and every dog praises its own tail. Except to paralyse India, these ten men had to come to Colaba, sit at a restaurant called Leopold, operational since 1867 and begin the go slow, of Indian economy.

In 2008 the whole world was facing the start of the recession, India wasn't. The Bombay Stock Exchange had reached its peak in January 2008. The fall of Global Markets had no impact on India's economy. However after 26/11, India began a go slow. The internet, if not for other reasons, have brought the emergence of various cities in India, but Mumbai is still the economic capital of India. Mumbai, unlike New York is the capital of Indian media, housing, "Bollywood." A combination of New York and L. A. Shut it down, an economy shall stand shut and Bollywood.

Ravi for some reason being part of the security establishment landed up being at the forefront of affairs, at the time of the entry of the four terrorist, let me say these gay charlies, walking with machine guns, going to the most prestigious place of Mumbai the lobby of the Taj Mahal hotel. Why prestigious since it's the only five star hotel since 1903 in Mumbai.

Yes the Trident has to be added besides Nariman House.

The September 11 attacks, wasn't a failed mission. The Mumbai 26/11 attacks, definitely a failed mission. There was a failed mission which took place, as far as the World Trade Center.

ADHOCACY

The car bombing which took place on February 26, 1993 in the basement.

After the 26/11 Jalianwallah Bagh massacre, there was a threat to Ravi's Life. If Ravi had a threat, so did Radhika and Mrs.Sonal Modi Joseph and Rohan. For everyone in India the 26/11 attacks ended after 3½ days. Some lost their lives and some lost their kith and kin. But Radhika, Mrs.Sonal Modi Joseph and Rohan was in a constant dilemma. The only family in India, which was in a a constant dilemma, since Ravi had received calls from terrorists threatening to take his life . A threat to his life, is a threat to his immediate family.

No other family in India has gone though the 26/11 attacks for seven months after the attack.

Yes there have definitely been, a lot of loss to a lot of families, but a differentiation has to be held.

Unfortunately the human mind, which is the conscious only, has the ability to comprehend, what is visible. Everything has to have a reason, is how the conscious mind runs, its day to day business. Where was the reason, for The Josephs's the only family to go through seven months of suffering.

"What is the suffering?. Did Ravi die?" is what Rohan was asked, by the bank thugs.

This is exactly how the conscious mind functions. It has to see a physical wound. Only then one is said to be, suffering.

India was paralyzed for three and a half days, but being paralyzed for seven months is something which is not perceivable.

The biggest psychological difficulty is being captive and yet not and yet eligible to be captive, like Kevin Costner in the movie Fugitive.

If something was to happen to Ravi, the onus would be on Rohan to take care of Radhika. Ravi and Radhika had just received blessings from lord Ram in the form of a beautiful baby Jyoti. Jyoti would have been without a father, in the first year of her birth.

There are customs and usuages of Lex Loci, which cannot change because of religion. That is of the Karta system. Just because Rohan's mother, a Hindu, that didn't mean the Karta system applied, since Mr.Righteous was Christian. Under any Christian Law, which is Cannon law, there is no Karta system. But the law of the land Lex Loci applied and Rohan became the Karta of the family. Therefore the onus would lie on Rohan.

A coralary, which would remind Rohan of the flick 'Sholay'. The only flick which ran at Minerva Theatre, for 5 consecutive years and which Rohan has watched umpteen times and will for,

"Yeh dosti, hum nahi chodege, chodege dum magar tera saatna chodege."

To Rohan these words are and will always mean his friendship with his friend India. Which having the holocaust of the security threats and the banks playing tantrums by April though it wasn't banks it was the thugs. The occurrence crept, was life worth carrying on, with this relationship, with this friend of his, India. Yes it was. Since Rohan had already been a Chupa Rustom, nearly to be resticated from school, a PNG having, a case lying in abeyance about the fate of advocates and those having an L.L.B. degree and that of every citizen of India and all other exigencies put together. Rohan could not betray his mother India, nor his friend, by carrying out the cowardly act of suicide. Since the banks wanted to see physical calamity and the case was still in abeyance.

It was only when, the Pakistani government accepted that Ajmal Kasab is a Pakistani that the security threats stopped.

But did it?

The Arguments in Supreme Court

"It must be remembered that there is nothing more difficult to plan, nothing more doubtful of success, nor more dangerous to manage than the creation of a new system. For the initiation, has the enmity of all, who would profit by the representation of the old institutions and merely lukewarm defenders in those who would gain, by the new ones. The hesitation of the latter arises in part from the general scepticism of mankind, which does not really believe in an innovation until experience proves its value."

Niccolo Machiaveli
Western Political Thinker

The matter now in Supreme Court in the form of a Special Leave Petition, commonly known as SLP, under its Civil Appellate Jurisdiction. The situation outside the Supreme Court was chaos and outside every High Court and Magistrate Courts, and were devoid of advocates in the Court rooms, though a miniscule amount did function. It would remind one of the non cooperation movement, by Mahatma Gandhi against the British. It has never been realized that if the Courts come to a standstill the whole country would come to a standstill, since the administration offices and the police would function but no Magistrates would be hearing cases. People would be languishing in jail, since no bail applications would be heard.

The country was functioning, but a silent civil revolution was taking place. The ministers could not sit as Magistrates, as they were not qualified to do so. Nor could anyone sit as a Magistrate, unless appointed by the due process of law.

With such a situation a Full Bench of 15 judges was constituted. This was put forward by the President of India. An act, which she felt the need for, as justice to the people. Since the situation could turn into an emergency at any point of time. It was the Executive and the Judiciary. Since the Judiciary is not appointed by the Prime Minister but by the President, for the first time, Parliament had no say in the matter.

The President Her Excellency Shrimati Sonali Srivasta was of the opinion that the people of India, should not be hurt in any manner that at any point of time, the people of India should not feel the President did not do everything for a non encumberant trial. It was her decision and on her recommendation that the Chief Justice of India R. J. Setalwad constituted a Full Bench of 15 judges.

Rohan began his arguments with, "Your Lordships, through its work, spread over half a century, the Supreme Court has gained the respect of all citizens and has emerged as a vigilante of democracy and liberty. Your forceful intervention has steered the ship, the State during many storms, without causing peril to it. With great patience, sageness, prudence, sagaciousness your Lordships of this Honourable Apex Court has held the balance between civil liberty, order and reform. Your contribution by watering the roots and stabilizing the basic values of our supreme law and life as well has been both imaginative as well as a practice. Your Lordships, have enhanced the legal profession of the country, in the unity of the nation. I the petitioner along with all these, whose signatures I have, request your Lordships, to do the same in this petition too."

"Your Lordships, have already decided this issue in the case of Dr. Haniraj L. Chulani. However in the present appeal, the Appellants do not put forward, the question of excessive legislative power. The question which is put forward is the whole situation of the country, which needs to be taken into consideration. All Acts are enacted in respect to the country. If any Act is against the very social situation of the country, due to every Indian being subjected to the three language syndrome, the situation arises that rule 1(I) of the Bar Council of Maharashtra & Goa framed under Section 28 (2) read with Section 24(1)(e) whereby Rule 1(I) doesn't violate the Articles of the Constitution, but violates the Preamble, the social situation. One cannot change the social situation of the country. Just as Parliament cannot amend the Preamble of the Constitution as held in the Keshavananda Bharati case. The social situation of the country your Lordships, is a process which flows from hundreds of years and cannot be changed by one Act of Parliament."

"Before I go any further, your Lordships, these are my submissions.

(1) It is not the rule making power which the Appellant disputes. But it violates various laws embedded in our system, Common law, Principles of Equity and Good Conscience, Custom Law.

ADVOCACY

(2) As far as Statute law is concerned being the Advocates Act 1961 the same doesn't stand above the Preamble of the Constitution of India.

(3) Article 29 (1) of the Constitution states any section of the citizens residing in the territory of India or any part thereof having a distinct language, script or culture of its own shall have the right to conserve the same. The people of India being multi linguistic, multi religious, multi cultural thereby having a distinctive work culture being multi professional, has the right to practice the same.

(4) The Parliament's power to enact an Act does not extend to damaging or destroying or abrogating the essential features of the Constitution, which are embedded in the Preamble of the Constitution, that is liberty of thought, expression, belief, faith and worship being the genus and its species being multi professionalism.

(5) The constituent of Indian citizens being, multi lingual, multi religious and multi cultural and thereby multi professional is not a phenomena of today. The ingredient dates back to the days of the Aryan Civilization and through the caste system even before the Constitution was enacted.

(6) The Supremacy of the Preamble of the Constitution of India as held by this Honourable Apex Court in the Keshavananda Bharati case, whereby the basic structure of the Constitution cannot be vicissituded under any circumstance, has to be upheld in the present case too before your Lordships.

(7) The guarantee of basic human rights to all its citizens to ensure, justice, social, economic and political, liberty of thought, expression, belief, faith and worship and equality of status of opportunity. These are rights stated in the Preamble. All these above rights make Indian society, a multi professional society, even before the enactment of the Constitution.

(8) Parliament under democracy is an insurance company who under the insurance companies enactment being the Constitution of India, has to abide by the Preamble.

(9) The policy holders, the citizens of India are supreme and Parliament under any circumstances has to abide by the contract signed between the insurance company Parliament and the policy holders the citizens of India. The policy of the citizens of India is the Preamble of the Constitution which cannot be amended under any circumstance.

(10) In a Constitution, what is left unsaid, is as important as, what is said, what is implied, is as much a part of the instrument, as what is expressed. What is left unsaid that Indian society is multi professional and what is implied is that India is multi professional, which is as much a part of the instrument, The Constitution of India.

(11) The Preamble of the Constitution is the contract between the policy holders, the policy holders the citizens of India and Parliament. The policy guarantees the diversities and that it shall be protected. The same has also been

guaranteed under Article 29(1) of the Constitution. The species of the genus being multi professionalism has to be accepted. If not it would amount to, only parents of Indian society being accepted and the children being left out as Persona Non Grata the species.

(12) The power to alter or destroy the basic structure of the Constitution the Preamble is an ultimate legal sovereignity and that sovereignity rest with the people. But the people are not associated with the law making process at all. Parliament when enacting the Advocates Act 1961 cannot be equated with the people and Parliament's will is definitely not the peoples will.

(13) There were four advocates which were involved with our independence. Mahatma Gandhi, Pandit Jawaharlal Nehru, Sardar Vallabhai Patel, Quad-i-azam Mohammed Ali Jinnah, though the creation of Pakistan happened. They happened to be advocates from well to do families and were Barristers at law. It is these advocates who brought the tyranny of the Parliament, the British to its knees and gained independence. Similarly it is the advocates today, who has to keep the supreme Parliament in check and balances which otherwise it would amount to a dictatorship, in disguise of a cloak called Parliament. Though Parliament till date has not wronged the people of India as the People of India themselves elect those in Parliament. The same would apply with regards to the British Rule.

(14) Unlimited power in the hands of Parliament, is like signing a death warrant, except its execution is to

happen at a later date. The only overseer is an advocate to safeguard the policy holders, the citizens from the absolute tyranny of Parliament. In the words of W.B. Yeats "No government has the right, whether to flatter fanatics or in mere vagueness of mind to forge an instrument of tyranny and say it will never be used."

(15) The various psychiatric institutions across the world having given the opinion and findings that Indian society is multi and pluralistic in nature and that multi professionalism is a species of the genus of multi linguism, multi religious and multi cultural society.

(16) Advocates across the country having sent their submissions, with their physical signatures in support of the petition.

(17) The Advocates having filed the case for being allowed to practice, as sales tax practitioners which amounts to, a want to be able to practice law as well as that of an accountant.

(18) The pending amount of matters to be disposed off in Court, a backlog of cases, which should not be dragged on, for want of a sustainable income from litigants to Advocates.

(19) Indian society being multi and pluralistic in nature, can take anything in small doses. The Advocates Act due to the impugned rule administers only one big dose advocacy. Only those who can take one big dose succeed.

Rohan endeavoured to be as emphatic as possible and went on with his arguments. "It would be prudent to explain the work of genetics and DNA your Lordships. Genetics play an important role in the societal situation. Each person is unique, but he or she inherits some characteristics and even appearance from his or her parents. We all know your Lordships that the study of how characteristics are passed on, from one parent to an offspring, is known as genetics and it affects all forms of Life and the legal profession."

"At the center of this process is the DNA (deoxyribonucleic acid) molecule, which exists inside every living cell and contains a complex chemical code that controls the way in which life forms are put together and operate. DNA is composed of genes, and DNA in turn makes up chromosomes. All these microscopic structures lives, in the nuclei of cells."

"Your Lordships, let us look at, what genes do as far as rules made under section 28(2) of the Advocates Act. A gene your lordship is a basic unit of inheritance, a small segment of a DNA molecule. There are about 100,000 genes in each of the 46 human chromosomes. Genes contains the instructions, which control cell activities. Therefore genes help to determine the characteristic of an organism. Genes is the basic unit of inheritance and there being around 100,000 genes in chromosomes. For the Advocates Act to apply, rules made under section 28 rule 2 it would have to alter these very genes, which have been passed on from generations. For instance at every stage in Indian history, be it from the Aryan (Vedic) period right to the present day, there have been a clear and distinct fact that multiple languages has always been a means of communication in the Indian subcontinent.

With three languages, being the medium of communication of Indian society today. We Indians, have the ability to practice three professions simultaneously, at any given point of time."

"Your Lordships, let us see, what heredity has got to do, with the impugned rule. Heredity is the transmission of characteristics, from one generation to another, such as size, shape and colour, are determined by genes passed on by parents. Therefore the characteristics of the multiple language syndrome, has passed on through generations. Therefore as Indian citizens, we have the genetics and heredity passed on through generations of speaking multiple languages. The same theory applies, as far as religion and culture is concerned. Had the various invasions, not taken place of India and their subsequent integration into the Indian diaspora, we would have not had such a strong multi language, religion and culture syndrome. For instance your Lordships, I would not be speaking English, had the British not have conquered India. It is this syndrome, which makes an Indian, able to adapt and practice multi professions. For instance, being an Advocate in the morning and a businessman in the afternoon and a doctor in the evening. As an Indian, your Lordships, I speak to the Taxi driver in Hindi, the court clerk in Marathi and to your Lordships in English. In no other country this happens. This is the life, of every citizen of India. Whether in Delhi, Chennai, Kolkatta, Bangalore, Hyderabad, Pune and all other cities, towns, villages of India including the city of Mumbai, is subject to the multiple language syndrome. Only, if we Indians are allowed to do things in multiples, would we be able to live our lives to the fullest and the lives as Indians to the fullest. Since your Lordships, I might migrate to another country, become a citizen of that country or be a non resident Indian. But then the question of advocacy doesn't come in."

At this particular point of time advocate general appearing for the government intervened Mr. Harsh Sinha, "Your Lordships, do not need to go into what has happened in the Vedic period as we are not living in the Vedic period . . . . "

Before Mr. Sinha could go forward, the Chief Justice cut him short, "Mr. Sinha this is not a normal ordinary civil case. This is with regards to every advocate on strike and Courts being boycotted, at this very moment as I speak and people languishing in jail, since their bail applications are not being heard and a grave law and order situation, in every part of the country. The Appellant here is advocating his first case and the first case is here in this Court. I give you directions not to interrupt the Appellant for whatever reason, without permission from this Court and if you do, it has to have grave relevance to importance. You will have your turn, to reply to the Appellant. We put forward, the same to the Appellant too, at the time of reply to your submissions. Does this Court have your agreement?"

Mr. Sinha and Rohan both stated in unison, "Yes your Lordships."

For Rohan it felt like school as if, saying present miss.

"You may carry on," said the Chief Justice.

"Your Lordships, let us look at what Memetics, has to do with the impugned rule. Humans often copy each other, from the time we are small, to taking to chewing tobacco or smoking it, to adults using a blackberry mobile. Family, community and society, influence their behavioural pattern. For instance, a person who is a rice eater from the south, who doesn't eat wheat. His siblings will have the same habit of eating rice. His siblings may grow up and eat outside, but they shall always eat rice at home and want to eat rice at home. The same is the case of one from the north of India, where wheat is concerned. To understand this pattern, it is essential to understand the study of memes, Memetics. Memes are essentially the cultural equivalent that is transmitted, from one person to another, much as genes transmit hereditary information, from one person to his or her progeny."

"Your Lordships, through the study of Memetics, it is found Memetics has three qualities fecundity, fidelity and longevity. Fecundity being it should be easy to replicate. Fidelity being copies of it should be accurate. The third longevity, it should have long life. The multi lingual, religious and cultural syndrome fits all three."

"The concept of multiplicity, pluralistic nature in our society has traveled as water rushes down the mountain. It is the first thing that travels to, an offspring of a parent. The way a child says 'mama' or 'dada' or' mummy or 'daddy' or 'dad' or' mom' or 'ma', is taught to the child by the parents of the child, right to the point, when he grows up."

"With the influence of radio, television and the media the child is, further subjected to various languages, strengthening the concept of multiplicity and pluralistic nature in the child's life, with their being no negativity in doing so. For instance, a father telling his son to learn Malayalam, Gujarati and Konkani and Marathi, the child gets subjected to an acceptance, that multiplicity and a pluralistic nature is an accepted norm. This multiplicity and pluralistic nature in society, becomes a way of life and a behavioral pattern of our society, right from hutmen dwellers, to the middle class, to the upper middle class, to the affluent. All are subjected to the multiplicity syndrome of Indian society."

"There is no denial that law is universally described, as an honourable profession and that as an advocate and officer of justice and friend of Court and as we say in legal parlance, 'amicus curiae.' An advocate is an integral part of the administration of justice. The legal profession is a monopolistic profession in character and this monopoly inherits high traditions, which its members are expected to keep an uphold."

"But your Lordships, these factors cannot be an end in itself. It's the progress of the country and the present situation of advocates across the country, which is more important than the monopolistic requirement of the legal profession. With India having the second largest amount of advocates in the world after United States and when we take into consideration the population, we have more advocates than the United States. Besides, all those who have an L.L.B. degree are advocates, who are not allowed to advocate. It would not be right to live with a, 'Pardah.' The monopoly in front when, at the back of the Pardah one doesn't have a decent meal to eat. Unless he has, he shall cling onto cases which he has."

"Your Lordships, the impugned rule is violative of Article 19(1) Right to work and Article 14 Right to equality but both have clauses to protect the impugned rule from a nulity. The impugned rule of the Advocate's Act refraining advocates from carrying on any other profession besides legal and barring those from carrying on any other profession, while enrolling themselves to the Bar, would amount to a nullity, since law is made for the smooth sailing of the vessel society and its progress whose basic structure is, as given in the Preamble of the Constitution being multiplicity and pluralistic in nature and such a section hinders the progress of society and thereby India as a whole."

"To make rules for entry has been entrusted by the legislature, to the chosen representatives of the legal practitioners, who would know the requirements of the states concerned, where the Bar Council functions and the need of the litigating public residing in the state and in the light of the setting up of Courts in the state. The same doesn't amount to unfettered power, so as to amount to total effacement of the legislative control. However the impugned rule amounts to hindering the progress of the country as a whole. The reason being Indian society has the ingredient of the multiplicity syndrome and which will always have, a want of carrying out two or more professions, by the citizens of India. It is like speaking Malayalam and Punjabi or Bhojpuri and Bengali or Gujarati and Oriya. In fact such a rule causes the disintegration of society and the country at large. Since the country being multi lingual, there fore restraining a citizen of India from being able to speak Punjabi, Marathi, Telegu, Bengali, Tamil, Gujarati or any other regional language for that matter from where he hails, his regional society in reference to Memetics would cause a conflict and thereby not allowing the point of liberty, as engrained in the Constitution. It amounts to, once you are Hindu, I cannot practice Christianity or worship Allah or any other religion or vice versa. This would amount to a

ADHOCACY

tyranny. The only thing which Indians don't do in a multi format, multiplicity is where spouse relationships are concerned."

At this point the whole Court laughed and so did the judges. At times there a statements made in Court, which as humans one cannot refrain form having a chuckle. Rohan had just to wait till the Court became silent again. Something like what happens at Wimbledon and carry on, once the Court became silent, which he did.

"Parliament cannot, under any circumstance, abrogate the basic structure of the Constitution. The basic structure being that of human freedom, liberty and that engrained in the Preamble of the Constitution which every citizen of India has a right to enjoy."

"Just as the eminent jurist Sir Nana A Palkivala pointed out in the Golaknath case 'In a Constitution, what is left unsaid is as important as what is said, what is implied, is as much a part of the instrument, as what is expressed.' In the Indian Constitution it has been left unsaid that India is a multi professional country. The Preamble of the Constitution states, India is multi lingual, multi religious and multi cultural and safeguards the linguistic, regional and religious diversities. But out of being multi linguistic, religious, cultural the genus, comes the species of being multi professional."

"To quote Sir Nani A Palkivala, "The Powers to destroy the basic structure of the Constitution is an attribute of ultimate sovereignty and that sovereignty rests with the people. But the people are not associated with the legislative process of law. Parliament cannot be equated with the people and Parliaments will, is certainly not the will of the people." The will of the people in this case, has already been shown all over the country, through protests in every part of the country, by lakhs of advocates signing this petition and endorsing it. The will of the people, is higher than the want of Parliament. The want of Parliament your Lordships, maybe is to keep the Judiciary not totally independent enough, whereby it doesn't question the acts of Parliament unlike the Federal Court of U.S.A. Parliament under no circumstance, can go against the basic structure of the Constitution being the Preamble, the will of the people."

It was the fourteenth day. Rohan was still standing. He had already discussed the Haniraj L. Chulani case, The Satish Kumar Sharma case, the cases filed by advocates filing writs to be allowed to act as chartered accountants.

With all his direct marketing skills, Rohan had to find out a way in which, the advocates situated all over India could be contacted. Advocates in rural India do not live an internet savvy life. In fact they do not need to. One, because they do not need to market themselves through the internet. Since advocates cannot advertise their services. Two, because the legal profession is like psychology it works under basis of 2+2=5=4. The computer and the internet work on the basis of 2+2=4. For example when a person is convicted of a crime and the whole country believes the convict to have committed a crime. The computer too will say the convict has committed a crime. Since majority wins. Just like Google will pop a site which is the most visited. But the advocate for the convict will be saying no, the convict has not committed a crime. Even though the convict has committed the crime. The very prominent example is that of Ajmal Kasab the lone terrorist caught in the 26/11 attacks on the Trident, Nariman Point and Taj Mahal Hotel in Mumbai.

The only way to contact the advocates, in every state was the Indian Post. Once upon a time, a lone ranger the Indian Post. No one could deliver an article but the Indian Post. But due to letters not reaching their destination, due to lost in transit or return to sender, the concept of courier came up, since even if the article or document did reach the desired person or party it reached them after, for example where an invitation to an event is concerned, after the event. But there was no courier which could reach every nook and corner of the country but the Indian Posts and no courier, which could deliver at Rs. 4. The obvious winner was the Indian Posts.

The next important task in database marketing is that once decided, to do a mailer, is procuring data. Procuring the names and addresses of advocates, situated all over India was a tedious task. But, if Rohan was a direct marketer, he definitely had to find a solution. This wasn't rocket science. Rohan went about contacting a database agency in every city. When he contacted them, each and every agency obliged. It is a human phenomenon, when you genuinely ask, people will go out of their way, to give it to you. Unfortunately people do not genuinely ask. It is like common sense is not so common. All these agencies, found the list of advocates listed with the Bar Council of their state. All Rohan did was contact a Direct Marketing Association and they set the ball in motion.

Data with names and addresses of advocates, of all the states began to pour in his inbox. Having received the data, the endorsement mailer had to be printed and sent out. Printing and sending them out wasn't a problem. The problem was money. To print the mailer and the amounts for postage, which was a huge amount, Rohan had to take personal loans from private sector banks and foreign banks and had to mortgage his house.

Rohan sent out 10 lakh mailers, with a request to give a copy to their colleagues. The cost of each mailer was Rs. 4 and was sent under Book Post. The cost for printing the mailer and the cost for the envelope came to another Rs. 2. The reason being there were two envelopes one, which was for sending the mailer and the other for receiving the mailer. In postage terms it is called 'Business Reply Envelope,' in normal parlance, it is called prepaid envelope. A new registration was not needed, that of IBTC Ltd. was used.

The reason behind the sending of physical mailers was, the fact that cases, are fought physically in Court, therefore advocates will respond to physical mailers. But the main reason being on each of the mailer a court fee stamp of Rs. 5 needed to be affixed.

"Your Lordships, in the words of the Honourable Mr. Justice V.K. Khare retd. ex Chief Justice Of India, "The Judiciary of this country has consistently endeavoured to respect the expectation of society in upholding the, 'Rule of Law,' and dispensing matters concerning law and justice to all. With the passage of time, increasing public opinion on matters concerning law has facilitated its development. Societal expectation from the Judiciary, have considerably increased with the increase of public awareness of their rights." It is this public awareness, which is being jeopardized and society expects the Judiciary, to uphold the rule of law, the Preamble of the Constitution, as much as what is said, as much as what is not said." Rohan carried on with his arguments.

"In the context of this petition, it is important to unearth, the development of law in India. The roots and ramifications of the justice system in India, remained encapsulated in Sruti (word of mouth) and Smriti (memory) for considerable period of time in ancient India, after the decline of the Harrapan Civilization in 1500 B. C."

"Subsequently the textual tradition began around the 3rd century B.C. and took a concrete form, in the later historical period."

"Transformation from the oral tradition, to the textual form, resulted in recording and processing the system of justice originated since the Rig Vedic time. In subsequent phases, more pragmatic treatism on law and justice were written, in the form of Dharmasastras. In course of time, the system of law influenced the social, political and economic affairs of the state. Kautilya's Arthasastra gives a good account, of Rajdharma of the time."

"There is no doubt that the administration of justice in India, is based on our wisdom of our ancient tenets imbibed in the oral and feudal tradition and it is important to note that the present ramifications, show the integration of multiple elements, from different cultural streams in the course of history. Introduction of the democratic set up in India in the 20th century, resulted in an integrated framework, for the system of Justice. Which, is the need for accountability, to ensure normative behaviour of the people of India."

"3000 years before the Christian era, artifacts show some rule of law through seals. In around 3000 B.C. Arthasastra, the earliest document, engulfing the theory of jurisprudence as part of the practical governance, such as Vyavahara transactions between two parties and Vivada or disputes, are enshrined in the 3rd chapter of the Arthasastra"

"Ashokan Edicts 300-183 B.C. inscribed in Brahmi script on rock surface and pillars, reveal the rule of law of the Mauryan empire, for the first time in Indian History. These are, the first written records of law and administration."

"From the above, your Lordships, it is clear that law is an ever evolving subject. What was applicable in ancient times, is not applicable now such as Sati. However, what has been applicable from ancient times and still applicable today becomes law, without any statutory recognition, sanction or enactment, that is Indian society being multi and pluralistic in nature. It is, in the light of the present situation, being the people's will and not that of Parliament for which advocates from all over the state have submitted their endorsement and with an application for an order in favour of the Appellants granting prayer (a) and (b) in absolute."

"Law has to be seen in the context of what is applicable today, since law keeps changing with time and the times has changed, whereby advocates should not be deprived of being able to carry out, which is part and parcel of Indian society being multi and pluralistic in nature."

The amount of replies Rohan received of the mailer sent out, were overwhelming. All ten lakh mailers were not received. An amount of 965,483 were received. Obviously some were lost in transit, some did not respond and some were returned to the sender. But in the history of database marketing, never was a

96.5% result received. The normal estimated result of database marketing is only 0.5 to 1. %.

Besides the 9,65,483 mailers Rohan received an amount of another 23,37,293 through those who copied the submission and couriered or posted the same through their own cost. No advocate would stand up and make an application to Court of such a sort. Yes there was the Dr. Haniraj L.Chulani case but for the advocates to send their submission, application would put them against the present system. Which made it easier for them to send it and the fact was, they believed in the petition. There were applications received through the official site of the case www.fiteforuright.law. The domain. law was appropriate. This had everything to do with law and the right of the people of India, which is engrained in the basic structure of the Constitution, the Preamble."

"Your Lordships, may take cognizance of the fact that Parliament in enacting the impugned rule of the Advocates Act, cannot assume a power not originally conferred by the Constitution. The Constitution has not granted the liberty to Parliament, to enact an Act or any provision which goes against the basic structure of the Constitution. The basic structure as engrained in the Preamble."

"To allow the impugned rule, would be granting the power to enact a section which would go against the basic structure of the Constitution, making the Constitution a creature of Parliament, when Parliament is a creature of the Constitution. It is like putting the cart, before the horse. The Constitution is the will of the people, its master, the people. Your Lordships, sit

Reoferron Martin

in judgment, with a duty to keep the Legislature and Executive in check. What is sought is only one particular section of an Act and not Parliament not the Executive. Since Parliament and the Executive is for the benefit of the people. It is exactly what is sought by this petition."

"It is imperative your Lordships, to arm the advocates of this country who from the applications received from lakhs of advocates, those who have an L L. B. degree and are not allowed to practice, the legal profession and still being received. It is the will of the people, that they want to be armed with the weapon, of being able to carry out the paradigm shift formula, that of being able to practice the legal profession and be able to practice another profession or a business. It is their submission that they want to get free from the slavery of having to fend for finance for their daily living."

Rohan was interrupted. "Your Lordships, may please note my learned friend is insinuating that advocates are slaves," by the fiery Advocate General.

"Counsel you are aware that in the Supreme Court this is just not allowed. You can put whatever you want in your arguments in reply. What we shall not accept is such interruption for something which on the face of it, counsel for the Appellants have not insinuated advocates are slaves," said Mr. Justice M. R. Lohia commenting at Harsh's harsh statement, is what Rohan called it.

Rohan felt good having been called counsel for the Appellants when he was party in person. The right wordings would have been, the Appellant. It might have seemed, which was confirmed later, that he didn't look or argue as a party in person but just another senior advocate, who forgot his gown and his Geneva Bands and was reprimanded by their Lordships for absent mindedness. Though, it happened, everyday of the case.

It was a great boon, for him. All his life, he had hated people interrupting him. Advocate General Mr. Harsh Sinha was a huge 9 foot tall stouted man. He had risen to the top, because of his legal acumen and won many battles for the government. He himself came from a wealthy family, who owned a resort in Manali, had a knitting establishment in Chandigarh and many other businesses all over India. But a fact that was, a Sagittarius was he, a horse that went straight to the point with blinkers. He had won many cases, because of the straight to the point attitude and never say die, where an argument is concerned. The straight to the point was, catch everything the opponent says and hit it with an, "aah", like Monica Seles would do, to every ball of Steffi Graf or Gabriela Sabatini. Even if the ball was out, Sinha would hit it, though with accuracy, to hit the ball divisively in the other court, where the opponent couldn't hit the ball back. In this case it was Rohan.

Mr. Sinha wasn't a Leo like Napoleon, but the fact that he had arisen to great a height like Napoleon surely made him have Leo traits. Not that Sagittarius doesn't rise, but a mix of both is a lethal combination, where the legal profession is concerned. When unearthed, it was found that his father, the great influencer Mr. Ashitosh Sinha was a Leo. Sinha had received great accolades, since he had never lost a single matter, when he was not the Advocate General. But even as Advocate General his track record was exceptional, a won run of 80%. Everyone knew that this matter for him was an open and shut case. Even though, peaceful agitations and strikes were taking place all over India.

Rohan had already accepted the fact that Sinha was going to kill him, in the duel with his aah. Knowing of the saying, take care of the pennies, the pounds will take care of themselves, resounded in Rohan's head. That was exactly Sinha's motto, like any Sagittarius and to hit every new submission with an aah.

Normally in a game of sport, the professional players, such as players of the Indian cricket team, World Cup soccer players, NBA players and other sports, all watch other players of opponents and gauge how they play. Observing their weak and plus points and try to defeat them, on their weak points and to avoid doing anything that would help the opponent exercise his plus point. Here Rohan was advocating for the first time. He had sat in all the Court rooms of the Bombay High Court. Original side, as well as Appellate. Rohan had seen various legal luminaries flown down to Mumbai, from various cities to argue cases. But he had no idea, of his opponent, who had arisen to the post of Advocate General from the High Court at Delhi. This wasn't the case of Shivaji the Maratha, against Aurangzeb the Moghul. It would definitely be the Mahatma, Pandit, Sardar and Quad-i-Azam against the British, if one wants to look at it, in a perspective. Though, it wasn't. It was Rohan advoccating a cause and the Constitution, the people of India against the one impugned rule enacted by Parliament which needed to be struck down as ultra virus of the Preamble of the Constitution. Unfortunately there was nothing in the Preamble, which stated that Indian Society is multi professional.

"Your Lordships, it is important to go into the question of what is Common law. Before the invasion of England by William the Conqueror. England was comparatively a primitive country. Very much as what we could call India at some stage, whether before the British or after the British, the stage can be left to ones perception. Travel and other means of communication, were very difficult and different customs, even different modes of dress and speech prevailed in different parts of England. In a similar manner, travel and other means of communication, were very difficult and different customs, languages, beliefs, were prevalent in India and still is."

"After the Norman conquest, a strong central government came into being and this led to the rapid growth of a uniform system of law, which was common throughout England. In a similar manner after the conquest of India, by the British, a strong central government came into being and this led to the rapid growth of a uniform system and which is still applicable today. Since our first Prime Minister Pandit Jawaharlal Nehru alongwith Parliament then, did not feel the need to change the law administered through the Acts prevalent, at the time of gaining independence, even though the British was no longer with the reigns of the country and the Acts were enacted by the British."

"Thus the term Common law, in its original sense was used by English lawyers to mean, that part of the law, which applied throughout England, as opposed to different local customs and usages, which applied to particular areas. The legislation of the Advocates Act amounts to that part of law, which applies throughout the country."

"The introduction of a circuit system, a system whereby judges went around the country administering justice, helped the process of uniforming law. As far as the impugned rule, Parliament nor the Bar council has checked psychologically whether it is apt, to enact such a rule with regards to Indian Society."

"The Process brought into being Common Law, not by imposing a new and uniform system of law on the people, but by molding into one, the different local customs and usages. This is exactly what is sought by the petition, not to change the Advocates Act but to allow prayer (a) and prayer (b) whereby an advocate can practice another profession, as long as the same is not contrary to any law, besides the legal profession. Since Parliament has not taken into consideration that Indian society is multi and pluralistic in nature."

"Not all branches of Common Law, owe their origin to local customs and usages. But your Lordships, the profession of law definitely owes its origin, to local customs and usages. Otherwise advocates would not be wearing a black coat and a gown alongwith their Geneva Bands, but would come to Court in black Bermuda shorts, a white T-shirt and a white scarf instead of their bands."

"The Principles of Equity is important to be delved on. The term equity in its widest sense means natural justice. But its technical or narrow sense means those principles of natural justice and good conscience, which were administered by the Chancery Courts in England. It is this principle, which the Appellent seeks to be applied with regards to this petition. The Common Law Courts merely declared and enforced the customs of the land and Acts passed by Parliament. The Bar Council has merely declared and enforced the Act passed by Parliament but not considered the custom of Indian society being multi and pluralistic in nature."

"However great the hardships to the claimant, they could not and did not deal with matters, which were outside the scope of the law administered by them. Similarly your Lordships, the Bar Council of Maharashtra & Goa, however great the hardship faced by advocates and those with L.L.B degrees but not practicing law, have not and could not act, violative of the impugned rule of the Advocates Act, since it is outside the scope of law administered by them. Similarly your Lordships, have not passed a judgement violative of the said impugned rule, since it would be outside the scope of law administered by yourselves in the Dr. Chulani's case. Therefore as Appellants it is evident that inordinate and excessive power has not been given to the Bar Council, but Parliament has acted without taking into consideration Indian Society as multi and pluralistic in nature However the point of Indian Society being pluralistic in nature was not brought to Parliament either. For which no encumberance has been done by Parliament."

"Common Law was rigid and narrow. There were many wrongs, for which no common law action could be brought and in many cases, a right was recognized by law, but the Common Law Courts had no means, by which they could compel the wrong doer to carry out, the orders of the Court. In a similar manner there is no action, which can be brought about, as far as the impugned section is concerned. However the Constitution of India has recognized the fact, that Indian society is multi lingual, multi religious and multi cultural in the Preamble and thereby in silence, has accepted India as multi professional. The impugned rule cannot be declared ultra virus of Article 14, Article 19 (1) and Article 29(1) because of the clauses as held in the Dr. Chulani's case. However it stands ultra vires of the Preamble."

"Thus in many cases of Common Law, recognition of rights, did not provide adequate remedy and its procedure was, often defective. In a similar manner, the right as granted by the Preamble that Indian society is multi and pluralistic in nature, the same is not recognized by the Advocates Act and there is no adequate remedy for such a right."

"A practice developed of petitioning the king in council, to exercise his extraordinary judiciary powers, known as the King's prerogative. In a similar manner the Appellant have petitioned your Lordships, through this petition, who have the same prerogative powers as the King's prerogative and to exercise your extraordinary judicial powers."

"The King in turn referred such petitions to the 'Keeper of the conscience'. The Lord Chancellor, who was also a priest. It is with this very view point of the Keeper of the Conscience that the Appellant has come before your Lordships to ensure that right, since there is no written but implied right, as far as the petition is concerned engrained in the Preamble of the Constitution."

"As a number of these petitions increased, the Court of Chancery was brought into being independent of the King in Council. The Court of Chancery administered the set principles of justice equity and good conscience. In this petition your Lordships, are on the same bench as the Chancery Courts and a judgment entailing, justice, equity and good conscience is sought terming the impugned rule as ultra vires of the Preamble of the Constitution, which guarantees basic human rights to all Indian citizens to ensure justice, social, economic, political, liberty of thought, expression, belief, faith and worship and equality of status and opportunity. Whereby expressing the fact that India is multi lingual, multi religious and multi cultural and thereby multi professional."

"Equity as administered by the Court of Chancery supplemented Common Law. It enforced new rights unknown to Common Law. It brought new remedies for enforcement of Common Law rights, for example, specific performance of contracts, injunctions to prevent or restrain an injury, the appointment of a receiver of property, to prevent a defendant from destroying or parting with the same, during the pendency of an action and in ordering amounts to be taken. In this petition too, we seek your intervention in recognizing the right embedded in the Preamble of the Constitution that Indian society is multi professional. Just as new remedies were brought about for Common Law rights, this petition seeks the remedy too, for accepting Indian society as multi professional and declaring the impugned rule as ultra vires of the Preamble of the Constitution of India."

"The Chancery Court had intervened, to supply defects of Common Law procedure, as this brought into being new procedures, for example, ordering discovery of documents and ordering evidence to be taken 'de bene esse,' when a witness was not available to give evidence at the hearing of the action or on account of ill health or old age or absence from England. The Chancery Courts, being Courts of justice, equity and good conscience, had gone to such varied lengths, whereby evidence could be given de bene esse. The same is sought, from this Honourable Court to go to the length of recognizing Indian Society, as multi in nature, in a de bene esse mode, since Society as a witness is absent from India and cannot deport before your Lordships, is to be construed."

"For some centuries, these two distinct systems of justice, continued to be administered in two independent Courts. As neither the Common Law Courts had the power to grant complete relief, parties had to often go to one Court to another. For example Common Law Courts had no power to order specific performance of a contract, for instance the party, who committed a breach of contract, could not be ordered to carry out his promise, but could only be ordered to pay damages. While the Equity or Chancery Courts had no powers to award damages, though they could in a proper case, order specific performance. In some cases the Equity Courts granted an injunction, to prevent the enforcement of a judgement of the Common Law Courts, on the ground that the judgement had been obtained unfairly. The anomalies at last led to the passing of the Judicature Acts 1873 and 1875 these two systems were finally brought together under one administration. One Supreme Court of Judicature was established, administering both law and equity. The Supreme Court was divided into the High Court of Justice and the Supreme Court of Appeal. You your Lordships, are the Supreme Court of Appeal and therefore this Appeal has been filed, whereby your Lordships, recognize that the impugned rule doesn't enhance the legal profession of law, but is causing a hindrance in its progress and is an anomaly, being in conflict of the Preamble of the Constitution and just as the anomalies, between the Common Law Courts and Equity, Chancery Courts brought about the passing of the Judicature Acts 1873 and 1875. A judgement is sought from your Lordships, to plug the anomaly of the impugned rule, being ultra vires of the Preamble of the Constitution."

"Let us take into consideration your Lordships, Statule Law. The term Statute Law refers to the law made by Parliament. All Acts of Parliament are recognized in its Statute book and this is called Statute Law, which is called, "written law". While Common Law is called, "unwritten law," because it is not officially written down anywhere in any particular book. It is to be found scattered among judicial decisions."

"As Parliament is the supreme law making authority. Statute Law prevails over both Equity and Common Law in case of conflict. Many of the rules of Common Law as well as Equity have found their way in the Statute book and have been modified from time to time. Indian Society your Lordships is multi and pluralistic in nature, is common throughout India and therefore it is Common Law. Application of justice, equity and good conscience by your Lordships would term the impugned rule as ultra vires of Common Law and justice equity and good conscience. But the impugned rule is a section of Statute Law which shall prevail over Common Law and Equity. But many of the rules of Common Law and Equity have become Statute Law. The fact that Indian Society is multi professional, will become part of Statute Law at some point of time, whether your Lordships, pass an order today or not. But it is the endeavour of the Appellant to make your Lordships, see the anomaly and give your Lordships, the ground to exercise your powers as the

Supreme Court. Since Suo Motto your Lordships, are not armed to take action in such a matter. Parliament has been given wide powers to amend the Constitution under Article 354 and can even amend the Fundamental rights. But as laid down in the Keshavanda Bharati case, the basic structure of the Constitution, being the Preamble, that Indian Society is multi lingual, multi religious and multi cultural as a genus and its species being Indian Society a multi professional one."

"The first Courts to be established by the British in India, were the Mayor's Courts in the three Presidency towns of Calcutta, Madras and Bombay. This was in the 18th century. The chambers establishing these Courts introduced into jurisdiction English Common Law and Statule Law in force at the time so far as they were applicable to Indian circumstances. Therefore it is sought through this petition, the rule laid down and applied by the Mayor's Courts in the 18th century that even though Statule Law being the Advocates Act exists, what is applicable to Indian circumstances need to be applied, that of Indian Society being multi and pluralistic in nature."

"Your Lordships, in the case of Advocate General of Bengal v/s Surnomoyer Desgee (1894) 9 M.CA 387. The ratio of the case as held being the Supreme Charters applied the English Law not in its entirety, but as nearly as the circumstances of the place and of the inhabitants admit. The citizens of India have already accepted Indian Society as multi and pluralistic in nature in the Preamble. The Statute Law, the Advocates Act needs to be viewed as an English Statute to comprehend the impact of the impugned rule."

ADHOCACY

"In the case of Waghela v/s Sheik Masludin (1887) 14 I. A. 89 at page 96. The ratio held being that there is no express provision, for the administration of Common Law and Equity as regards to Courts in India. They have been established mostly by legal Acts. Each of such Acts containing a provision, which required these Courts, in the absence of any specific enactment or usage applicable to the case, to act according to equity and good conscience. The expression was held by the Judicial Committee of the Privy Council, to mean the rules of English Law, so far as they are applicable to Indian Society and circumstances. Even though there being a statute enacted, being the Advocates Act the impugned rule should be applicable to Indian society and circumstances. The impugned rule is definitely not applicable to Indian Society and circumstances. Which amounts to the rule being ultra vires, not only of the Preamle of the Constitution of India, but of the people of India. The people of India being higher than the Preamble of the Constitution, it's master."

"In the case of Mayor of Lyons v/s The East India Co (1836) I M. I. A 75. The ratio held being that the Courts in India will not apply English Law which is so special in their origin, as to be inapplicable to different circumstances of this country India. Therefore law has to apply, after taking into consideration the different circumstances, prevalent in the country. The circumstances prevalent is, that Indian Society is multi and pluralistic in nature. Therefore the impugned rule shall be ultra vires, not only of the Preamble of the Constitution, but society as a whole. Indian Society being the people of India living in every state, city, town and locality of India. Since administration of justice, is the bedrock on which society stands and it is through advocates that the people of India receive justice, not Parliament. Since Parliament enacts, but it is advocates who protects an aggrieved person on a case to case basis."

"Let us look at the relevance of Custom law, as far as this petition is concerned. Sir John Salmond in his book, 'Jurisprudence,' states that custom is the embodiment of the principles which have commended themselves to the national conscience as principles of truth, justice and public utility. The fact that any rule has the sanction of custom, raises the presumption that it requires the sanction of law also. The custom of Indian Society, being multi and pluralistic in nature, has received the sanction of law through the Preamble, which therefore silently states Indian Society as multi professional, which is a constituent derived, from being multi lingual, religious and multi cultural. This custom applies through out India. Just as your Lordships, have been the protector with regards to the basic structure of the Constitution in the Keshavananda Bharati case. The same is sought, from your Lordships, in this Appeal too, the protection of what is implied in the Preamble that Indian Society is a multi professional society."

"Your Lordships, in order that a custom should be valid at law and have a binding effect. It must conform to certain requirements. The essentials of a valid custom are:

(1) It must be ancient and it should have existed for so long a time that the memory of man runneth not to the contrary. In English Law by legal fiction, thememory of man is supposed to reach as far back to the reign of Richard I. In India there is no such limit. Since the caste system dates

back to the Aryan age, Indian Society being multi and pluralistic in nature dates back to then.

(2) It must be certain and not ambigious. The custom of Indian Society being multi and pluralistic in nature is certain, since the Preamble states so.

(3) It must be reasonable. The Advocates Act has already accepted the reasonability of multi professionalism by allowing one who is a sleeping director to practice the profession of law.

(4) It should not be opposed to morality and public policy. The Constitution of India guarantees equality and right to work. Therefore multi professionalism is a part of public policy.

(5) It must not be expressly forbidden by legislation. The custom of multi professionalism, where advocates are concerned has been expressly forbidden by legislation. But your Lordships this is the crux of the petition, that how can a legislation expressly forbid something, which is expressly granted in the Preamble of the Constitution of India, through an implication.

(6) It must be invariable and continuous. There is no question that Indian Society was multi and pluralistic in nature, and will be and the only part which Parliament cannot amend, of the Constitution is the basic structure of the Constitution, the Preamble.

Your Lordships, Indian Society being multi and pluralistic in nature is an Indian custom, law of the land and is binding on all those residing in India and the Parliament. It has been granted by the Preamble through an implication and by which your Lordships, are bound."

"It is important your Lordships, to see how mercantile law evolved and its relevance to this petition. The Law Merchant or, 'Lex Mecatoria,' is based to a great extent on conventional customs or usages of merchants and traders. With the progress of trade and commerce a collection of legal principles grew up in England having their foundation in the customs and practices of merchants."

"In the middle ages each class of merchants or artisans had its own guild or union, some of them wielding considerable influence. In those days, these usuges were ascertained and enforced, by guild councils and at courts held at fairs, where much of the international trade in those days carried on. In course of time, the courts of law began to recognize these usages and eventually they became part of Common Law."

"In a similar manner, through this petition it is sought, the recognition that Indian Society is multi professional, as a species of the genus, of being multi lingual, multi religious and multi cultural. If your Lordships, do not accept Indian society as multi professional then for arguendo, it would amount to in this situation that the courts have accepted, the parents of India being multi lingual, multi religious and not the children being multi professional."

"In the beginning, there has been a reluctance, to recognize foreign languages and customs but later, a broader outlook developed. Your Lordships, have been reluctant earlier as far as recognition, that Indian society is multi professional and therefore the judgement in the Dr.Chulani's case was passed.

But just as the English Courts in the matter of Lex Mercatoria began to take a broader outlook, the Appellant seeks for your Lordships, to take a broader outlook."

"During the 17th and 18th centuries the Law Merchant was gradually absorbed into Common Law and the concept of Indian Society being multi professional, will be absorbed into Common Law of India. These acts of integration in English Courts, then was mainly due to two great judges, Lord Mansfield known as the father of Mercantile law and Lord Ellenborough. The fact that Chief Justice Lord Mansfield being an enlightened man, who could read and write foreign languages and therefore had the knowledge of works of law, by continental authors of different periods and appreciated the homogeneity and interdependence between the usages and practices of English and Continental Merchants. The Appellant seek, from your Lordships, to be enlightened persons like the Chief Justice of then of the English Courts, but not as far as Continental languages is concerned, but the psychological aspect of the species, of the genus, of Indian Society, being multi professional in nature."

"In the case of Goodwin v/s Roberts (1875) L.R. Ex 337. The ratio held, that the Law Merchant is neither more nor less the usages of merchants and traders in the different departments of Trade ratified by decisions of Courts of Law, which upon such usages, being passed before them, have adopted them as settled law, with a view to the interests of trade and public convenience. The Court proceeds on the well known principle of law, that with the reference to transactions in different departments of trade, the Court of Law in giving effect to the contracts and dealings of the parties, will assume that the latter, have dealth with each other on the footing of any custom or usage prevailing in the particular department. By this process, what was before, has become engulfed upon, or incorporated into Common Law, and may be said to form part of it."

"Similarly at a later date it shall be accepted that Indian Society is multi professional. Since Indian Society is multi lingual and multi religious and multi cultural and this shall be ratified at some later stage by the Courts, if not today through this petition. It will become settled law, at some later stage, with a view to the progress of India as a whole and for public convenience and for progress of every Indian citizen. Just as what was usage earlier and unsanctioned by legislation was engulfed into Common Law, in the same manner Indian Society being multi and pluralistic in nature, therefore multi professionalism at some later date will become part of Common Law and Statute Law. Just as the Law Merchant is not a fixed and stereotyped body of law, incapable of expanding. Similarly the legal profession is not fixed and stereotyped profession not capable of expanding. The legal profession is an ever growing body of law, modifying itself with certain limitations, according to the changing times."

With Rohan standing on his feet the hearing had gone to its 28th day. Various other judgements of various Courts, were put forward. Various opinions given by various institutions from the US, UK, France, Germany, Australia stating that due to Indian Society being pluralistic and multi in nature as a genus, the species of which is multi professionalism.

The documents of the various advocates throughout India, who had sent their submissions was placed before their Lordships. The amount of submissions were little less than

ADHOCACY

113 million. Never in the history of India, did a particular case receive 113 million people attached as respondents in a form of a submission. These were only advocates who had all put the necessary court fee stamp on each. There was another set of those that had simply attached themselves by saying they vote for prayer (a) and (b) of the petition to be granted. Those who simply had an L.L.B. degree and could not practice the profession of law. The amount of those on the site www.fiteforyourite.law had reached 200 million people. They believed in the petition. They believed the petition would sprout liberty. They believed the petition would bring freedom."

It was time for Rohan's final submission.

"The state of advocacy is, as held in the Sanjiv Datta case and is important to be pointed out here. As stated in the case, "It can be described as unfortunate both for the legal profession and the administration of justice. It becomes, therefore our own duty to bring to the notice of the members of the profession, that it is in their hands, to improve the quality of service, they render both to the litigants and the public and to the Courts and to brighten their image in society. Some members of the profession have been adopting perceptibly a casual approach, to the practice of the profession, as is evident from their absence, when the matters are called out, the filling of incomplete and in accurate pleadings, many a time, even illegible and without personal check and verification, the non payment of court fees and process fees, the failure to remove office objections, the failure to take steps to serve the parties at all. They do not realize the seriousness of these acts and omissions. They do disservice to the litigants and create an embarrassing situation in the Court leading to avoidable unpleasantness and delay in disposal of matters. This augurs ill for the health of the judicial system."

"The legal profession is a solemn and serious occupation. It is a noble calling and all who belong to it, are its honourable members. Although, the entry to the profession can be had, by acquiring merely the qualification of technical competence, the honour as a professional has to be maintained by its members, by their exemplary conduct, both in and outside the Court. The legal profession is different from other professions, in that what the lawyers do, affects not only an individual but the administration of justice, which is the foundation of a civilized society. Both as a leading member, of the intelligentsia, of the society and as a responsible citizen, the lawyer has to conduct himself as a model for others, both in his professional and in his private and public life. The regard for the legal and judicial system in this country, is in no small measure, due to the timeless role played by the stalwarts in the profession, to strenghten them. They took their profession seriously and practiced it with dignity, deference and devotion. If the profession is to survive, the judicial system has to be vitalized. No service will be too small, in making the system efficient, effective and credible. The casualness and indifference with which some members practice the profession, are certainly not calculated to achieve that purpose to enhance the prestige either of the profession or of the institution, they are serving. If people loose confidence in the profession, on account of the defiant ways of some of its members, it is not only the profession which will suffer, but also the administration of justice as a whole. The present trend unless checked, is likely to lead to a stage, when the system will be found wrecked from within, before it is wrecked form outside. It is for the members of the profession, to introspect and take the corrective steps in time and also spare the Courts the unpleasant duty. We say no more."

"Your Lordships, yourselves have stated, what the situation of the profession of advocacy is. It is an unfortunate situation both for the legal profession and the administration of justice. Bringing to the notice of the members, doesn't solve the problem since it is in your Lordships, hands, to improve the quality of service, by freeing not only the advocates, but all those with an L.L.B. degree from the cage of being able to practice another profession, besides legal and from not being able to practice the legal profession, since they have an L.L.B. degree and carry on practicing whatever other profession they are practicing. If this Honourable Court is of the opinion that positive disservice is done to litigants which is also contempt of Court, embarrassing situations are created in Court, which could be avoided, which has been causing delay in disposal of matters. The Apex Court cannot accuse the advocates when they are in a cage, since the society, which they have been brought up in, is multi and pluralistic in nature, but the profession of law has caught them and put them in the singular cage, which your Lordships, through petitions such as the Dr. Chulani's case and others such as Satish Kumar Sharma v/s Bar Council of Himachal Pradesh Air 2001 S.C. 509 have kept them in the cage still, though they have petitioned, stating they want to come out. On one side your Lordships state ill health is being caused by the advocates and on the other hand, they have to remain in this singular jail. The legal profession is a solemn and serious occupation only when the advocates are not in the singular jail. Its definitely a noble calling with regards to Mahatma Gandhi or Pandit Jawaharlal Nehru fighting for independence even though they were jailed by the British. But with the Advocates Act, advocates not being allowed to practice another profession, they are in a singular jail, whether the profession is a noble calling or that they are honourable members of the profession, if one is in jail, one is in jail. One can't be half in jail and half out. It would be meaningless to a person from a society, which is multi and pluralistic in nature, put in the singular jail and ask him to still keep his honour as a professional and demand exemplary conduct, should be maintained both in and outside Court. It is right that what lawyers do, affects not only an individual but the administration of justice, which is the foundation of a civilized society. If it is the foundation of a civilized society, then the lacunae needs to be plugged of keeping advocates in the singular jail. Yes it does show, since advocates are on strike in every state of India, but a peaceful strike and have appealed to the people of India to bear with the strike. Though in every state, the strike is not peaceful. Lawyers cannot themselves be asked to be, as role models when they themselves are in the singular jail. If your Lordships, state that society has the right to expect the conducting of oneself as a role model, then advocates too, have the right of release from the singular jail. It would make no difference, if one who is in the singular jail, whether his profession is held in high esteem or not. An advocate is not a philanthropic nor is the legal profession a philanthropic profession. If an advocate is not able to sustain himself, he will wear his life jacket. If the profession is to survive, as your Lordships, have stated, the judicial system needs to be vitalized. How? The only way is to first free the advocates from the singular jail. Then the system will be vitalized."

"As your Lordships, have stated that if the present trend unless checked is likely to lead to a stage, when the system will be found wrecked from within, before it is wrecked from outside. It is for your Lordships, to introspect and take the corrective steps in time. Whether your Lordships do or do not, Indian Society will remain multi and pluralistic in nature. I say no more" and Rohan sat down.

Forty six days had passed. Rohan had put forward what could have been put. No arguments were put forward with regards to right to equality or right to work where Articles of the Constitution was concerned. Those were already thwarted by earlier case law. Rohan didn't see any inclination that the match was tilting in his favour. Maybe because Mr. Sinha and Rohan didn't have any volleys from which to gauge.

What would be lost? Would be only by Rohan, his house and his office and his car would go to the banks, it was mortgaged to. It really, didn't matter. But what can be gained, would be, by every citizen of India. How could Rohan not bother and be selfish, the ratio 1: 1.15 Billion people. It was time for Attorney General Mr. Harsh Sinha.

Advocate General Of India
Mr. Harsh Sinha

Argument's by Rohan were simply thwarted by Sinha, on the basis that Parliament is the supreme law making body and the Advocates Act having been enacted stands supreme. He made submissions that the legal profession requires a full time submission and would not countenance an advocate riding two horses or more at the same time. When he made that statement, Rohan had to mumble to himself, *"When we Indians speak, two or three or four languages at the same time, we are riding two three and four horses at the same time? He needs to go back to school and learn some common sense or simply see the epic Mahabharata, which I saw on television, when in school. When you want to ride, two three and four horses at a time and if you do, it is called a chariot."*

"The fact that the statement was made by Sinha, that the legal profession is a full time profession was absurd, since advocates were standing outside that very moment of Magistrates Courts asking passerbys for cases and the same time shouting Notary Notary Notary. If the legal profession is a full time profession, then why were petitions being filed by advocates, to be able to file returns for clients, with regard to sales tax, if their hands were tied with legal work. I am yet to see doctors outside hospitals or clinics saying fracture fracture fracture or chartered accountants, saying tax filing, tax filing, tax filing."

Sinha stated that if Rohan was allowed to practice the legal profession and his business, it would be a precedent that would be applicable, to the whole territory of India.

"Jack ass that is exactly what I want," was what was going on in Rohan's mind. It didn't make a difference, where Rohan was concerned. Whether Rohan wins or looses the case and loose his office and house to the banks. He had failed umpteen times in his life. To him failure, was only with regards to the conscious mind. To the subconscious, there is no word called failure. Rohan believed that if the light bulb has to illuminate the world for a 100 years and even today and every new invention shall be from the prototype of Thomas A Edison, failure has to be experienced after which there is only light. Failure will only lead to the light bulb, but it is about finishing the race. Only if the race is finished, will one see the fruit, the light bulb. Failure by the hare to the tortoise doesn't finish the race.

Sinha said that, "I would be neither here nor there."

"When I speak four different languages in one sentence, I am neither here nor there. Then would I be hanging in thin space? I am in Mumbai sorry Delhi Supreme Court and not in Timbuk 1 Timbuk2 or Timbik3 at the same time," Rohan was murmuring to himself.

Whenever Rohan murmured to himself it would remind him of, *"tell me what you thinking, tell what you are thinking,"* is what one of his girlfriends would say, even though his answer would be, *"I am not thinking anything."* But she wouldn't give up, with, *"That can't be."* Which would make Rohan's mind drift to the saying of another girlfriend, *"There has to be a reason for everything."* Rohan would always reply, *"That there hasn't to be a reason for everything."*

Rohan was trying to find a reasoning of sitting in the Supreme Court fighting the SLP.

Sinha's contention was that an awkward situation would be created for Rohan's business and his clients.

"Unfortunately he must have had cider that day, since it only enhances the dignity of me as an advocate and me being in business, since then I will be given a genius tag. Otherwise as an advocate, I remain an advocate only. But being an advocate and a businessman is like a genius, who would be like a receiver of a double promotion in school, with the next class being too timid for me to handle at school." Rohan was a known murmurer and could not stop.

Sinha made a statement stating, "I would have to travel and shall not be able to attend Court causing inconvenience to his clients and unpleasantness to Court."

"He must have had another swig of cider. Adultery is a crime. Let us put a check on all hotel rooms, if adultery is being committed. He said my attention would be divided. When adultery is being committed, it is not rape but consensual sex. If two people want to have consensual sex and want to commit adultery it is their prerogative. A crime or a wrong, is a wrong only once it is committed. This Sinha was saying, that just because two people one married boy and one not married girl are together they are going to commit adultery under all circumstances, if inferred." this was Rohan and his wandering mind with reason.

He put it, "The Appellant would be in a dilemma, whether to attend a business meeting or attend to his legal profession and work for preparing cases for the next day in Court."

Mr Sinha was being laughed at, by the whole country. Every businessman who has multiple businesses is never in a dilemma, as to whether to attend a business meeting of one of his companies in the evening and preparing for another business meeting in the morning and the same would apply to a surgeon or a urologist. *"Practicing of a profession is done by the subconscious and not the conscious. It is like driving a car. Either you know how to drive or you don't. No one would want to sit in a car with someone who says he can drive, has a licence but is still wondering which gear to change to. Half pregnant is not an acceptability norm, either one is or one is not. As far as driving, who says one cannot drive a bike in the morning, a car in the afternoon and a lorry the next day, if one has a licence or not, but knows how to. Where advocacy is concerned one needs a licence to practice, a Sanad and that was exactly what the petition was about, liberty."*

As an advocate Rohan may be required, to spend his evenings and even late nights, for making witnesses ready, for examination in Court the next day and under these circumstances, if Rohan was a practicing advocate and a businessman and if he had to give his attention to a business emergency, it would be difficult to make a choice, is what Sinha had put forward.

It reminded Rohan of Marie Antoniette of the French Revolution *"If such a situation arose, I would simply go out and buy cake for my clients, though her right words would be* "Le theme est quete", *by making another advocate appear for me, with higher legal acumen than me, for that hearing in Court,"* was Rohan's answer, though in Rohan's mind.

"The Appellant's business or his clients would suffer, one of the two and that the Appellant would be torn between two conflicting loyalties," is what Sinha said.

"This amounts to convicting a person, even before he has committed a crime. First rule of law 'no man shall be convicted without being heard' stood violated by his submission. When an Indian speaks two languages, he is never torn between conflicting loyalties. It comes naturally to Indians."

He submitted that, "The Appellants would be such a person, aspiring to have simultaneous enrolment, both as a lawyer and a businessman and will be like a 'Trishanku' of yore who will neither be in heaven nor on earth."

"This amounts to all Indians are like Trishankus. When they speak two three and four languages. When one, as an Indian practices Hinduism, Budhism, Sikhism, the Muslim religon, the Parsi religon, Catholicism, when practicing the cultures of Kashmiri, Punjabi, Bengali, Keralite, Maharashtrian, Gujarati, Lucknowi, Chenaite, Orissan and all the other states put together, one doesn't become a Trishanku of yore, but an Indian. It would amount to, what the Catholics say 'souls in purgatory.' I am an Indian and I speak multiple languages, practice multiple religions and cultures. I am from earth and not a Trishanku of yore or a soul in purgatory because I go to Mumbadevi Temple and do darshan and go to Church on Sundays on that same day, one after another."

Sinha put forward that, "It would be axiomatic, that the Appellant would have to stay up the night, for preparing cases to be argued the next day and that he would have to face examination everyday in Court and that he would have to spend time with his clients, after Court working and in order to bring out his best, he would have to give his whole hearted attention to the legal profession."

"In school, college, students give six examinations in a row. If they have studied the subjects the examinations is a cakewalk. If not, it is a harrow. The legal profession is like one subject, the question paper, you do not know, you are either competent to answer or you are not. What you have studied is law and what comes as a question paper is facts. If you have studied law, you should be able to take on any question paper."

Sinha put forward that, "Advocates has to burn the midnight oil."

"I am sure Sinha had not done his homework. No machine can work at full ballast without a break. If the human machine an advocate, has to, on certain occasions, one is already trained in giving examinations right from school. If the legal profession is a full time profession, then at any given point of time, all advocates in the whole country should be engaged in work during Court hours. In other words, there should be no advocate outside any Magistrate Court in the whole of India not engaged in burning the day oil appearing in Court. If they were a student in school, it would amount to bunking class. But it would amount to bunking class, if there was class. In this context advocates were outside Magistrates Courts and were not bunking Court class. Since there was no Court class."

Sinha stated that, "Such a rule was enacted, for ensuring full time attention of legal practitioners, towards their profession and with a view to bringing out their best, so that they can fulfill their role as a legal officer of Court and can give their best in the administration of justice."

"Do all legal practitioners give full time attention to the legal profession? They can't because they have been trained not to, since

Indian Society is pluralistic and multi in nature. Fulfilling their role as an officer of the Court is one thing. But here, the situation amounts to, that a person who drinks alcohol, chews tobacco or smokes it or enjoys paan, the rule amounts to stating that the advocate has to accept and do all acts that is required for the legal profession that they do not smoke or chew tobacco or drink alcohol or enjoys paan when they actually do. If they do, they do and it has to be accepted. You can stop one from smoking or drining or enjoying paan in particular area, but totally is cutting liberty, if it is part of ones society. A similar ratio would be like stopping one from speaking his regional language like Marathi totally. Practicing of two professions enhances oneself and would never amount to a vice, such as smoking or drinking alcohol or enjoying paan," was what Rohan thought to himself. Obviously drinking of alocohol or smoking cigarettes cannot be equated with that of practicing two professions, but Rohan had to look at all angles of the triangle in front of him, to obtain liberty.

"The impugned rule, for not allowing other professionals to enter the Bar, when he doesn't want to give up the other profession or business, doesn't amount to an unreasonable restriction on the fundamental rights. If prayer (a) and (b) of the petition is granted then it would hinder the unflinching devotion expected by the legal practitioner from its members," is what Sinha said.

"The question of unflinching devotion would be nullified, since advocates are fighting cases to do work of sales tax practitioners and cost accountants. All these professions, sales tax practitioners, chartered accountants, engineers, doctors, architects are FMCP (fast moving consumer professions). These professions have constant work, just like an FMCG product has constant sale. But an advocate doesn't get regular work. At times he gets and at times he doesn't."

Sinha kept harping that, "The classification has a reasonable means to the object sought, namely the efficiency of advocates and better administration of justice."

"The fact is that, one side the Apex Court makes a statement, of advocates taking a total callousness attitude to the profession. At the same time, the advocates search for work outside the Magistrates Courts all over India and advocates are filing Writs for carrying out work of cost accountants and sales tax practitioners. When would salvation be achieved?"

It was time for the final rejoinder to be given.
Do or die, Rohan's was not to question why.

If he was a noble knight.

Nani A Palkivala

Advocate General Harsh Sinha, had given his reply to Rohan's arguments and submissions. Loosing in the battle made Rohan know, what his actions was to be, do or die and not question why. How to convince their Lordships was a mystery.

"Your Lordships, India has not witnessed a greater jurist than Sir Nani A.Palkivala. He will always be revered and shall always remain standing tall in the annuls of the legal profession. A figure every advocate would like to aspire to, just like every Hindu mother would like her son to become like lord Ram, a Muslim mother would like her son to become like Prophet Mohammed, every Sikh mother would like her son to become like Sant Guru Gobind Sing Ji and every Catholic mother would like her son to become like Lord Jesus. Unfortunately idealism has no say in reality," Rohan began his rejoinder.

Sir Nani A. Palkivala was a Capricorn born on 16.1.1920. But as relcoach.com would put it, as a cusp between Capricorn and Aquarius. In 1936 he passed his matriculation exams with the highest marks in English. In 1937 he had passed his FYA with the highest marks in Persian. In 1950 he passed B.A. with honours in English. In 1942 he passed M.A with honours in English. In 1943 he passed his first L.L.B. exam with first class first. In 1944 he passed his second L.L.B. exam with first class first. In 1946 he passed the Advocate (O.S.) examination with the highest marks in every individual paper. In 1949 he was a part time professor, at Government Law College.

"It is important to note your Lordships, that at every stage right from matriculation, Sir Nani A. Palkivala had achieved the highest marks for instance in English, Persian and stood first class first in the L.L.B. exam of the 1st year 2nd year and got the highest marks, in every individual paper, on the advocate (O.S.) examination. A feat I wonder how many have done."

It is why Rohan calls Sir Nani the Nani of the legal profession. At the time of choosing the name for Sir Nani they definitely got his name right.

"In 1950 Sir Nani Palkivala published his book 'The Law and Practice of Income Tax.' In 1956 he was appointed member of the law commission and was entrusted with the task of recasting the Indian income Tax Act."

Sir Nani was destined to be an advocate and change the face of law totally. Sir Nani wanted to be a lecturer and applied for the post, but did not get through, since a lady advocate had applied and had the teaching qualification. It definitely would be said, as fortunately, which Sir Nani did not have. Otherwise a legal stalwart might have been lost. Sir Nani had wanted to be a civil servant. In 1942 the World War II was on and written examinations were being held in Delhi. Sir Nani definitely thought he would get the highest marks and top the examination. He had beckoned his fortune twice, but since he was not suppose to be a civil servant, he was rejected on medical grounds and then Delhi was engulfed by some contagious disease and therefore did not send his application.

Had Sir Nani to have become a lecturer, the whole of India would not have received the lectures he has given, as the lectures he would have given, would find themselves confined to an institution and not India. If Sir Nani would have become a civil servant, he wouldn't have been fighting against the government in many cases, since he would have been working for the government. If any of the above happened, India would not have its Sir Nani of the legal profession, nor would for instance such as, the first Writ of Mandamus been issued against the government. Nor would Rohan have filed the petition.

In Sir Nani's own words "I share the faith of Malcolm Mulleridge that in all the larger shaping of life, there is already a plan into which one has no choice but to fit." This is exactly the point which flashed in front of Rohan, that from the time Rohan had that argument with his uncle Quentin, an engineer attached to oil companies in the Gulf, from time to time and had come down to India after the Iraq invasion of Kuwait that, "I will not be an advocate outside Court, begging for work and if be, I shall change the face of Advocacy totally," and here Rohan was advocating for the change in the Supreme Court.

It was absurd then, that a boy in his first year of college, making a statement of sorts to a renowned engineer, sought by many reputed oil companies in the Gulf, besides being the most difficult person to argue with.

"He should have been an advocate, not an engineer," is what Rohan would say.

Maybe Rohan was to change the face of Advocacy totally. It was, as if as a person in coma, before dying, revives for the last time. That statement which Rohan made, that he would change

ADHOCACY

the face of Advocacy was, as if it was a Fatwaah, which was already written and nothing could be done about it. The will was written and Rohan had no choice but to fit in it.

Just like Sir Nani had written an essay in March 1945 praising Sir J.R.D. Tata and 16 years later landed up being a director with the Tatas.

Which ever way one might look at it, the day Rohan made that statement, that he will change the face of Advocacy to uncle Quentin and that one will not find advocates outside Courts begging for work, it was the Fatwaah. The doors of heaven began to work and whatever he did, from that time or happened in his life, was correlated to the final act to be done. It was written, that the face of Advocacy was going to change and Rohan was going to be the torch bearer. The flame was lit then.

Like Sir Nani Palkivala who had changed the face of law. A similar feat was being fought to be achieved. Whether achieved or not, won was all upto the 15 judges before whom Rohan stood. If a similar feat was to be achieved, similar acts had to be carried out. Therefore just like Sir Nani Palkivala who fought the case of Ram v/s Advani pertaining to the Bombay Land Acquisition Act which came up before the Honourable Mr. Justice N. H. Bhagwati. Rohan had to do similarly.

Sir Nani Palkivala was assessing his senior in the case. The then advocate general M. P. Amin had given his reply. Just as in this particular case Mr. Sinha had given his reply to Rohan's arguments. Sir Nani was asked to give his rejoinder in the case. Sir Nani's rejoinder was with totally new arguments, which is not allowed as far as the procedure adhered to. That advocate general, in that particular case did not object. Rohan hoped Mr.

Sinha would not. Since here the situation was a taint of a shade darker or lighter. It was Rohan who had put forth the arguments in opening and was going to give the rejoinder.

However the situation did not allow Sinha to object. Since the argument put forth now, was no longer about the Advocates Act but solely on violation of Article 14 of the Indian Constitution, Right to Equality.

In that particular petition, the first writ of Mandamus was issued against the government. Rohan hoped to achieve a judgment in favour of the Appellant, in this petition that being Rohan himself. Since Sir Nani could fight battles for the citizens of India against the legislature or government excesses. Why not Rohan?

"Keeping in mind your Lordships, what Sir Nani Palkivala said that there is already a larger shaping of life and I just have to fit in. I would have sat down long ago, but for my conviction that in this Court no case is lost till the last word is spoken." Rohan made the statement and felt as if their Lordships acknowledged and appreciated his bravery.

Everything about Rohan was already in the open he had lost everything. His house and his office was mortgaged. The first to the Pecuniary Loan Company of which he had not paid the EMIs for ten months. The second to the Rabitat Loan Company. They had already sent the the 60 days notice under the Sir Phirowing Securitization Act. *"An Act which is unconstitutional since it doesn't give a chance to be heard, except by depositing half the amount to be paid,"* was what Rohan thought about the Act. Which basically amounts to being convicted, before being given a trial

ADHOCACY

or being heard. In fact to Rohan the Securitization Act wasn't totally unconstitutional, since the same would apply to Car Loans except the tenure and amounts would differ. But to Rohan all this didn't matter since whatever had taken place where the banks were concerned was done "NOT" by the banks. It was done as the rumour had it, to stop Rohan from filing the SLP in Supreme Court.

"Your Lordships Sir Nani Palkivala was hired by J. R. D. Tata on 1st April 1961 as one of the Directors of Tata Industries Ltd. the managing agency of the Tata group. At that time he was also a director of a small private limited company Favre Leuba Co Ltd, a subsidiary of the famous Swiss watchmaker, and a director of ICICI where he served for 18 years from 28th October 1959 to 27th September 1977. It is known, as legal advisor to the Tata group his involvement was full time and he was given a dispensation to continue his practice." Rohan continued with his arguments.

For the first time there was a hush, a lull and when you hear this hush or lull you can be sure some tables have turned. Rohan had heard this hush, many a times at the High Court and many a times when Harsh Sinha gave his reply. But this was Rohan arguing the case, in Supreme Court. All the arguments till date had gone against Rohan. But there seemed to be a change in tide and that now being, was being heard. Whenever one brings out abstract things, it is very difficult for the conscious mind to perceive it. After all the Court is the mandir of the conscious mind. All Rohan's arguments till date have been on the abstract level. Which made it very easy, for the advocate general to thwart it. The judges too had no choice but to accept it.

"Your Lordships, in 1963 Sir Nani Palkivala was appointed as a director on the Central Board of Reserve Bank Of India to fill the vacancy, caused by the death of K.C. Mahindra and was appointed when the board was reconstituted in January 1966 for a four year term. This your Lordships would agree with me is a blatant violation of the Advocates Act. However the eminent Sir Nani Palkivala was allowed to be a director and was given a dispensation to continue his practice. This is a blatant violation of Article 14 of the Constitution, "Right to Equality."

Justice R. J. Setalvad at this juncture interrupted "It would be prudent, if not acting prudent to ask, counsel do you term yourself as a Nani Palkivala?"

Rohan wasn't flabbergasted being asked a comparison, since he had apprehended he would have been asked such a question. Besides being called Counsel, when he wasn't one.

His reply was, "Your Lordships, under no circumstance would I term myself as Sir Nani Palkivala. He is a soul, which has given many souls life, right to the point of the first Writ of Mandamus being issued against the government and advocating for our very own dynamic ex Pime Mnister Mrs. Indira Gandhi. A man, who could finish reading a book, in half an hour. An act, which only one other person can do, being Thomas Edison. Obviously there are others, of whom I am not aware off. He stood first from his matriculation examination in 1936 right to the advocates examination in 1946. Whereas I on the other hand, has failed many examinations. In fact it has taken me, nine long years to pass the L.L.B. examination. I cannot be made to sit alongside Sir Nani Palkivala and a comparison made. However

ADHOCACY

your Lordships, there is one point, which is similar between Sir Nani Palkivala and me that being I am an Indian citizen. Just like Sir Nani Palkivala and with an L.L.B. degree under Article 14 of the Constitution of India, all citizens are guaranteed equality and therefore the dispensation given to Nani Palkivala, the Appellant Rohan Joseph is entitled to, the same and under no circumstance, can your Lordships deny me that right."

There were voices Rohan could hear at the back. In Court voices you can accept as good or bad. It was Rohan in possession of the lecturn, to decide whether they were good or bad. The Court room is like a cricket match, where the bowler and the batsman is the advocate for the defendant and the plaintiff. The judge the umpire and the fielders are the others connected with the case like the litigants. If a six is hit, the whole stadium uproars. If out the whole stadium will still uproar. In the Court room, if a point is drilled, there will be voices from the back, whether a six is hit or out, decision is not the umpires but one with the lectern. Except here, if out, there is no leaving the field, there is no term called leave. As an advocate batting has to be done for all the eleven players. Since in Court, the battle is never lost, till the last batsman has got out. Till the last word is said unlike cricket, where another batsman can take your place.

Mr. Sinha bolted in at that time, "The petitioner your lordship cannot make statements that your lordship cannot deny him a right. The right he is seeking is not granted, under the Advocates Act under reasonable restriction and your Lordships have already decided the question in Dr. Chulani's case which is now a precedent applicable throughout the territory of India."

Sinha was only protecting his reputation, hitting every ball with an aah. Every advocate in Court makes the statement that, "This Court cannot deny him a right." But Sinha had to hit it, with all the Saginess in him.

"Mr. Sinha it is upto us, to decide whether the petitioner is directing us or not. No one can direct us, to do anything, as far as this case is concerned, carry on Petitioner," Chief Justice R. J. Setalvad said setting the scores right.

With Mr. Sinha sitting down and directions given to Rohan to carry on with his arguments, Rohan did, "Your Lordships, coming back to where I left off. In 1969, Sir Nani Palkivala joined the board of Nocil Ltd. It is pertinent to mention a statement made by Sir Nani Palkivala to Mr. Justice Yeshwant Chandrachud, the Honourable Ex Chief Justice of India, being, "Yeshwant, I am to become a director on the condition that I can work as an independent lawyer, exactly how I am doing now." From this, your Lordships, it is a accepted fact, that Sir Nani Palkivala was a director as far as the Tata group of companies, as well as other companies and institutions and a practicing advocate. Which is a blatant violation of the Advocates Act, as well as Article 14 of the Constitution where the Appellant is concerned. For arguendo, the said dispensation given to Sir Nani Palkivala would amount to that one has to be a lawyer first, prove his potential and metal as an advocate to receive a dispensation. If one is a businessman or a doctor, he has to stop being a businessman or a doctor, become an advocate, prove his potential and only then can he practice the medical profession or that of his business."

ADHOCACY

Rohan took a break to have a sip of water. There were voices in whispers, it seemed apparent that those present understood the underlying road taken in the arguments.

"Your Lordships, it would be accepted and construed that Sir Nani Palkivala's becoming a director of the Tata group never affected his performance, on the volume of work as an independent lawyer." From this statement the view taken by their Lordships in the Dr. Chulani's case is that law is a full time profession shall stand abrogated."

Justice T. A. Rehmaan interrupted, "So, are you putting forward the argument that every advocate has the same acumen as Nani Palkivala, since if an order is passed dismissing the petition in favour of the Appellant it will be a precedent applicable to the whole of India?"

Again a similar question as Chief Justice R. J. Setalvad.

"Your Lordships, it is not a matter of advocates having the acumen of Sir Nani Palkivala. But that each and every advocate or aspiring advocate is equal under the eyes of law, under Article 14 of the Indian Constitution and should have an equal opportunity to strive to become as Sir Nani Palkivala. To be able to emulate him in whatever way possible and for that should be given an equal opportunity for doing so, which is guaranteed under Article 14 of the Constitution. If every advocate, who is not already successful or successful and your Lordships, will agree success is a relative term, puts a benchmark for himself to emulate Sir Nani Palkivala O.I%, the amount of advocates it might take, might be a certain amount of hundreds for another Sir Nani Palkivala," was Rohan's reply.

"Which will change the face of Advocacy and those who have become Adhocracy," is what Rohan said to himself. Rohan was always known to have funny thoughts.

"Your Lordships Sir Nani Palkivala joined the board of the two major companies, Tata Motors (then called Tata Engineering and locomotive Co. Ltd.) in 1970 and the flagship Tata Steel (then called Tata Iron and Steel Co.Ltd.) He became Vice-Chairman in December 1971. As time passed, he became a director of all major Tata Group companies in India, including Tata chemicals, Tata Hydro, Indian Hotels, Voltas and Tata Exports. He was even part of the management of the International companies, Tata Ltd. London, Tata Incorporated New York, Tata International Ag Zug Switzerland. The Advocates Act doesn't allow a practicing advocate to be a director or be part of the management of a company. But Sir Nani Palkivala was a director of not just one company, your Lordships, but several companies. But in the present petition, your Lordships, the Bar Council has not allowed the Appellant to manage his own company International Business Traveller's Club Ltd. being a family business, started by Appellant's father. This is a blatant violation of Article 14 of the Indian Cconstitution."

Knowing that Rohan did have a point and there being pin drop silence and the same can be eerie. In times like these, hearing of third party sounds was important, if Rohan wanted to stay alive. The Supreme Court is a totally air conditioned Court and all Rohan could hear was the sound of the air conditioner's ducts, even though the air conditioner's ducts could not be heard. Whether it was his brain or reality, it made no difference. Rohan was standing before 15 judges hearing his petition. Never

ADHOCACY

in the history of the Supreme Court was a bench of 15 judges convened. In the Golaknath case, a bench comprising of 11 judges was convened. In the Kehavananda Bharati case, a bench comprising of 13 judges was convened. Then again there wasn't a case heard, which could change the face of advocacy, besides changing the lives of each and every citizen.

Sir Nani Palkivala had in many cases, fought against the government. He could do since his livelihood did not come from the profession of advocacy and that, because he was a director of various companies was a view which Rohan had. If a doctor's only livelihood is from one patient or lets take a hypothetical figure as ten patients, there is all likelihood, that the doctor may do everything possible, for those ten patients to keep getting sick or to remain sick for as long as possible the doctor can, as long as the patient doesn't die.

Judges are good people and there is an affinity with those wearing the same gown, not that they are not to those who are not wearing the same gown, but it's due to affinity. Rohan wasn't even an advocate. All he could do was wear his usual black coat, with a black tie, though he would have loved to wear his tweeties, a white shirt with his pin stripped trousers to look as advocatish as possible, since he was party in person. The Court room looked like a fashion show. As if Rohan was promoting an Armani suit. Rohan wasn't, he was promoting the change of the face of advocacy besides promoting his usual Linen Arrow suit.

There are very few cases which are fought in the Supreme Court as party in person, this was one of them. Till now the case was a loosing battle and so Rohan carried on, "Your Lordships in 1980 Sir Nani Palkivala became Chairman of Tata Exports. For 25 years Sir Nani Palkivala had been the Chairman of Tata Consultancy Services. At the same time Sir Nani Palkivala was a practicing advocate, however the Appellant's application to enrollment to the Bar stands rejected. Besides the Appellants application, there have been a huge amount of applications which have been rejected. By 1970 Sir Nani Palkivala was part of, if not every major decision of the Tata Group. This amounts to participation of the management of the company. The only difference your Lordships is, the participation in the management was done by Sir Nani Palkivala and not the Appellant, even though the Constitution of India guarantees equality under Article 14. Is this equality?"

"It is imperative to note that at a time when Sir Nani Palkivala was an active director of the Tata Group of companies and on the board of ICICI Ltd. he was Counsel lawyer for our very own dynamic ex Prime Minister Indira Gandhi and whose case was fought in this Supreme Court. The only period when Sir Nani Palkivala was not practicing the legal profession and director of various companies was in the year 1977 to 1979 when he was appointed as India's Ambassador to the United States. All this period, Sir Nani Palkivala was an advocate and an active director of various companies. Though Sir Nani Palkivala was given a dispensation, the same is a blatant violation of the Advocates Act. But due to a dispensation the rule as far as the Advocates Act stands neutralized. However the dispensation doesn't neutralize the violation of Article 14 of the Constitution.

ADHOCACY

Whereby the Appellant is entitled to a similar dispensation." Rohan said and sat down.

Rohan had never in his weirdest day dreams, thought that he would be arguing a case of this magnitude, in the Supreme Court. For the first time in the history of the Supreme Court and all other Courts of India, was a case being aired on all public news channels. The Right to information Act had made many things possible, such as judges of the Supreme Court disclosing their assets. The channels flight to fancy, made it possible for the proceedings to be aired. The Parliament's proceedings are being aired and since the case was not a case being held in camera, was being aired.

There were 4 advocates, Mahatma Gandhi the father of the nation, Pandit Jawahar Lal Nehru, Sardar Vallabhbhai Patel and Quad e Azam Mohammed Ali Jinnah. One might ask about Quad e Azam Mohamed Ali Jinnah and the inference should be held, where Pakistan is concerned. Then it was about the Independence from the rule of the British and it is again but about one simple section, one simple rule and not the whole Advocates Act and not against the Government or Parliament.

In China 19 of 20 cabinet ministers have been Civil Engineers all at one point of time. A point that stuck to Rohan's mind about the four advocates who fought for Independence. Mahatma Gandhi, Pandit Jawaharlal Nehru, Sardar Vallabhbhai Patel and let us put it Quad e Azam Mohammed Ali Jinnah with reference to Pakistan have been, the Sir Nani Palkivala's of the British era. It is important for the advocates to do the check and balance, a task given to them by the Indian Constitution on the basis of the Judiciary being given the term as Independent.

Critics might say that Rohan having filed the SLP was against Parliament, critics will always be critical and be people that owe their allegiance to cynicalism, where their bread is buttered to criticize. Parliament till date has never enacted any Act or acted in a manner which is wrong, as long as whatever was asked was done, which is elect them whereby they enacted Acts, which they have enacted through the mandate given by the people of India. No one can hold God responsible for non receipt unless asked. Rohan filing the SLP was only doing the act of asking. They, the ministers, become as people, who have been entrusted the day to day activities, of whom the people of India are the owners of the company, India. The company of India is owned by the shareholders the people of India and just as in the case of Independence, the shareholders the people of India have every right to ask and Rohan was the torch bearer.

The ratio that was put forward for the proceedings of the case to be aired was that every citizen had a right to know the arguments of Rohan Joseph in totality. The Supreme Court could not accommodate each and every advocate of India nor every person, who had passed, even the first L. L. B. exam, since they are considered as aspiring advocates, nor every citizen of India for advocates are those who assist in the administration of justice involving every citizen of India and administration of justice would affect the whole of India.

At first there was a hue and cry of the declaration of assets of the judges by the Supreme Court of India. But later the judges did declare their assets. The Chief Justice in this case, had no choice and granted permission to news channels, to upload the proceedings of the case. For the first time the drama of the Court was being aired. A reality show, it was and an understanding of the proceedings would take place if there was an understanding of Court proceedings by those watching.

Every High Court of all sates had a peaceful set of advocates who did believe in the petition. They boycotted Court proceedings in a peaceful manner. They were followers of the father of the nation. There were others who protested outside Parliament, Supreme Court, High Courts and Magistrate Courts. The advocates who normally would be found stating to passerbys "Notary Notary Notary" realized the importance of the petition. They realized this petition could free them from the bondage and instead of standing outside a Magistrates Court everyday, could do something substantial and hold an office and when they did have a case, they could appear at the Magistrates Courts, but with a big if, the Supreme Court passes an order in the Appellant's favour. Every Magistrates Court witnessed a silent protest. If not with placards, with a simple black flag on their shirts.

Now the lives of lakhs of advocates, those who passed their L.L.B. exam and those as citizens of India were on the fence, sitting with a wait and watch, a want to be free. It was all left to the verdict of the 15 judges. The judgement was to be given after a gap of 15 days.

Hai Ram, Vayuguru madad, O Jesus Help,

Ya Ali Madat

Salvation

The judgement was passed. The verdict was given in open Court, the operational part. The judgement ran into 5842 pages. One of the longest judgements in the world. The case lasted for 91 days, one of the longest in the history of the Apex Court.

"It is our view that from the submissions of the Appellants, Indian Society is multi and pluralistic in nature. There is an implication of the same which can be inferred from the Preamble of the Constitution. Therefore prayer (a) and (b) of the petition stands granted in absolute terms. The impugned Rules of the Bar Council of Maharashtra and Goa made under Rule 2 of section 28 of The Advocates Act 1961 doesn't stand abrogated, as the same is not ultra vires of any provisions of the Constitution of India. However the Bar Council of Maharashtra and Goa is hereby directed to accept the application of the Appellant's enrolment to the Bar. The Bar Council of Maharashtra and Goa is further directed, to make guidelines to ensure that practicing advocates are allowed to practice another profession or carry on a business, besides the legal profession, after an undertaking is given, that no activity, profession or business, being carried out besides the legal profession, shall be violative of any law for the time being in force. Those advocates desiring to practice another profession or business besides the legal profession and those enrolling to the Bar and who desires to practice another profession or carry on a business shall do so on furnishing a fixed deposit of Rs 10000/—which shall remain with the Bar council's possession. The interest of the same shall go to the Bar council. In the event of the advocate carrying out any activity violative of any law for the time being in force, the fixed deposit shall stand transferred in the name of the Bar Council. The fixed deposit shall have to be issued by a Nationalised Bank. The above shall be subject to the approval of the Bar Council of Maharasthra and Goa and an application will have to be made detailing the profession or business being carried out in a format which the Bar Council shall have to formulate. The substantive part shall be delivered later. The Petition stands dismissed. No order as to costs."

Signed

R.J. Setalvad
Chief Justice Supreme Court of India

Rohan was a pauper, since he practically owned nothing at the point of time of the judgement being delivered. There were crackers outside every Court in India. Usually the only time crackers are lit, is when India has won a cricket match, a politician has won an election, new year's eve, when someone is getting married or just got married or at Diwali. Rohan would say the legal profession won, it was a new beginning for the legal profession and the legal profession was getting married to the masses on Diwali.

The judgemnt directing the Bar Council of Maharashtra and Goa to accept Rohan's application for enrolment did not give him immense joy, as the fact that every advocate practicing in Magistrates Courts can do, exactly what he has been thought from childbirth, speak multiple languages, one law, the other whichever profession or business they prefer.

A fund was set up by Ramesh Poojari, an advocate from Delhi practicing in the Delhi High Court. The judgement, exhilerated his life straight away. Since he came from a business family, with legal roots. But being the only son, he could not take part in the management of his business. Besides being a practicing advocate he was an architect, by profession. He knew that Rohan's office and his house were going to be taken over by the banks due to non payment. To save someone who thought saved him, a fund was set up by him called, "The Save Rohan Fund." Each advocate who felt a difference due to the judgement was asked to put or send a draft or cheque payable at Delhi of only Rs. 10. If a cheque was sent and not payable at Delhi the bank charges itself would be Rs. 150.

In a span of 15 days a receipt of Rs. 88,76,68,870 was received USD 19725974. The fund was thrown open to everyone. Since the judgement did not affect only the practicing advocates, those with an L.L.B. degree but not practicing the legal profession, but every citizen of India. Every citizen of India realised their latent quality. Something which, they did not know. They were always of the opinion that one's calling is what they should do in life. A dawn that India has the highest amount of parental ascendance, because of the joint family concept. Which doesn't change, even though the siblings part and go and stay in different homes. Therefore as an Indian they realised they will always have qualities of their parents, whereby they being able to carry on the profession of their parents and another of their choice. An awakening to every Indian citizen.

The amount of Rohan's loans were in total Rs. 1,50,00,000 USD 333333 pending to be paid with regards to his office and his house and everyone else who he owed money. There was therefore a surplus amount of Rs.87,26,68,870/-. A huge amount in surplus. The name of the fund was changed to, 'Rohan Advocates Welfare Fund.' The Articles of Association was drawn up for the fund and the money was used for the welfare of advocates in need. The fund is growing at 200 crores when Rohan last checked and benefiting advocates from all sorts of calamities.

The paradigm shift took place that every Indian has multi professionalism engrained, began to be practiced, not only by advocates, L.L.B. degree holders, but by the citizens of India.

It was the people of India who had won. Every advocate can now aspire to be like Sir Nani A Palkivala.

Salvation achieved !

Disclaimer

Adhocacy has been written, on the basis of the various experiences of my life. Wherever real names of persons and places have been used, the same has been in correlation to reality, to events which have taken place, fused with fiction, to keep the authenticity and keep the fiction flavour. However where fiction has been infused, the names places and events that have been used, would amount to a coincidence to reality.

Every effort has been made to every part, in correlation to real places and events to make the book, as realistic as possible leading to the final Act 'Salvation.'

All data with regards to Sir Nani A Palkivala has been sourced through Public Forums. To me Sir Nani A Palkivala will always remain a mentor.

The Writ Petition in the High Court wasn't filed, nor was an appeal filed in Supreme Court. However all citations, which have been cited are authentic and if a Writ was filed, the road might have ended . . . . !

Rohan decides to fight to win a lottery.

Rohan fights to win a lottery.

Rohan wins a lottery.

Law……..!

Rohan decides to get married.

Rohan gets married.

To a long lost love. Found…………!

lissa Rodrigues

Lightning Source UK Ltd.
Milton Keynes UK
178100UK00001B/89/P